New Worlds For Old by H. G. Wells

A PLAIN ACCOUNT OF MODERN SOCIALISM

Fix two tables

Herbert George Wells was born on September 21st, 1866 at Atlas House, 46 High Street, Bromley, Kent. He was the youngest of four siblings and his family affectionately knew him as 'Bertie'.

The first few years of his childhood were spent fairly quietly, and Wells didn't display much literary interest until, in 1874, he accidentally broke his leg and was left to recover in bed, largely entertained by the library books his father regularly brought him. Through these Wells found he could escape the boredom and misery of his bed and convalescence by exploring the new worlds he encountered in these books.

From these humble beginnings began a career that was, after several delays, to be seen as one of the most brilliant of modern English writers.

Able to write comfortably in a number of genres he was especially applauded for his science fiction works such as *The Time Machine* and *War of the Worlds* but his forays into the social conditions of the times, with classics such as *Kipps,* were almost as commercially successful. His short stories are miniature masterpieces many of which bring new and incredible ideas of science fiction to the edge of present day science fact. Wells also received four nominations for the Nobel Prize in Literature

Despite a strong and lasting second marriage his affairs with other women also brought the complications of fathering other children. His writings and work against fascism, as well as the promotion of socialism, brought him into increasing doubts with and opposition to religion. His writings on what the world could be in works, such as *A Modern Utopia*, are thought provoking as well as being plausible, especially when viewed from the distressing times they were written in.

His diabetic condition pushed him to create what is now the largest Diabetes charity in the United Kingdom. Wells even found the time to run twice for Parliament.

It was a long, distinguished and powerfully successful career by the time he died, aged 79, on August 13th, 1946.

Index of Contents

INTRODUCTORY REMARKS

"Undiluted Atheism, theft and immorality.... I know of no language sufficiently potent to express fully my absolute detestation of what I believe to be the most poisonous doctrine ever put forward, namely Socialism."

HIS GRACE THE DUKE OF RUTLAND.

"Let all parties then unite to defeat this insidious Socialism which is threatening the country, and take immediate steps to expose and bring it to light. The country may truly be said to be sleeping over a veritable volcano which the next general election may precipitate, unless steps are taken at once to bring this nightmare into the light of day and force it out of its creeping nocturnal habits."

MR. DUDLEY S. A. COSBY in the Westminster Review .

"Many people think that it is possible to conduct a victorious campaign with the single watchword 'Down with Socialism.' Well, I am not fond of mere negatives. I do not like fighting an abstract noun. My objection to Anti Socialism as a platform is that Socialism means so many different things. On this point I agree with Mr. Asquith. I will wait before I denounce Socialism till I see what form it takes... Socialism is not necessarily synonymous with robbery. Correctly used, the word only signifies a particular view of the proper relation of the State to its citizens, a tendency to substitute public for private ownership, or to restrict the freedom of individual enterprise in the interests of the public. But there are some forms of property which we all admit should be public and not private, and the freedom of individual enterprise is already limited by a hundred laws. Socialism and Individualism,—I am not fond of these abstract phrases. There are opposing principles which enter in various proportions into the constitution of every civilized society. It is merely a question of degree. One community is more Socialistic than another. The same community is more Socialistic at one time than at another. This country is far more Socialistic than it was fifty years ago, and for most of the changes in that direction the Unionist or Tory Party is responsible."

LORD MILNER.

CHAPTER I

THE GOOD WILL IN MAN

The present writer has long been deeply interested in the Socialist movement in Great Britain and America, and in all those complicated issues one lumps together as "social questions." In the last few years he has gone into it personally and studied the Socialist movement closely and intimately at first hand; he has made the acquaintance of many of its leaders upon both sides of the Atlantic, joined numerous organizations, attended and held meetings, experimented in Socialist politics. From these inquiries he has emerged with certain very definite conclusions as to the trend and needs of social development, and these he is now rendering in this book. He calls himself a Socialist, but he is by no means a fanatical or uncritical adherent. To him Socialism presents itself as a very noble but a very human and fallible system of ideas and motives, a system that grows and develops. He regards its spirit, its intimate substance as the most hopeful thing in human affairs at the present time, but he does also find it shares with all mundane concerns the qualities of inadequacy and error. It suffers from the common penalty of noble propositions; it is hampered by the insufficiency of its supporters and advocates, and by the superficial tarnish that necessarily falls in our atmosphere of greed and conflict darkest upon the brightest things. In spite of these admissions of failure and unworthiness in himself and those about him, he remains a Socialist.

In discussing Socialism with very various sorts of people he has necessarily had, time after time, to encounter and frame a reply to a very simple seeming and a really very difficult question: "What is Socialism?" It is almost like asking "What is Christianity?" or demanding to be shown the atmosphere. It is not to be answered fully by a formula or an epigram. Again and again the writer has been asked for some book which would set out in untechnical language, frankly and straightforwardly, what Socialism is and what it is not, and always he has hesitated in his reply. Many good books there are upon this subject, clear and well written, but none that seem to tell the whole story as he knows it; no book that gives not only the outline but the spirit, answers the main objections, clears up the chief ambiguities, covers all the ground; no book that one can put into the hands of inquiring youth and say: "There! that will tell you precisely the broad facts you want to know." Some day, no doubt, such a book will come. In the meanwhile he has ventured to put forth this temporary substitute, his own account of the faith that is in him.[1]

[1] As I pass these proofs I am reminded that Mr. J. R. MacDonald has in the press Socialism (Jacks, Edinburgh)—a general account of the movement. From Mr. Kirkup's An Enquiry into Socialism and from Fabian Essays (the Fabian Society, London) a good idea of the general Socialist position may also be obtained.

Socialism, then, as he understands it, is a great intellectual process, a development of desires and ideas that takes the form of a project—a project for the reshaping of human society upon new and better lines. That in the ampler proposition is what Socialism claims to be. This book seeks to expand and establish that proposition, and to define the principles upon which the Socialist believes this reconstruction of society should go. The particulars and justification of this project and this claim, it will be the business of this book to discuss just as plainly as the writer can.

II

Now, because the Socialist seeks the reshaping of human society, it does not follow that he denies it to be even now a very wonderful and admirable spectacle. Nor does he deny that for many people life is even now a very good thing....

For his own part, though the writer is neither a very strong nor a very healthy nor a very successful person, though he finds much unattainable and much to regret, yet life presents itself to him more and more with every year as a spectacle of inexhaustible interest, of unfolding and intensifying beauty, and as a splendid field for high attempts and stimulating desires. Yet none the less is it a spectacle shot strangely with pain, with mysterious insufficiencies and cruelties, with pitfalls into anger and regret, with aspects unaccountably sad. Its most exalted moments are most fraught for him with the appeal for endeavour, with the urgency of unsatisfied wants. These shadows and pains and instabilities do not, to his sense at least, darken the whole prospect; it may be indeed that they intensify its splendours to his perceptions; yet all these evil and ugly aspects of life come to him with an effect of challenge, as something not to be ignored but passionately disputed, as an imperative call for whatever effort and courage lurks in his composition. Life and the world are fine, but not as an abiding place; as an arena—yes, an arena gorgeously curtained with sea and sky, mountains and broad prospects, decorated with all the delicate magnificence of leaf tracery and flower petal and feather, soft fur and the shining wonder of living skin, musical with thunder and the singing of birds; but an arena nevertheless, an arena which offers no seats for idle spectators, in which one must will and do, decide, strike and strike back—and presently pass away.

And it needs but a cursory view of history to realize—though all knowledge of history confirms the generalization—that this arena is not a confused and aimless conflict of individuals. Looked at too closely it may seem to be that—a formless web of individual hates and loves; but detach oneself but a little, and the broader forms appear. One perceives something that goes on, that is constantly working to make order out of casualty, beauty out of confusion; justice, kindliness, mercy out of cruelty and inconsiderate pressure. For our present purpose it will be sufficient to speak of this force that struggles and tends to make and do, as Good Will. More and more evident is it, as one reviews the ages, that there is this as well as lust, hunger, avarice, vanity and more or less intelligent fear to be counted among the motives of mankind. This Good Will of our race, however arising, however trivial, however subordinated to individual ends, however comically inadequate a thing it may be in this individual case or that, is in the aggregate an operating will. In spite of all the confusions and thwartings of life, the halts and resiliencies and the counter strokes of fate, it is manifest that in the long run human life becomes broader than it was, gentler than it was, finer and deeper. On the whole—and now a days almost steadily—things get better. There is a secular amelioration of life, and it is brought about by Good Will working through the efforts of men.

Now this proposition lies quite open to dispute. There are people who will dispute it and make a very passable case. One may deny the amelioration, or one may deny that it is the result of any Good Will or of anything but quite mechanical forces. The former is the commoner argument. The appeal is usually to what has been finest in the past, and to all that is bad and base in the present. At once the unsoundest and the most attractive argument is to be found in the deliberate idealization of particular ages, the thirteenth century in England, for example, or the age of the Antonines. The former is presented with the brightness of a missal, the latter with all the dignity of a Roman inscription. One is asked to compare these ages so delightfully conceived, with a patent medicine vendor's advertisement or a Lancashire factory town, quite ignoring the iniquity of mediæval law or the slums and hunger and cruelty of Imperial Rome.

But quite apart from such unsound comparisons, it is, we may admit, possible to make a very excellent case against our general assertion of progress. One can instance a great number of things, big and little, that have been better in past times than they are now; for example, they dressed more sumptuously and delightfully in mediæval Venice and Florence than we do—all, that is, who could afford it; they made quite unapproachably beautiful marble figures in Athens in the time of Pericles; there is no comparison between the brickwork of Verona in the twelfth century and that of London when Cannon Street Station was erected; the art of cookery declined after the splendid period of

Roman history for more than a thousand years; the Gothic architecture of France and England exceeds in nobility and quality and aggregated beauty, every subsequent type of structure. This much, one agrees, is true, and beyond disputing. The philosophical thought of Athens again, to come to greater things, was at its climax, more free, more finely expressed than that of any epoch since. And the English of Elizabeth's time was, we are told by competent judges, a more gracious and powerful instrument of speech than in the days of Queen Anne or of Queen Victoria.

So one might go on in regard to a vast number of things, petty and large alike; the list would seem overwhelming until the countervailing considerations came into play. But, as a matter of fact, there is hardly an age or a race that does not show us something better done than ever it was before or since, because at no time has human effort ceased and absolutely failed. Isolated eminence is no proof of general elevation. Always in this field or that, whether it was in the binding of books or the enamelling of metal, the refinement of language or the assertion of liberty, particular men have, by a sort of necessity, grasped at occasion, "found themselves," as the saying goes, and done the best that was in them. So always while man endures, whatever else betide, one may feel assured at this or that special thing some men will find a way to do and get to the crown of endeavour. Such considerations of decline in particular things from the standard of the past do not really affect the general assertion of a continuous accumulating betterment in the lot of men, do not invalidate the hopes of those who believe in the power of men to end for ever many of the evils that now darken the world, who look to the reservoirs of human possibility as a supply as yet scarcely touched, who make of all the splendour and superiorities of the past no more than a bright promise and suggestion for the unborn future our every act builds up, into which, whether we care or no, all our achievements pour.

Many evils have been overcome, much order and beauty and scope for living has been evolved since man was a hairy savage holding scarcely more than a brute's intercourse with his fellows; but even in the comparatively short perspective of history, one can scarcely deny a steady process of overcoming evil. One may sneer at contemporary things; it is a fashion with that unhappily trained type of mind which cannot appreciate without invidious comparison, so poor in praise that it cannot admit worth without venting a compensatory envy; but of one permanent result of progress surely every one is assured. In the matter of thoughtless and instinctive cruelty—and that is a very fundamental matter—mankind mends steadily. I wonder and doubt if in the whole world at any time before this an aged, ill clad woman, or a palpable cripple could have moved among a crowd of low class children as free from combined or even isolated insult as such a one would be today, if caught in the rush from a London Council school. Then, for all our sins, I am sure the sense of justice is quicker and more nearly universal than ever before. Certain grave social evils, too, that once seemed innate in humanity, have gone, gone so effectually that we cannot now imagine ourselves subjected to them; the cruelties and insecurities of private war, the duel, overt slavery, for example, have altogether ceased; and in all Western Europe and America chronic local famines and great pestilences come no more. No doubt it is still an unsatisfactory world that mars the roadside with tawdry advertisements of drugs and food; but less than two centuries ago, remember, the place of these boards was taken by gibbets and crow pecked, tattered corpses swinging in the wind, and the heads of dead gentlemen (drawn and quartered, and their bowels burnt before their eyes) rotted in the rain on Temple Bar.

The world is now a better place for a common man than ever it was before, the spectacle wider and richer and deeper, and more charged with hope and promise. Think of the universal things it is so easy to ignore; of the great and growing multitude, for example, of those who may travel freely about the world, who may read freely, think freely, speak freely! Think of the quite unprecedented numbers of well ordered homes and cared for, wholesome, questioning children! And it is not only that we have this increasing sea of mediocre well being in which the realities of the future are engendering, but in the matter of sheer achievement I believe in my own time. It has been the cry of the irresponsive man since criticism began, that his own generation produced nothing; it is a cry that I hate and deny. When the dross has been cleared away and comparison becomes possible, I am convinced it will be admitted that in the aggregate, in philosophy and significant literature, in architecture, painting and scientific research, in engineering and industrial invention, in statecraft, humanity and valiant deeds, the last thirty years of man's endeavours will bear comparison with any other period of thirty years whatever in his history.

And this is the result of effort; things get better because men mean them to get better and try to bring betterment about; this progress goes on because man, in spite of evil temper, blundering and vanity, in spite of indolence and base desire, does also respond to Good Will and display Good Will. You may declare that all the good things in life are the result of causes over which man has no control, that in pursuit of an "enlightened self interest" he makes things better inadvertently. But think of any good thing you know! Was it thus it came?

III

And yet, let us not disguise it from ourselves, for all the progress one can claim, life remains very evil; about the feet of all these glories of our time lurk darknesses.

Let me take but one group of facts that cry out to all of us—and will not cry in vain. I mean the lives of little children that are going on now—as the reader sits with this book in his hand. Think, for instance, of the little children who have been pursued and tormented and butchered in the Congo Free State during the last year or so, hands and feet chopped off, little bodies torn and thrown aside that rubber might be cheap, the tyres of our cars run smoothly, and that detestable product of political expediency, the King of the Belgians, have his pleasures. Think too of the fear and violence, the dirt and stress of the lives of the children who grow up amidst the lawless internal strife of the Russian political chaos. Think of the emigrant ships even now rolling upon the high seas, their dark, evil smelling holds crammed with humanity, and the huddled sick children in them—fleeing from certain to uncertain wretchedness. Think of the dreadful tale of childish misery and suffering that goes on wherever there are not sane factory laws; how even in so civilized a part of the world as the United States of America (as Spargo's Bitter Cry of the Children tells in detail) thousands of little white children of six and seven, ill fed and often cruelly handled, toil without hope.

And in all agricultural lands too, where there is no sense of education, think of the children dragging weary feet from the filthy hovels that still house peasants the whole world over, to work in the mire and the pitiless winds, scaring birds, bending down to plant and weed. Even in London again, think just a little of the real significance of some facts I have happened upon in the Report of the Education Committee of the London County Council for the year 1905.

The headmaster of one casually selected school makes a special return upon the quality of the clothing of his 405 children. He tells of 7.4 per cent. of his boys whose clothing was "the scantiest possible—e.g. one ragged coat buttoned up and practically nothing found beneath it; and boots either absent or represented by a mass of rags tied upon the feet"; of 34.8 per cent. whose "clothing was insufficient to retain animal heat and needed urgent remedy"; of 45.9 per cent, whose clothing was "poor but passable; an old and perhaps ragged suit, with some attempt at proper underclothing—usually of flannelette"; thus leaving only 12.8 per cent. who could, in the broadest sense, be termed "well clad."

Taking want of personal cleanliness as the next indication of neglect at home, 11 per cent. of the boys are reported as "very dirty and verminous"; 34.7 per cent. whose "clothes and body were dirty but not verminous"; 42.5 per cent, were "passably clean, for boys," and only "12 per cent. clean above the average."

Eleven per cent. verminous; think what it means! Think what the homes must be like from which these poor little wretches come! Better, perhaps, than the country cottage where the cesspool drains into the water supply and the hen house vermin invades the home, but surely intolerable beside our comforts! Give but a moment again to the significance of the figures I have italicized in the table that follows, a summarized return for the year 1906 of the "Ringworm" Nurses who visit the London Elementary Schools and inspect the children for various forms of dirt disease.

Departments.	Number of children examined.	Clean.	Partially	Verminous.	Number of children cleansed.
Boys .	34,345	32,726	847	1,139	
Girls .	36,445	22,476	4,426	12,003	
Infants .	42,140	6,675	2,661	29,675	
Mixed .	5,855	4,886	298	897	
Special .	977	624	133	296	
Total .	119,762	67,387	8,365	44,010	

Does not this speak of dirt and disorder we cannot suffer to continue, of women ill trained for motherhood and worked beyond care for cleanliness, of a vast amount of preventable suffering? And these figures of filth and bad clothing are paralleled by others at least equally impressive, displaying emaciation, under nutrition, anæmia and every other painful and wretched consequence of neglect and insufficiency. These underfed, under clothed, undersized children are also the backward children; they grow up through a darkened, joyless childhood into a grey, perplexing, hopeless world that beats them down at last, after servility, after toil, after crime it may be and despair, to death.

And while you grasp the offence of these facts, do not be carried away into supposing that this age is therefore unprecedentedly evil. Such dirt, toil, cruelty have always been, have been in larger measure. Don't idealize the primitive cave, the British hut, the peasant's cottage, damp and windowless, the filth strewn, plague stricken, mediæval town. In spite of all these crushed, mangled, starved, neglected little ones about the feet of this fine time, in spite of a thousand other disorders and miseries almost as cruel, the fact remains that this age has not only more but a larger percentage of healthy, happy, kindly treated children than any age since the world began; that to look back into the domestic history of other times is to see greater squalor and more suffering.

Why! read the tombstones and monuments in any old English church, those, I mean, that date from earlier than 1800, and you will see the history of every family, of even the prosperous county families, laced with the deaths of infants and children. Nearly half of them died. Think, too, how stern was the upbringing. And always before these days it seemed natural to make all but the children of the very wealthy and very refined, fear and work from their earliest years. There comes to us too, from these days, beautiful furniture, fine literature, paintings; but there comes too, much evidence of harsh whippings, dark imprisonments and hardly a children's book, hardly the broken vestige of a toy. Bad as things are, they are better—rest assured—and yet they are still urgently bad. The greater evil of the past is no reason for contentment with the present. But it is an earnest for hoping that our efforts, and that Good Will of which they are a part and outcome, may still go on bearing fruit in perpetually dwindling misery.

It seems to me that the whole spirit and quality of both the evil and the good of our time, and of the attitude not simply of the Socialist but of every sane reformer towards these questions, was summarized in a walk I had a little while ago with a friend along the Thames Embankment, from Blackfriars Bridge to Westminster. We had dined together and we went there because we thought that with a fitful moon and clouds adrift, on a night when the air was a crystal air that gladdened and brightened, that crescent of great buildings and steely, soft hurrying water must needs be altogether beautiful. And indeed it was beautiful; the mysteries and mounting masses of the buildings to the right of us, the blurs of this coloured light or that, blue white, green white, amber or warmer orange, the rich black archings of Waterloo Bridge, the rippled lights upon the silent flowing river, the lattice of girders and the shifting trains of Charing Cross Bridge—their funnels pouring a sort of hot edged moonlight by way of smoke—and then the sweeping line of lamps, the accelerated run and diminuendo of the Embankment lamps as one came into sight of Westminster. The big hotels were very fine, huge swelling shapes of dun dark grey and brown, huge shapes seamed and bursting and fenestrated with illumination, tattered at a thousand windows with light and the indistinct, glowing suggestions of feasting and pleasure. And dim and faint above it all and very remote was the moon's dead wan face veiled and then displayed.

But we were dashed by an unanticipated refrain to this succession of magnificent things, and we did not cry, as we had meant to cry, how good it was to be alive! We found something else, something we had forgotten.

Along the Embankment, you see, there are iron seats at regular intervals, seats you cannot lie upon because iron arm rests prevent that, and each seat, one saw by the lamplight, was filled with crouching and drooping figures. Not a vacant place remained, not one vacant place. These were the homeless, and they had come to sleep here. Now one noted a poor old woman with a shameful battered straw hat awry over her drowsing face, now a young clerk staring before him at despair; now a filthy tramp, and now a bearded, frock coated, collarless respectability; I remember particularly one ghastly long white neck and white face that lopped backward, choked in some nightmare, awakened, clutched with a bony hand at the bony throat, and sat up and stared angrily as we passed. The wind had a keen edge that night even for us who had dined and were well clad. One crumpled figure coughed and went on coughing—damnably.

"It's fine," said I, trying to keep hold of the effects to which this line of poor wretches was but the selvage; "it's fine! But I can't stand this."

"It changes all that we expected," admitted my friend, after a silence.

"Must we go on—past them all?"

"Yes. I think we ought to do that. It's a lesson, perhaps—for trying to get too much beauty out of life as it is—and forgetting. Don't shirk it!"

"Great God!" cried I. "But must life always be like this? I could die—indeed, I would willingly jump into this cold and muddy river now, if by so doing I could stick a stiff dead hand through all these things—into the future; a dead commanding hand insisting with a silent irresistible gesture that this waste and failure of life should cease, and cease for ever."

"But it does cease! Each year its proportion is a little less."

I walked in silence, and my companion talked by my side.

"We go on. Here is a good thing done, and there is a good thing done. The Good Will in man—"

"Not fast enough. It goes so slowly—and in a little while we too must die—"

"It can be done," said my companion.

"It could be avoided," said I.

"It shall be in the days to come. There is food enough for all, shelter for all, wealth enough for all. Men need only know it and will it. And yet we have this!"

"And so much like this!" said I....

So we talked and were tormented.

And I remember how later we found ourselves on Westminster Bridge, looking back upon the long sweep of wrinkled black water that reflected lights and palaces and the flitting glow of steamboats, and by that time we had talked ourselves past our despair. We perceived that what was splendid remained splendid, that what was mysterious remained insoluble for all our pain and impatience. But it was clear to us the thing for us two to go upon was not the good of the present nor the evil, but the effort and the dream of the finer order, the fuller life, the banishment of suffering, to come.

"We want all the beauty that is here," said my friend, "and more also. And none of these distresses. We are here—we know not whence nor why—to want that and to struggle to get it, you and I and ten thousand others, thinly hidden from us by these luminous darknesses. We work, we pass— whither I know not, but out of our knowing. But we work—we are spurred to work. That yonder— those people are the spur—for us who cannot answer to any finer appeal. Each in our measure must do. And our reward? Our reward is our faith. Here is my creed to night. I believe—out of me and the Good Will in me and my kind there comes a regenerate world—cleansed of suffering and sorrow. That is our purpose here—to forward that. It gives us work for all our lives. Why should we ask to know more? Our errors—our sins—to night they seem to matter very little. If we stumble and roll in the mud, if we blunder against each other and hurt one another——"

"We have to go on," said my friend, after a pause.

We stood for a time in silence.

One's own personal problems came and went like a ripple on the water. Even that whisky dealer's advertisement upon the southern bank became through some fantastic transformation a promise, an enigmatical promise flashed up the river reach in letters of fire. London was indeed very beautiful that night. Without hope she would have seemed not only as beautiful but as terrible as a black panther crouching on her prey. Our hope redeemed her. Beyond her dark and meretricious splendours, beyond her throned presence jewelled with links and points and cressets of fire, crowned with stars, robed in the night, hiding cruelties, I caught a moment's vision of the coming City of Mankind, of a city more wonderful than all my dreaming, full of life, full of youth, full of the spirit of creation....

CHAPTER II

THE FUNDAMENTAL IDEA OF SOCIALISM

The fundamental idea upon which Socialism rests is the same fundamental idea as that upon which all real scientific work is carried on. It is the denial that chance impulse and individual will and happening constitute the only possible methods by which things may be done in the world. It is an assertion that things are in their nature orderly, that things may be computed, may be calculated upon and foreseen. In the spirit of this belief Science aims at a systematic knowledge of material things. "Knowledge is power," knowledge that is frankly and truly exchanged—that is the primary assumption of the New Atlantis which created the Royal Society and the organization of research. The Socialist has just that same faith in the order, the knowableness of things and the power of men in co operation to overcome chance; but to him, dealing as he does with the social affairs of men, it takes the form not of schemes for collective research but for collective action and the creation of a comprehensive design for all the social activities of man. While Science gathers knowledge, Socialism in an entirely harmonious spirit criticizes and develops a general plan of social life. Each seeks to replace disorder by order.

Each of these systems of ideas has, of course, its limits; we know in matters of material science that no calculated quantity is ever exact, no outline without a fogging at the edge, no angle without a curve at the apex; and in social affairs also, there must needs always be individuality and the unexpected and incalculable. But these things do not vitiate the case for a general order, any more than the different sizes and widths and needs of the human beings who travel prevent our having our railway carriages and seats and doors of a generally convenient size, nor our sending everybody over the same gauge of rail.

Now Science has not only this in common with Socialism that it has grown out of men's courageous confidence in the superiority of order to muddle, but these two great processes of human thought are further in sympathy in the demand they make upon men to become less egotistical and isolated. The main difference of modern scientific research from that of the middle ages, the secret of its immense successes, lies in its collective character, in the fact that every fruitful experiment is published, every new discovery of relationships explained. In a sense scientific research is a triumph over natural instinct, over that mean instinct that makes men secretive, that makes a man keep knowledge to himself and use it slyly to his own advantage. The training of a scientific man is a training in what an illiterate lout would despise as a weakness; it is a training in blabbing, in blurting things out, in telling just as plainly as possible and as soon as possible what it is he has found. To "keep shut" and bright eyed and to score advantages, that is the wisdom of the common stuff of humanity still. To science it is a crime. The noble practice of that noble profession medicine, for example, is to condemn as a quack and a rascal every man who uses secret remedies. And it is one of the most encouraging things for all who speculate upon human possibility to consider the multitude of men in the last three centuries who have been content to live laborious, unprofitable, and for the most part quite undistinguished lives in the service of knowledge that has transformed the world. Some names indeed stand out by virtue of gigantic or significant achievement, such names as Bacon, Newton, Volta, Darwin, Faraday, Joule; but these are but the culminating peaks of a nearly limitless Oberland of devoted toiling men, men one could list by the thousand. The rest have had the smallest meed of fame, small reward, much toil, much abandonment, of pleasure for their lot. One thing ennobles them all in common—their conquest over the meanness of concealment, their systematic application of energy to other than personal ends!

And that, too, Socialism pre eminently demands. It applies to social and economic relationships the same high rule of frankness and veracity, the same subordination of purely personal considerations to a common end that Science demands in the field of thought and knowledge. Just as Science aims at a common organized body of knowledge to which all its servants contribute and in which they share, so Socialism insists upon its ideal of an organized social order which every man serves and by which every man benefits. Their common enemy is the secret thinking, self seeking man. Secrecy, subterfuge and the private gain; these are the enemies of Socialism and the adversaries of Science. At times, I will admit, both Socialist and scientific man forget this essential sympathy. You will find specialized scientific investigators who do not realize they are, in effect, Socialists, and Socialists so dull to the quality of their own professions, that they gird against Science, and are secretive in policy. But such purblind servants of the light cannot alter the essential correlation of the two systems of ideas.

Now the Socialist, inspired by this conception of a possible frank and comprehensive social order to which mean and narrow ends must be sacrificed, attacks and criticizes the existing order of things at a great number of points and in a great variety of phraseology. At all points, however, you will find upon analysis that his criticism amounts to a declaration that there is wanting a sufficiency of CONSTRUCTIVE DESIGN. That in the last resort is what he always comes to.

He wants a complete organization for all those human affairs that are of collective importance. He says, to take instances almost haphazard, that our ways of manufacturing a great multitude of necessary things, of getting and distributing food, of conducting all sorts of business, of begetting and rearing children, of permitting diseases to engender and spread are chaotic and undisciplined, so badly done that here is enormous hardship, and there enormous waste, here excess and degeneration, and there privation and death. He declares that for these collective purposes, in the satisfaction of these universal needs, mankind presents the appearance and follows the methods of a mob when it ought to follow the method of an army. In place of disorderly individual effort, each man doing what he pleases, the Socialist wants organized effort and a plan. And while the scientific man seeks to make an orderly map of the half explored wilderness of fact, the Socialist seeks to make an orderly plan for the half conceived wilderness of human effort.

That and no other is the essential Socialist idea.

But do not let this image mislead you. When the Socialist speaks of a plan, he knows clearly that it is impossible to make a plan as an architect makes a plan, because while the architect deals with dead stone and timber, the statesman and Socialist deal with living and striving things. But he seeks to make a plan as one designs and lays out a garden, so that sweet and seemly things may grow, wide and beautiful vistas open and weeds and foulness disappear. Always a garden plan develops and renews itself and discovers new possibilities, but what makes all its graciousness and beauty possible is the scheme and the persistent intention, the watching and the waiting, the digging and burning, the weeder clips and the hoe. That is the sort of plan, a living plan for things that live and grow, that the Socialist seeks for social and national life.

To make all this distincter I will show the planlessness of certain contemporary things, of two main sets of human interests in fact, and explain what inferences a Socialist draws in these matters. You will then see exactly what is meant when we deny that this present state of affairs has any constructive plan, and you will appreciate in the most generalized form the nature of the constructive plan which Socialists are making and offering the world.

CHAPTER III

THE FIRST MAIN GENERALIZATION OF SOCIALISM

I

The first—the chief aspect of social life in relation to which the Socialist finds the world now planless and drifting, and for which he earnestly propounds the scheme of a better order, is that whole side of existence which is turned towards children, their begetting and upbringing, their care and education. Perpetually the world begins anew, perpetually death wipes out failure, disease, unteachableness and all that has served life and accomplished itself; and to many Socialists, if not to all, this is the supreme fact in the social scheme. The whole measure of progress in a generation is the measure in which the children improve in physical and mental quality, in social co ordination, in opportunity, upon their parents. Nothing else matters in the way of success if in that way the Good Will fails.

Let us now consider how such matters stand in our world at the present time, and let us examine them in the light of the Socialist spirit. I have already quoted certain facts from the London Education Committee's Report, by which you have seen that by taking a school haphazard—dipping a ladle, as it were, into the welter of the London population—we find more than eighty in the hundred of the London children insufficiently clad, more than half unwholesomely dirty—eleven per cent. verminous—and more than half the infants infested with vermin! The nutrition of these children is equally bad. The same report shows clearly that differences in clothing and cleanliness are paralleled with differences in nutrition that are equally striking.

"The 30 boys of the lowest class showed considerable failure to reach the average weight for their age of the school; the average shortage per boy for his age being as much as .7 kilogram. The effect upon weight was more striking than upon height, as the average failure in height was one centimetre. The 141 boys of the next class worked out at exactly the average. The 49 well clad boys showed an average excess per age weight of .54 kilogram and age height of 1.8 centimetres."

And who can doubt the amount of mental and moral dwarfing that is going on side by side with this physical shortage?

Now, it may be argued that this is not a fair sample of our general population, that these facts have been culled from a special section of the population, that here we are dealing with the congestion of London slums and altogether exceptional conditions. This is not so. The school examined was not from a specially bad district. And it happens that the entire working class population of one typical English town, York, has been exhaustively studied by Mr. B. S. Rowntree, and here are some facts from his result that quite confirm the impression given by the London figures.

"It was quite impossible to make a thorough examination of the physical condition of all the children, but as they came up to be weighed and measured, they were classified under the four headings, 'Very Good,' 'Good,' 'Fair,' or 'Bad,' by an investigator whose training and previous experience in similar work enabled her to make a reliable, even if rough, classification....

"'Bad' implies that the child bore physical traces of underfeeding and neglect.

"The numbers classified under the various heads were as follows:—

BOYS.

	Very Good, per cent.	Good, per cent.	Fair, per cent.	Bad, per cent.
Section 1 (poorest)	2.8	14.6	31.	51.6
Section 2 (middle)	7.4	20.1	53.7	18.8
Section 3 (highest)	27.4	33.8	27.4	11.4

GIRLS.

Section 1 (poorest)	2.1	14.6	31.	52.3
Section 2 (middle)	7.5	21.2	50.4	20.9
Section 3 (highest)	27.2	38.	23.1	11.7

"It will be seen that the proportion of children classed as 'very good' in Section 3 is about ten times as large as in the poorest section, and that more than half of the children in the poorest section are classed as 'bad.'

"These 'bad' children presented a pathetic spectacle, all bore some mark of the hard conditions against which they were struggling. Puny and feeble bodies, dirty and often sadly insufficient clothing, sore eyes, in many cases acutely inflamed through continued want of attention, filthy heads, cases of hip disease, swollen glands—all these and other signs told the same tale of privation and neglect. It will be noticed that the condition of the children in Section 2 (middle class labour) comes about half way between Sections 1 and 3. In considering the above table it must of course be remembered that there was no absolute standard by which each child could be judged, but the broad comparison between the different classes is unimpeachable. The table affords further evidence of serious physical deterioration amongst the poorest section of the community."

And if York and London will not satisfy, let the reader take Edinburgh, whose Charity Organization Society has produced an admirable but infinitely distressing report of the physical conditions of the school children there. It gives a summary account of the homes of fourteen hundred children in one of the Edinburgh Elementary Schools, selected because it represented a fair mixture of prosperous and unprosperous people. I take the first ten entries of this list just as they come, representing thirty eight children, and they are a fair sample of the whole list. No amount of writing could make these little thumbnail sketches of the reality of domestic life among our population to day more impressive than they are, thus barrenly given.

"1. A bad home. Woman twice married; second husband deserted her six or seven years ago and she now keeps a bad house in which much drinking and rioting goes on. Daughter on stage sends 10/ a week, son is out of work. A son is in an institution. All as filthy as is the house. The food is irregular. Two children have had free dinners from school this and last winter, clothes were also given for one each time. The boy attends regularly. The woman is a hard drinker, and gets money in undesirable ways. The eldest child has glands, neck; hair not good but clean; fleabitten. The second child, adenoids and tonsils. Housing: five in one room. Evidence from Police, School Charity, Headmistress, School Officers and Doctors.

"2. The drinking capacity of this family cannot be too much emphasized. The parents can't agree, and live apart, the man allowing 7/6 a week when girl is with mother, and 5/ when she comes to him. She is verminous and very badly kept. Mother can't get charing, as she lives in so bad a neighbourhood, so means to move; at present she keeps other women's babies at 6d. a day each. Elder boy out of work, a tidy lad, reads in Free Library. One child has died. Housing: three in one room. House not so very untidy. Evidence from Police, Church and Officer.

"3. A miserable family and in very wretched circumstances. Father deserts home at intervals, but last time seemed 'sent back by providence,' as the works in the town he was in were burnt down. Children starving in his absence; one had pneumonia, and died since of the effects. The eldest child has adenoids; the second, urticaria; lice, bad; clothes full of pediculi. Housing: six in two rooms. Mother hard working, does her best, but has chronic bronchitis; does not keep house over tidy. The two elder boys are very idle, tiresome fellows, and worry the father a great deal. They improved and found work during the year following the visit, in which time the father got into decent work in the City. The S. P. C. C. branch had to interfere on behalf of small children. Three dead since marriage, when parents were at ages 23 and 20. Food good when there is any. School gave free dinners and clothes to two. Evidence from Police, S. P. C. C. branch, School Charity, Parish Sister, Employer, Headmistress, School Officer and Doctors.

"4. The father a complete wreck through intemperate and fast living; speculation first brought him down. Was later moved to hospital, where he died. Had worked on railway a little time. Mother hard working, works out, home untidy owing to her being out so much. She pays rent regularly, and does her best. An elder boy groom, fed and clad by his master, sends home what he can. Eldest boy does odd jobs, but seems a wastrel. Parish gave 7/6 after father ill, and feeds four children now. Winter of visit school dined five free daily, and clothed three, and previous winter three had free dinners and two had clothes. A school boy earns. The twins are delicate. There are two lodgers. The eldest child very dirty; the second, glands; the third, knock kneed, pigeon chest; very feeble, enlarged radices. Three children have died. Housing: nine in three rooms. Evidence from Police, Poor Law Officer, Parish Sister, School Charity, Army Charity, Children's Employment, School Officer, Factor, Pawnbroker and Doctors.

"5. The mother, a nice, clean, tidy woman, doing pretty well by the children. They kept a little shop for a time, and she used to do a day's charing now and then, but has too many babies now. Parents married at 21 and 18 respectively; two children dead and another expected. He reads papers a good deal, gets them out of trains. This is his first spell of regular work. Two boys sell papers, and a Mission gives cheap meal. Food none too plentiful. One child gets free dinners. The eldest child has glands; impetigo; thin and badly nourished. The second, glands, hair lice and nits bad. The third, boils on neck, glands, thin. The fourth, glands. Housing: eight in two rooms. They are in two thrift societies. Evidence from School master, Police, Parish Sister, Club, Army Charity, Charity School, Pawnbroker and Doctors.

"6. Father works in a shop in daytime, and in a public house at night. Rather soft; but wife industrious and energetic and does her best. Children well fed and regular at school. Two children have enlarged tonsils. They get no help, and belong to two thrift societies. One of six children dead in ten years of married life. Housing: seven in two rooms. Evidence from Police, Doctors, Society, Church, Mission, Club, Headmistress, Charity School and Pawnbrokers.

"7. A family where parents are much given to drink; father invalided and being helped by a Sick Society, 3/ a week, and Parish 5/ a week. Housing: five in two rooms. They are in a burying club. Children fleabitten. Two have died. Food is rather scanty. Wife very quarrelsome and drunken. The boys play truant often. Two were given free food and clothes two winters ago, and this winter one has free dinners and clothes given. A Mission has given cheap clothes. Evidence from School master, Police, Poor Law Officer, C.O.S. branch, Church, School Charity, Sick Society, Children's Employment, Factor, School Officer, Charity School, Pawnbroker and Doctors.

"8. Fairly decent family; mother washes out, and man has very early work. He drinks, and his employment is somewhat irregular. A son in the country on a farm, and two dead. They were married at 21 and 18. The food is erratic, the children getting 'pieces' at dinner time, or free school dinners; or when mother comes home, soup with her. The children are rather neglected, and the police give the parents an indifferent character. The eldest child has Eustacian catarrh and nasopharyngitis; glands. The second, enlarged uvula. Housing: four in two very small rooms. Evidence from School master, Police, Parish Sister, Church, Factor and Doctors.

"9. Father an old soldier without a pension, who reads novels. All the small children were found eating a large meal of ham and eggs and strong tea after 8 p.m., he in bed at the time. They have lapsed from thrift society membership. They are extremely filthy and the man drinks. A Mission sells them meal cheap. Wife 18 at marriage and one child died. They feed pretty largely but unhealthily, and eat 'pieces' at lunch time. At time of visit, though very dirty, they were tidier than ever found before. The eldest child has chronic suppuration and large perforation of ear. Housing: five in two rooms. Evidence from Police, Parish Sister, Factor, Soldiers' Society, Charity School and Doctors.

"10. The man a carter, who drank to a certain extent, and died some months after visit, when a Charity gave her help. She had an illegitimate child and two others. He was careless, and both neglected church going. No medical evidence. Housing: five in two rooms. Evidence from Police, two Churches, Parish Sister, Employer and Charity School."

II

Now to the Socialist, as to any one who has caught any tinge of the modern scientific spirit, these facts present themselves simply as an atrocious failure of statesmanship. Indeed, a social system in which the mass of the population is growing up under these conditions, he scarcely recognizes as a State, rather it seems to him a mere preliminary higgledy piggledy aggregation of human beings, out of which a State has to be made. It seems to him that this wretched confusion of affairs which repeats itself throughout the country wherever population has gathered, must be due to more than individual inadequacy; it must be due to some general and essential failure, some unsoundness in the broad principles upon which the whole organization is conducted.

What is this general principle of failure beneath all these particular cases?

In any given instance this or that reason for the failure of a child may be given. In one case it may be the father or mother drinks, in another that the child is an orphan, neglected by aunt or stepmother, in another that the mother is an invalid or a sweated worker too overwrought to do much for him, or, though a good hearted soul, she is careless and dirty or ignorant, or that she is immoral and reckless, and so on and so on. Our haphazard sample of ten Scotch cases gives instances of nearly all these alternatives. And from these proximate causes one might work back to more general ones, to the necessity of controlling the drink traffic, of abolishing sweating, of shortening women's hours of labour, of suppressing vice. But for the present argument it is not necessary to follow up these special causes. We can make a wider generalization. For our present analysis it is sufficient to say that one more general maladjustment covers every case of neglected or ill brought up children in the world, and that is this, that with or without a decent excuse, the parent has not been equal to the task of rearing a civilized citizen. We have demanded too much from the parent, materially and morally, and the ten cases we have quoted are just ten out of ten millions of the replies to that demand. Of fifty two children born, fourteen are dead; and of the remainder we can hardly regard more than thirteen as being tolerably reared.

Is it not obvious then that, unless we are content that things should remain as they are, we must put the relations of parent to child on some securer and more wholesome footing than they are at the present time? We demand too much from the parent, and this being recognized, clearly there are only two courses open to us. The first is to relieve the parents by lowering the standard of our demand; the second is to relieve them by supplementing their efforts.

The first course, the Socialist holds, is not only cruel and unjust to the innocent child, but an entirely barbaric and retrogressive thing to do. It is a frank abandonment of all ideas of progress and world betterment. He puts it aside, therefore, and turns to the alternative. In doing that he comes at once into harmony with all the developmental tendencies of the last hundred years. For a hundred years there has been going on a process of supplementing and controlling parental effort.

A hundred years or so ago, the parent was the supreme authority in a child's destiny—short only of direct murder. Parents were held responsible for their children's rearing to God alone; should they fail, individual good hearted people might, if they thought proper, step in, give food, give help—provided the parents consented, that is, but it was not admitted that the community as a whole was concerned in the matter. Parents (and guardians in the absence of parents) were allowed to starve their children, leave them naked, prey upon their children by making them work in factories or as chimney sweeps and the like; the law was silent, the State acquiesced. Good hearted parents, on the other hand, who were unsuccessful in the world's affairs, had the torment of seeing their children go short of food and garments, grow up ignorant and feeble, their only hope of help the chancy kindliness of their more prosperous neighbours and the ill organized charities left by the benevolent dead.

Through all the nineteenth century the irresistible logic of necessity has been forcing people out of the belief in that state of affairs, has been making them see the impossibility of leaving things so absolutely to parental discretion and conscience, has been forcing them towards a constructive and organizing, that is to say towards a Socialist attitude. Essentially the Socialist attitude is this, an insistence that parentage can no longer be regarded as an isolated private matter; that the welfare of the children is of universal importance, and must, therefore, be finally a matter of collective concern. The State, which a hundred years ago was utterly careless of children, is now every year becoming more and more their Guardian, their Over Parent.

To day the power of the parents is limited in ways that would have seemed incredible a hundred years ago. In the first place they must no longer unrestrictedly use their very young children to earn money for them in toil and suffering. A great mass of labour legislation forbids them. In the next place their right to inflict punishment or to hurt wantonly has been limited in many ways. The private enterprises of charitable organizations for the prevention of cruelty and neglect has led to a growing system of law in this direction also. Nor may a parent now prevent a child getting some rudiments of an education.

Between the parent and Heaven now, in addition to the more or less legalized voluntary interference of well disposed private people, there do appear certain rare functionaries who—while they interfere not at all between good and competent parents and their children, do, in certain instances, save a parental default from its complete fruition. There are the school attendance officer and the sanitary inspector. Then there are—in the London County Council area—the "Ringworm" nurses, who examine the children systematically and by means of certain white and red cards of remonstrance and warning intimidate the parent into good behaviour or pave the way for a prosecution. Everywhere there is the factory inspector—and in certain cases the police. All these functionaries and "accessory consciences" have been thrust in between the supremacy of the parent and the child within the century.

So much the Socialist regards as all to the good, as all in the direction of that great constructive plan of organized human welfare at which he aims. And they all amount to a destruction, so much with this and so much with that, of the independence of the family, an invasion of the old moral isolation of parent and child.

But while a number of people (who haven't read the Edinburgh Charity Organization Society's Report) are content to regard these interventions as "going far enough," the Socialist considers these things as only the beginning of the organization of the welfare of the nation's children. You will notice that all these laws and regulations at which we have glanced are in the nature of prohibitions or compulsions; few have any element of aid. By virtue of them we have diminished the power of the inferior sort of parents to do evil by their child, but we have done little or nothing to increase and stimulate their powers to do good. We may prevent them doing some sorts of evil things to the child; they may not give it poisonous things, or let it live in morally or physically contagious places, but we do not insure that they shall give it wholesome things—better than they had themselves. We must, if our work is ever to reach effectual fruition, go on to the logical completion of that process of supplementing the parent that the nineteenth century began.

Consider, for instance, the circumstances of parentage among the large section of the working classes whose girls and women engage in factory labour. In many cases the earnings of the woman are vitally necessary to the solvency of the family budget, the father's wages do not nearly cover the common expenditure. In some cases the women are unmarried, or the man is an invalid or out of work. Consider such a woman on the verge of motherhood. Either she must work in a factory right up to the birth of her child—and so damage its health through her strain and fatigue,[2] or she must give up her work, lose money and go short of food and necessities and so damage the coming citizen. Moreover, after the child is born, either she must feed it artificially and return to work (and prosperity) soon, with a very great risk indeed that the child will die, or she must stay at home to nourish and tend it—until her landlord sells her furniture and turns her out!

[2] *The facts of the case are put very clearly, and quite invincibly, by Miss Margaret Macmillan in* Infant Mortality. *See also* The Babies' Tribute to the Modern Moloch, *by F. Victor Fisher. (Twentieth Century Press, 1d.) These are small polemical tracts. The case is treated fully, authoritatively and without bias in* Infant Mortality *by Dr. G. Newman.*

Now it does not need that you should be a Socialist to see how cruel and ridiculous it is to have mothers in such a dilemma. But while people who are not Socialists have no remedy to suggest, or only immediate and partial remedies, such, for example, as the forbidding of factory work to women who are about to be or have recently been mothers—an expedient which is bound to produce a plentiful crop of "concealment of birth" and infanticide convictions—the Socialist does proffer a general principle to guide the community in dealing not only with this particular hardship, but with all the kindred hardships which form a system with it. He declares that we are here in the presence of an unsound and harmful way of regarding parentage; that we treat it as a private affair, that we are still disposed to assume that people's children are almost as much their private concern as their cats, and as little entitled to public protection and assistance. The right view, he maintains, is altogether opposed to this; parentage is a public service and a public duty; a good mother is the most precious type of common individual a community can have, and to let a woman on the one hand earn a living as we do, by sewing tennis balls or making cardboard boxes or calico, and on the other, not simply not to pay her, but to impoverish her because she bears and makes sacrifices to rear children, is the most irrational aspect of all the evolved and chancy ideas and institutions that make up the modern State. It is as if we believed our civilization existed to make cheap cotton and tennis balls instead of fine human lives.

The Socialist takes all that the nineteenth century has done in remedial legislation as a mere earnest of all that it has still to do. He works for a consistent application of the principle that England, for example, tacitly admitted when she opened her public elementary schools and compelled the children to come in; the principle that the Community as a whole is the general Over Parent of all its children; that the parents must be made answerable to the community for the welfare of their children, for their clear minds and clean bodies, their eyesight and weight and training; and that, on the other hand, the parents who do their duty well are as much entitled to collective provision for their needs and economic security as a soldier, a judge or any other sort of public servant.

III

Now do not imagine the case for the State being regarded as the Over Parent, and for the financial support of parents is based simply upon the consideration of neglected, underfed, undereducated and poverty blighted children. No doubt in every one of the great civilized countries of the world at the present time such children are to be counted by the hundred thousand—by the million; but there is a much stronger case to be stated in regard to that possibly greater multitude of parents who are not in default, those common people, the mass of our huge populations, the wives of the moderately skilled workers or the reasonably comfortable employees, of the middling sort of people, the two, three and four hundred pounds a year families who toil and deny themselves for love of their children, and do contrive to rear them cleanly, passably well grown, decent minded, taught and intelligent to serve the future. Consider the enormous unfairness with which we treat them, the way in which the modern State, such as it is, trades upon their instincts, their affections, their sense of duty and self respect, to get from them for nothing the greatest social service in the world.

For while the least fortunate sort of children have at any rate the protection of the police and school inspectors, and the baser sort of parent has all sorts of public and quasi public helps and doles, the families that make the middle mass of our population are still in the position of the families of a hundred years ago, and have no help under heaven against the world. It matters not how well the home of the skilled artisan's wife or the small business man's wife has been managed—she may have educated her children marvellously, they may be clean, strong, courteous, intelligent—if the husband gets out of work or suffers from business ill luck or trade depression, or chances to be killed uninsured, down they all go to want. Such insurance as they are able to make, and it needs a tremendously heavy premium to secure an insurance that will not mean a heavy fall of income with the bread winner's death—must needs be in a private insurance office, and there is no effectual guarantee for either honesty or solvency in that. In most of the petty insurance business the thrifty poor are enormously overcharged and overreached. Rumour has been busy, and I fear only too justly, with the financial outlook of some of the Friendly Societies upon which the scanty security of so many working class families depends. Such investments as the lower and middle class father makes of surplus profits and savings must be made in ignorance of the manœuvres of the big and often quite ruthless financiers who control the world of prices. If he builds or trades, he does so as a small investor, at the highest cost and lowest profit. Half the big businesses in the world have been made out of the lost savings of the small investor; a point to which I shall return later. People talk as though Socialism proposed to rob the thrifty industrious man of his savings. He could not be more systematically robbed of his savings than he is at the present time. Nowhere beyond the limit of the Post Office Savings' Bank is there security—not even in the gilt edged respectability of Consols, which in the last ten years have fallen from 114 to under 82. Consider the adventure of the thrifty well meaning citizen who used his savings bank hoard to buy Consols at the former price, and now finds himself the poorer for not having buried his savings in his garden. The middling sort of man saves for the sake of wife and child; our State not only fails to protect him from the adventures of the manipulating financier, but it deliberately avoids competition with banker, insurance agent and promoter. In no way can the middle class or artisan parent escape the financier's power and get real security for his home or his children's upbringing.

Not only is every parent of any but the richest classes worried and discouraged by the universal insecurity of outlook in this private adventure world, but at every turn his efforts to do his best for his children are discouraged. If he has no children, he will have all his income to spend on his own pleasures; he need only live in a little house, he pays nothing for school, less for doctor, less for all the needs of life, and he is taxed less; his income tax is the same, no bigger; his rent, his rates, his household bills are all less....

The State will not even help him to a tolerable home, to wholesome food, to needed fuel for the new citizens he is training for it. The State now a days in its slow awakening does show a certain concern in the housing of the lowest classes, a concern alike stimulated and supplemented by such fine charities as Peabody's for example, but no one stands between the two hundred a year man and his landlord in the pitiless struggle to get. For every need of his children whom he toils to make into good men and women, he must pay a toll of owner's profits, he must trust to the anything but intelligent greed of private enterprise.

The State will not even insist that a sufficiency of comfortable, sanitary homes shall be built for his class; if he wants the elementary convenience of a bathroom, he must pay extra toll to the water shareholder; his gas is as cheap in quality and dear in price as it can be; his bread and milk, under the laws of supply and demand, are at the legal minimum of wholesomeness; the coal trade cheerfully raises his coal in mid winter to ruinous prices. He buys clothes of shoddy and boots of brown paper. To get any other is nearly impossible for a man with three hundred pounds a year. His newspapers, which are supported by advertisers and financiers, in order to hide the obvious injustice of this one man fight against the allied forces of property, din in his ears that his one grievance is local taxation, his one remedy "to keep down the rates"—the "rates" which do at least repair his roadway, police his streets, give him open spaces for his babies and help to educate his children, and which, moreover, constitute a burthen he might by a little intelligent political action shift quite easily from his own shoulders to the broad support of capital and land.

If the children of the decent skilled artisan and middle class suffer less obviously than the poorer sort of children, assuredly the parents in wearing anxiety, in toil and limitation and disappointment, suffer more. And in less intense and dramatic, but perhaps even more melancholy ways, the children of this class do suffer. They do not die so abundantly in infancy, but they grow up, too many of them, to shabby and limited lives; in Britain they are still, as a class, extraordinarily ill educated—many of them still go to incompetent, understaffed and ill equipped private adventure schools—they are sent into business prematurely, often at fourteen or fifteen, they become mechanical "respectable" drudges in processes they do not understand. They may escape want and squalor for a while, perhaps, but they cannot escape narrowness and limitation and a cramped and anxious life. If they get to anything better than that, it is chiefly through almost heroic parental effort and sacrifice.

The plain fact is that the better middle class parents serve the State in this matter of child rearing, the less is their reward, the less is their security, the greater their toil and anxiety. Is it any wonder then that throughout this more comfortable but more refined and exacting class, the skilled artisan and middle class, there goes on something even more disastrous, from the point of view of the State, than the squalor, despair and neglect of the lower levels, and that is a very evident strike against parentage? While the very poor continue to have many children who die or grow up undersized, crippled or half civilized, the middle mass, which can contrive with a struggle and sacrifice to rear fairly well grown and well equipped offspring, which has a conscience for the well being and happiness of the young, manifests a diminishing spirit for parentage, its families fall to four, to three, to two—and in an increasing number of instances there are no children at all.

With regard to the struggling middle class and skilled artisan class parent, even more than to the lower poor, does the Socialist insist upon the plain need, if only that our State and nation should continue, of endowment and help. He deems it not simply unreasonable but ridiculous that in a world of limitless resources, of vast expenditure, of unparalleled luxury, in which two million pound battleships and multi millionaires are common objects, the supremely important business of rearing the bulk of the next generation of the middling sort of people should be left almost entirely to the unaided, unguided efforts of impoverished and struggling women and men. It seems to him almost beyond sanity to suppose that so things must or can continue.

IV

And what I have said of the middle class parent is true with certain modifications of all the classes above it, except that in a monarchy you reach at last one State subsidized family—in the case of Britain a very healthy and active group, the Royal family—which is not only State supported, but also beyond the requirements of any modern Socialist, State bred. There are enormous handicaps at every other social level upon efficient parentage, and upon the training of children for any public and generous end. Parentage is treated as a private foible, and those who undertake its solemn responsibilities are put at every sort of disadvantage against those who lead sterile lives, who give all their strength and resources to vanity and socially harmful personal indulgence. These latter, with an ampler leisure and ampler means, determine the forms of pleasure and social usage, they "set the fashion" and bar pride, distinction or relaxation to the devoted parent. The typical British aristocrat is not parent bred, but class bred, a person with a lively sense of social influences and no social ideas. The one class that is economically capable of making all that can be made of its children is demoralized by the very irresponsibility of the wealth that creates this opportunity. This is still more apparent in the American plutocracy, where perhaps half the women appear to be artificially sterilized spenders of money upon frivolous things.

No doubt there is in the richer strata of the community a certain proportion of families with a real tradition of upbringing and service; such English families as the Cecils, Balfours and Trevelyans, for example, produce, generation after generation, public spirited and highly competent men. But the family tradition in these cases is an excess of virtue rather than any necessary consequence of a social advantage; it is a defiance rather than a necessity of our economic system. It is natural that such men as Lord Hugh and Lord Robert Cecil, highly trained, highly capable, but without that gift of sympathetic imagination which releases a man from the subtle mental habituations of his upbringing, should idealize every family in the world to the likeness of their own—and find the Socialist's Over Parent of the State not simply a needless but a mischievous and wicked innovation. They think—they will, I fear, continue to think—of England as a world of happy Hatfields, cottage Hatfields, villa Hatfields, Hatfields over the shop, and Hatfields behind the farmyard—wickedly and wantonly assailed and interfered with by a band of weirdly discontented men. It is a dream that the reader must not share. Even in the case of the rich and really prosperous it is an illusion. In no class at the present time is there a real inducement to the effectual rearing of trained and educated citizens; in every class are difficulties and discouragements.

This state of affairs, says the Socialist, is chaotic or indifferent to a sea of wretchedness and failure, in health, vigour, order and beauty. Such pleasure as it permits is a gaudy indulgence filched from children and duty; such beauty—a hectic beauty stained with injustice; such happiness—a happiness that can only continue so long as it remains blind or indifferent to a sea of wretchedness and failure.

Our present system of isolated and unsupported families keeps the mass of the world beyond all necessity painful, ugly and squalid. It stands condemned, and it must end.

V

Let me summarize what has been said in this chapter in a compact proposition, and so complete the statement of the First Main Generalization of Socialism.

The ideas of the private individual rights of the parent and of his isolated responsibility for his children are harmfully exaggerated in the contemporary world. We do not sufficiently protect children from negligent, incompetent, selfish or wicked parents, and we do not sufficiently aid and encourage good parents; parentage is too much a matter of private adventure, and the individual family is too irresponsible. As a consequence there is a huge amount of avoidable privation, suffering and sorrow, and a large proportion of the generation that grows up, grows up stunted, limited, badly educated and incompetent in comparison with the strength, training and beauty with which a better social organization could endow it.

The Socialist holds that the community as a whole should be responsible, and every individual in the community, married or single, parent or childless, should be responsible for the welfare and upbringing of every child born into that community. This responsibility may be entrusted in whole or in part to parent, teacher or other guardian—but it is not simply the right but the duty of the State— that is to say of the organized power and intelligence of the community—to direct, to inquire, and to intervene in any default for the child's welfare.

Parentage rightly undertaken is a service as well as a duty to the world, carrying with it not only obligations but a claim, the strongest of claims, upon the whole community. It must be provided for like any other public service; in any completely civilized State it must be sustained, rewarded and controlled. And this is to be done not to supersede the love, pride and conscience of the parent, but to supplement, encourage and maintain it.

VI

This is the first of the twin generalizations upon which the whole edifice of modern Socialism rests. Its fellow generalization we must consider in the chapter immediately to follow.

But at this point the reader unaccustomed to social questions will experience a difficulty. He will naturally think of this much of change we have broached, as if it was to happen in a world that otherwise was to remain just as the world is now, with merchants, landowners, rich and poor and all the rest of it. You are proposing, he may say, what is no doubt a highly desirable but which is also a quite impossible thing. You propose practically to educate all the young of the country and to pay at least sufficient to support them and their mothers in decency—out of what? Where will you get the money?

That is a perfectly legitimate question and one that must be answered fully if our whole project is not to fall to the ground.

So we come to the discussion of material means, of the wherewithal, that is to say to the "Economics" of Socialism. The reader will see very speedily that this great social revolution we propose necessarily involves a revolution in business and industry that will be equally far reaching.

The two revolutions are indeed inseparable, two sides of one wheel, and it is scarcely possible that one could happen without the other.

Of course the community supports all its children now—the only point is that it does not support them in its collective character as a State "as a whole." All the children in the world are supported by all the people in the world, but very unfairly and irregularly, through the intervention of that great multitude of small private proprietors, the parents. When the parents fail, Charity and the Parish step in. If the reader will refer to those ten cases from Edinburgh I have already quoted in Chapter III., § 1, he will note that in eight out of the ten there comes in the eleemosynary element; in the seventh case especially he will get an inkling of its waste. A change in the system that diminished (though it by no means abolished) this separate dependence of children upon parents, each child depending upon those "pieces" from its particular parental feast, need not necessarily diminish the amount of wheat, or leather, or milk in the world; the children would still get the bread and milk and boots, but through different channels and in a different spirit. They might even get more. The method of making and distribution will evidently have to be a different one and run counter to currently accepted notions; that is all. Not only is it true that a change of system need not diminish the amount of food in the world; it might even increase it. The Socialist declares that his system would increase it. He proposes a method of making and distribution, a change in industrial conditions and in the conventions of property, that he declares will not only not diminish but greatly increase the production of the world, and changes in the administration that he is equally convinced will insure a far juster and better use of all that is produced.

This side of his proposals we will proceed to consider in our next chapter.

CHAPTER IV

THE SECOND MAIN GENERALIZATION OF SOCIALISM

I

We have considered the Socialist criticism of the present state of affairs in relation to the most important of all public questions, the question of the welfare and upbringing of the next generation. We have stated the general principle of social reconstruction that emerges from that criticism. We have now to enter upon the question of ways and means, the economic question. We have to ask whether the vision we have conjured up of a whole population well fed, well clad, well educated—in a word, well brought up—is, after all, only an amiable dream. Is it true that humanity is producing all that it can produce at the present time, and managing everything about as well as it can be managed; that, as a matter of fact, there isn't enough of food and care to go round, and hence the unavoidable anxiety in the life of every one (except in the case of a small minority of exceptionally secure people), and the absolute wretchedness of vast myriads of the poorer sort?

The Socialist says, No! He asserts that our economic system is as chaotic and wasteful as our system of rearing children—is only another aspect of the same planlessness—that it does its work with a needless excess of friction, that it might be far simpler and almost infinitely more productive than it is.

Let us detach ourselves a little from our everyday habits of thinking in these matters; let us cease to take customary things for granted, and let us try and consider how our economic arrangements would strike a disinterested intelligence that looked at them freshly for the first time. Let us take some matter of primary economic importance, such as the housing of the population, and do our best to criticize it in this spirit of personal aloofness.

In order to do that, let us try to detach ourselves a little from our own personal interest in these affairs. Imagine a mind ignorant of our history and traditions, coming from some other sphere, from some world more civilized, from some other planet perhaps, to this earth. Would our system of housing strike it as the very wisest and most practical possible, would it really seem to be the attainable maximum of outcome for human exertion, or would it seem confused, disorderly, wasteful and bad? The Socialist holds that the latter would certainly be the verdict of such an impartial examination.

What would our visitor find in such a country as England, for example? He would find a few thousand people housed with conspicuous comfort and sumptuousness, in large, airy and often extremely beautiful homes equipped with every convenience—except such as economize labour—and waited on by many thousands of attendants. He would find next, several hundreds of thousands in houses reasonably well built, but for the most part ill designed and unpleasant to the eye, houses passably sanitary and convenient, fitted with bathrooms, with properly equipped kitchens, usually with a certain space of air and garden about them. And the rest of our millions he would find crowded into houses evidently too small for a decent life, and often dreadfully dirty and insanitary, without proper space or appliances to cook properly, wash properly or indeed perform any of the fundamental operations of a civilized life tolerably well—without, indeed, even the privacy needed for common decency. In the towns he would find most of the houses occupied by people for whose needs they were obviously not designed, and in many cases extraordinarily crowded, ramshackle and unclean; in the country he would be amazed to find still denser congestion, sometimes a dozen people in one miserable, tumble down, outwardly picturesque and inwardly abominable two roomed cottage, people living up against pigsties and drawing water from wells they could not help but contaminate. Think of how the intimate glimpses from the railway train one gets into people's homes upon the outskirts of any of our large towns would impress him. And being, as we assume, clear minded and able to trace cause and effect, he would see all this disorder working out in mortality, disease, misery and intellectual and moral failure.

All this would strike our visitor as a very remarkable state of affairs for reasonable creatures to endure, and probably he would not understand at first that millions of people were content to regard all this disorder as the permanent lot of humanity. He would assume that this must be a temporary state of affairs due to some causes unknown to him, some great migration, for example. He would suppose we were all busy putting things right. He would see on the one hand unemployed labour and unemployed material; on the other, great areas of suitable land and the crying need for more and better homes than the people had, and it would seem the most natural thing in the world that the directing intelligence of the community should set the unemployed people to work with the unemployed material upon the land to house the whole population fairly and well. There exists all that is needed to house the whole population admirably, the building material, the room, the unoccupied hands. Why is it not being done?

Our answer would be, of course, that he did not understand our difficulties; the land was not ours to do as we liked with, it did not belong to the community but to certain persons, the Owners, who either refused to let us build upon it or buy it or have anything to do with it, or demanded money we could not produce for it; that equally the material was not ours, but belonged to certain other Owners, and that, thirdly, the community had insufficient money or credit to pay the wages and maintenance and equipment of the workers who starved and degenerated in our streets—for that money, too, was privately owned.

This would puzzle our visitor considerably.

"Why do you have Owners?" he would ask.

We might find that difficult to answer.

"But why do you let the land be owned?" he would go on. "You don't let people own the air. And these bricks and timber you mustn't touch, the mortar you need and the gold you need—they all came out of the ground—they all belonged to everybody or nobody a little while ago!"

You would say something indistinct about Property.

"But why?"

"Somebody must own the things."

"Well, let the State own the things and use them for the common good. It owns the roads, it owns the foreshores and the territorial seas—nobody owns the air!"

If you entered upon historical explanations with him, you would soon be in difficulties. You would find that so recently as the Feudal System—which was still living, so to speak, yesterday—the King, who stood for the State, held the land as the Realm, and the predecessors of the present owners held under him merely as the administrative officials who performed all sorts of public services and had all sorts of privileges thereby. They have dropped the services and stuck to the land and the privileges; that is all.

"I begin to perceive," our visitor would say as this became clear; "your world is under the spell of an exaggerated idea, this preposterous idea there must be an individual Owner for everything in the world. Obviously you can't get on while you are under the spell of that! So long as you have this private ownership in everything, there's no help for you. You cut up your land and material in parcels of all sorts and sizes among this multitude of irresponsible little monarchs; you let all the material you need get distributed among another small swarm of Owners, and clearly you can only get them to work for public ends in the most roundabout, tedious and wasteful way. Why should they? They're very well satisfied as they are! But if the community as a whole insisted that this idea of private Ownership you have in regard to land and natural things was all nonsense—and it is all nonsense!—just think what you might not do with it now that you have all the new powers and lights that Science has given you. You might turn all your towns into garden cities, put an end to overcrowding, abolish smoky skies——"

"Hush!" I should have to interrupt; "if you talk of the things that are clearly possible in the world to day, they will say you are an Utopian dreamer!"

But at least one thing would have become clear, the little swarm of Owners and their claims standing in the way of any bold collective dealing with housing or any such public concern. The real work to be done here is to change an idea, that idea of ownership, to so modify it that it will cease to obstruct the rational development of life; and that is what the Socialist seeks to do.

II

Now the argument that the civilized housing of the masses of our population now is impossible because if you set out to do it you come up against the veto of the private owner at every stage, can be applied to almost every general public service. Some little while ago I wrote a tract for the Fabian Society about Boots;[3] and I will not apologize for repeating here a passage from that. To begin with, this tract pointed out the badness, unhealthiness and discomfort of people's footwear as one saw it in every poor quarter, and asked why it was that things were in so disagreeable a state. There was plenty of leather in the world, plenty of labour.

[3] *This Misery of Boots. It is intended as an introductory tract explaining the central idea of Socialism for propaganda purposes, and it is published by the Fabian Society, of 3 Clement's Inn, London, at 3d. That, together with my tract Socialism and the Family (A. C. Fifield, 44 Fleet Street, London, 6d.), gives the whole broad outline of the Socialist attitude.*

"Here on the one hand—you can see for yourself in any unfashionable part of Great Britain—are people badly, uncomfortably, painfully shod in old boots, rotten boots, sham boots; and on the other great stretches of land in the world, with unlimited possibilities of cattle and leather and great numbers of people who, either through wealth or trade disorder, are doing no work. And our question is: 'Why cannot the latter set to work and make and distribute boots?'

"Imagine yourself trying to organize something of this kind of Free Booting expedition and consider the difficulties you would meet with. You would begin by looking for a lot of leather. Imagine yourself setting off to South America, for example, to get leather; beginning at the very beginning by setting to work to kill and flay a herd of cattle. You find at once you are interrupted. Along comes your first obstacle in the shape of a man who tells you the cattle and the leather belong to him. You explain that the leather is wanted for people who have no decent boots in England. He says he does not care a rap what you want it for; before you may take it from him you have to buy him off; it is his private property, this leather, and the herd and the land over which the herd ranges. You ask him how much he wants for his leather, and he tells you frankly, just as much as he can induce you to give.

"If he chanced to be a person of exceptional sweetness of disposition, you might perhaps argue with him. You might point out to him that this project of giving people splendid boots was a fine one that would put an end to much human misery. He might even sympathize with your generous enthusiasm, but you would, I think, find him adamantine in his resolve to get just as much out of you for his leather as you could with the utmost effort pay.

"Suppose, now, you said to him: 'But how did you come by this land and these herds so that you can stand between them and the people who have need of them, exacting this profit?' He would probably either embark upon a long rigmarole, or, what is much more probable, lose his temper and decline to argue. Pursuing your doubt as to the rightfulness of his property in these things, you might admit he deserved a certain reasonable fee for the rough care he had taken of the land and herds. But cattle breeders are a rude violent race, and it is doubtful if you would get far beyond your proposition of a reasonable fee. You would, in fact, have to buy off this owner of the leather at a good thumping price—he exacting just as much as he could get from you—if you wanted to go on with your project.

"Well, then you would have to get your leather here, and to do that you would have to bring it by railway and ship to this country. And here again you would find people without any desire or intention of helping your project, standing in your course resolved to make every possible penny out of you on your way to provide sound boots for every one. You would find the railway was private property and had an owner or owners; you would find the ship was private property with an owner or owners, and that none of these would be satisfied for a moment with a mere fee adequate to their services. They too would be resolved to make every penny of profit out of you. If you made inquiries about the matter, you would probably find the real owners of railway and ship were companies of shareholders, and the profit squeezed out of your poor people's boots at this stage went to fill the pockets of old ladies, at Torquay, spendthrifts in Paris, well booted gentlemen in London clubs, all sorts of glossy people....

"Well, you get the leather to England at last; and now you want to make it into boots. You take it to a centre of population, invite workers to come to you, erect sheds and machinery upon a vacant piece of ground, and start off in a sort of fury of generous industry, boot making.... Do you? There comes along an owner for that vacant piece of ground, declares it is his property, demands an enormous sum for rent. And your workers all round you, you find, cannot get house room until they too have paid rent—every inch of the country is somebody's property, and a man may not shut his eyes for an hour without the consent of some owner or other. And the food your shoe makers eat, the clothes they wear, have all paid tribute and profit to land owners, cart owners, house owners, endless tribute over and above the fair pay for work that has been done upon them....

"So one might go on. But you begin to see now one set of reasons at least why every one has not good comfortable boots. There could be plenty of leather; and there is certainly plenty of labour and quite enough intelligence in the world to manage that and a thousand other desirable things. But this institution of Private Property in land and naturally produced things, these obstructive claims that prevent you using ground, or moving material, and that have to be bought out at exorbitant prices, stand in the way. All these owners hang like parasites upon your enterprise at its every stage; and by the time you get your sound boots well made in England, you will find them costing about a pound a pair—high out of reach of the general mass of people. And you will perhaps not think me fanciful and extravagant when I confess that when I realize this and look at poor people's boots in the street, and see them cracked and misshapen and altogether nasty, I seem to see also a lot of little phantom land owners, cattle owners, house owners, owners of all sorts, swarming over their pinched and weary feet like leeches, taking much and giving nothing and being the real cause of all such miseries."

III

Our visitor would not only be struck by the clogging of our social activities through this system of leaving everything to private enterprise; he would also be struck by the immense wastefulness. Everywhere he would see things in duplicate and triplicate; down the High Street of any small town he would find three or four butchers—mostly selling New Zealand mutton and Argentine beef as English—five or six grocers, three or four milk shops, one or two big drapers and three or four small haberdashers, milliners, and "fancy shops," two or three fishmongers, all very poor, all rather bad, most of them in debt and with their assistants all insecure and underpaid. He would find in spite of this wealth of competition that every one who could contrive it, all the really prosperous people in fact, bought most of their food and drapery from big London firms.

But why should I go on writing fresh arguments when we have Elihu's classic tract[4] to quote.

[4] Elihu's tracts are published by the Independent Labour Party at one penny each. The best are: Whose Dog Art Thou? A Nation of Slaves; Milk and Postage Stamps; A Corner in Flesh and Blood; and Simple Division.

"Observe how private enterprise supplies the streets with milk. At 7.30 a milk cart comes lumbering along and delivers milk at one house and away again. Half an hour later another milk cart arrives and delivers milk, first on this side of the street and then on that, until seven houses have been supplied, and then he departs. During the next three or four hours four other milk carts put in an appearance at varying intervals, supplying a house here and another there, until finally, as it draws towards noon, their task is accomplished and the street supplied with milk.

"The time actually occupied by one and another of these distributors of milk makes in all about an hour and forty minutes, six men and six horses and carts being required for the purpose, and these equipages rattle along one after the other, all over the district, through the greater part of the day, in the same erratic and extraordinary manner."

IV

Our imaginary visitor would probably quite fail to grasp the reasons why we do not forthwith shake off this obstructive and harmful idea of Private Ownership, dispossess our Landowners and so forth as gently as possible, and set to work upon collective housing and the rest of it. And so he would "exit wondering."

But that would be only the opening of the real argument. A competent Anti Socialist of a more terrestrial experience would have a great many very effectual and very sound considerations to advance in defence of the present system.

He might urge that our present way of doing things, though it was sometimes almost as wasteful as Nature when fresh spawn or pollen germs are scattered, was in many ways singularly congenial to the infirmities of humanity. The idea of property is a spontaneous product of the mortal mind; children develop it in the nursery, and are passionately alive to the difference of meum and tuum, and its extension to land, subterranean products and wild free things, even if it is under analysis a little unreasonable, was at least singularly acceptable to humanity.

And there would be admirable soundness in all this. There can be little or no doubt that the conception of personal ownership has in the past contributed elements to human progress that could have come through no other means. It has allowed private individuals in odd corners to try experiments in new methods and new appliances, that the general intelligence, such as it was, of the community could not have understood. For all its faults, our present individualistic order compared not simply with the communism of primitive tribes, but even with the personal and largely illiterate control of the mediæval feudal governments, is a good efficient working method. I don't think a Socialist need quarrel with the facts of history or human nature. But he would urge that Private Ownership is only a phase, though no doubt quite a necessary phase, in human development. The world has needed Private Ownership just as (Lester F. Ward declares[5]) it once needed slavery to discipline men and women to agriculture and habits of industry, and just as it needed autocratic kings to weld warring tribes into nations and nations into empires, to build high roads, end private war and establish the idea of Law, and a wider than tribal loyalty. But just as Western Europe has passed out of the phases of slavery and of autocracy (which is national slavery) into constitutionalism, so, he would hold, we are passing out of the phase of private ownership of land and material and food. We are doing so not because we reject it, but because we have worked it out, because we have learnt its lessons and can now go on to a higher and finer organization.

[5] Pure Sociology, p. 271 2, by Lester F. Ward. (The Macmillan Company, New York.)

There the Anti Socialist would join issue with a lesser advantage. He would have to show not only that Private Ownership has been serviceable and justifiable in the past—which many Socialists admit quite cheerfully—but that it is the crown and perfection of human methods, which the Socialists flatly deny. Universal Private Ownership, an extreme development of the sentiment of individual autonomy and the limitation of the State to the merest police functions, were a necessary outcome of the breakdown of the unprogressive authoritative Feudal System in alliance with a dogmatic Church. It reached its maximum in the eighteenth century, when even some of the prisons and workhouses were run by private contract, when people issued a private money, the old token coinage, and even regiments of soldiers were raised by private enterprise. It was, the Socialist alleges, a mere phase of that breaking up of the old social edifice, a weakening of the old circle of ideas that had to precede the new constructive effort. But with land, with all sorts of property and all sorts of businesses and public services, just as with the old isolated private family, the old separateness and independence is giving way to a new synthesis. The idea of Private Ownership, albeit still the ruling idea of our civilization, does not rule nearly so absolutely as it did. It weakens and falters before the inexorable demands of social necessity—manifestly under our eyes.

The Socialist would be able to appeal to a far greater number of laws in the nature of limitation of the owner of property than could be quoted to show the limitation of the old supremacy of the head of the family. In the first place he would be able to point to a constantly increasing interference with the right of the landowner to do what he liked with his own, building regulations, intervention to create allotments and so forth. Then there would be a vast mass of factory and industrial legislation, controlling, directing, prohibiting; fencing machinery, interfering on behalf of health, justice and public necessity with the owner's free bargain with his work people. His business undertakings would be under limitations his grandfather never knew—even harmless adulterations that merely intensify profit, forbidden him!

And in the next place and still more significant is the manifest determination to keep in public hands many things that would once inevitably have become private property. For example, in the middle Victorian period a water supply, a gas supply, a railway or tramway was inevitably a private enterprise, the creation of a new property; now, this is the exception rather than the rule. While gas and water and trains were supplied by speculative owners for profit, electric light and power, new tramways and light railways are created in an increasing number of cases by public bodies who retain them for the public good. Nobody who travels to London as I do regularly in the dirty, over crowded carriages of the infrequent and unpunctual trains of the South Eastern Company, and who then transfers to the cleanly, speedy, frequent—in a word, "civilized" electric cars of the London County Council, can fail to estimate the value and significance of this supersession of the private owner by the common weal.

All these things, the Socialists insist, are but a beginning. They point to a new phase in social development, to the appearance of a collective intelligence and a sense of public service taking over appliances, powers, enterprises, with a growing confidence that must end finally in the substitution of collective for private ownership and enterprise throughout the whole area of the common business of life.

V

In relation to quite a number of large public services it can be shown that even under contemporary conditions Private Ownership does work with an enormous waste and inefficiency. Necessarily it seeks for profit; necessarily it seeks to do as little as possible for as much as possible. The prosperity of all Kent is crippled by a "combine" of two ill managed and unenterprising railway companies, with no funds for new developments, grinding out an uncertain dividend by clipping expenditure.

I happen to see this organization pretty closely, and I can imagine no State enterprise west of Turkey or Persia presenting even to the passing eye so deplorable a spectacle of ruin and inefficiency. The South Eastern Company's estate at Seabrook presents the dreariest spectacle of incompetent development conceivable; one can see its failure three miles away; it is a waste with an embryo slum in one corner protected by an extravagant sea wall, already partly shattered, from the sea.

To day (Nov. 4, 1907) the price of the ordinary South Eastern stock is 65 and its deferred stock 31; of the London, Chatham and Dover ordinary stock 10 1/2; an eloquent testimony to the disheartened state of the owners who now cling reluctantly to this disappointing monopoly. Spite of this impoverishment of the ordinary shareholder, this railway system has evidently paid too much profit in the past for efficiency; the rolling stock is old and ageing—much of it is by modern standards abominable—the trains are infrequent, and the shunting operations at local stations, with insufficient sidings and insufficient staffs, produce a chronic dislocation and unpunctuality in the traffic that is exaggerated by the defects of direction evident even in the very time tables. The trains are not well planned, the connections with branch lines are often extremely ill managed. The service is bad to its details. It is the exception rather than the rule to find a ticket office in the morning with change for a five pound note; and, as a little indication of the spirit of the whole machine, I discovered the other day that the conductors upon the South Eastern trams at Hythe start their morning with absolutely no change at all. Recently the roof of the station at Charing Cross fell in— through sheer decay.... A whole rich county now stagnates hopelessly under the grip of this sample of private enterprise, towns fail to grow, trade flows sluggishly from point to point. No population in the world would stand such a management as it endures at the hands of the South Eastern Railway from any responsible public body. Out would go the whole board of managers at the next election. Consider what would have happened if the London County Council had owned Charing Cross Station three years ago. But manifestly there is nothing better to be done under private ownership conditions. The common shareholders are scattered and practically powerless, and their collective aim is, at any expense to the public welfare, to keep the price of the shares from going still lower.

The South Eastern Railway is only one striking instance of the general unserviceableness of private ownership for public services. Nearly all the British railway companies, in greater or less degree, present now a similar degenerative process. Years of profit sweating, of high dividends, have left them with old stations, old rolling stock, old staffs, bad habits and diminishing borrowing power. Only a few of these corporations make any attempt to keep pace with invention. It is remarkable now in an epoch of almost universal progress how stagnant the British privately owned railways are. One travels now a days if anything with a decrease of comfort from the 1880 accommodation, because of the greater overcrowding; and there has been no general increase of speed, no increase in smooth running, no increase in immunity from accident now for quite a number of years. One travels in a dingy box of a compartment that is too ill lit at night for reading and full of invincible draughts. In winter the only warmth is too often an insufficient footwarmer of battered tin, for which the passengers fight fiercely with their feet. An observant person cannot fail to be struck— especially if he is returning from travel upon the State railways of Switzerland or Germany—by the shabby looking porters on so many of our lines—they represent the standard of good clothing for the year 1848 or thereabouts—and by the bleak misery of many of the stations, the universal dirt that electricity might even now abolish. You dare not drop a parcel on any British railway cushion for fear of the cloud of horrible dust you would raise; you have to put it down softly. Consider, too, the congested infrequent suburban trains that ply round any large centre of population, the inefficient goods and parcel distribution that hangs up the trade of the local shopman everywhere. Not only in the arrested standard of comfort, but in the efficiency of working also are our privately owned railways a hopeless discredit to private ownership.

None of them, hampered by their present equipment, are able to adapt themselves readily to the new and better mechanism science produces for them, electric traction, electric lighting and so forth; and it seems to me highly probable that the last steam engines and the last oil lamps in the world will be found upon the southern railway lines of Great Britain. How can they go on borrowing new capital with their stock at the prices I have quoted, and how can they do anything without new capital? The conception of profit raising that rules our railways takes rather an altogether different direction; it takes the form of attempts to procure a monopoly even of the minor traffic by resisting the development of light railways, and of keeping the standard of comfort, decency and cleanliness low. As for the vast social ameliorations that could be wrought now, and are urgently needed now, by redistributing population through enhanced and cheapened services scientifically planned, and by an efficient collection and carriage of horticultural and agricultural produce, these things lie outside the philosophy of the Private Owner altogether. They would probably not pay him, and there the matter ends; that they would pay the community enormously, does not for one moment enter into his circle of ideas.

There can be little doubt that in the next decade or so the secular decay and lagging of the British railway services which is inevitable under existing conditions (in speed, in comfort, they have long been distanced by continental lines), the probable increase in accidents due to economically administered permanent ways and ageing stations and bridges, and the ever more perceptible check to British economic development due to this clogging of the circulatory system, will be of immense value to the Socialist propaganda as an object lesson in private ownership. In Italy the thing has already passed its inevitable climax, and the State is now struggling valiantly to put a disorganized, ill equipped and undisciplined network of railways, the legacy of a period of private enterprise, into tolerable working order.

VI

In a second great public service there is a perceptible, a growing recognition of the evil and danger of allowing profit seeking Private Ownership to prevail; and that is the general food supply. A great quickening of the public imagination in this matter has occurred through the "boom" of Mr. Upton Sinclair's book, The Jungle—a book every student of the elements of Socialism should read. He accumulated a considerable mass of facts about the Chicago stockyards, and incorporated them with his story, and so enabled people to realize what they might with a little imaginative effort have inferred before; that the slaughtering of cattle and the preparation of meat, when it is done wholly and solely for profit, that is to say when it is done as rapidly and cheaply as possible, is done horribly; that it is a business cruel to the beasts, cruel to the workers and dangerous to the public health. The United States has long recognized the inadequacy of private consciences in this concern, and while all the vast profits of the business go to the meat packers, the community has maintained an insufficient supply of underpaid and, it is said in some cases, bribable inspectors to look after the public welfare.

In this country also, slaughtering is a private enterprise but slightly checked by inspection, and if we have no Chicago, we probably have all its mean savings, its dirt and carelessness and filth, scattered here and there all over the country, a little in this privately owned slaughter house, a little in that. For what inducement has a butcher to spend money and time in making his slaughter house decent, sanitary and humane above the standard of his fellows? To do that will only make him poor and insolvent. Anyhow, few of his customers will come to see their meat butchered, and, as they say in the South of England, "What the eye don't see the heart don't grieve."

Many witnesses concur in declaring that our common jam, pickle and preserve trade is carried on under equally filthy conditions. If it is not, it is a miracle, in view of the inducements the Private Owner has to cut his expenses, economize on premises and wages, and buy his fruit as near decay and his sugar as near dirt as he can. The scandal of our milk supply is an open one; it is more and more evident that so long as Private Ownership rules the milk trade, we can never be sure that at every point in the course of the milk from cow to consumer there will not creep in harmful and dishonest profit making elements. The milking is too often done dirtily from dirty cows and into dirty vessels—why should a business man fool away his profits in paying for scrupulous cleanliness when it is almost impossible to tell at sight whether milk is clean or dirty?—and there come more or less harmful dilutions and adulterations and exposures to infection at every handling, at every chance at profit making. The unavoidable inefficiency of the private milk trade reflects itself in infant mortality—we pay our national tribute to private enterprise in milk, a tribute of many thousands of babies every year. We try to reduce this tribute by inspection. But why should the State pay money for inspection, upon keeping highly trained and competent persons merely to pry and persecute in order that private incompetent people should reap profits with something short of a maximum of child murder? It would be much simpler to set to work directly, employ and train these private persons, and run the dairies and milk distribution ourselves.

There is an equally strong case for a public handling of bakehouses and the bread supply. Already the public is put to great and entirely unremunerative expense in inspecting and checking weights and hunting down the grosser instances of adulteration, grubbiness and dirt, and with it all the common bakehouse remains for the most part a subterranean haunt of rats, mice and cockroaches, and the ordinary baker's bread is so insipid and unnutritious that a great number of more prosperous people now a days find it advantageous to health and pocket alike to bake at home. A considerable amount of physical degeneration may be connected with the general poorness of our bread. The plain fact of the case is that our population will never get good wholesome bread from the Private Owner's bakehouse, until it employs one skilled official to watch every half dozen bakers—and another to watch him; and it seems altogether saner and cheaper to abolish the Private Owner in this business also and do the job cleanly, honestly and straightforwardly in proper buildings with properly paid labour as a public concern.

Now, what has been said of the food supply is still truer of the trade in fuel. Between the consumer and the collier is a string of private persons each resolved to squeeze every penny of profit out of the coal on its way to the cheap and wasteful grate one finds in the jerry built homes of the poor. In addition there is every winter now, whether in Great Britain or America, a manipulation of the coal market and a more or less severe coal famine. Coal is jerked up to unprecedented prices, and the small consumer, who has no place for storage, who must buy, if not from day to day, from week to week, finds he must draw upon his food fund and his savings to meet the Private Owner's raised demands—or freeze. Every such coal famine reaps its harvest for death of old people and young children, and wipes out so many thousands of savings' bank accounts and hoarded shillings. Consider the essential imbecility of allowing the nation's life and the nation's thrift to be preyed upon for profit in this way! Is it possible to doubt that the civilized community of the future will have to resume possession of all its stores of fuel, will keep itself informed of the fluctuating needs of its population, and will distribute and sell coal, gas and oil—not for the maximum profit, but the maximum general welfare?[6]

[6] In Dakota, 1906 7, private enterprise led to a particularly severe coal famine in the bitterest weather, and the shortage was felt so severely that the population rose and attacked and stopped passing coal trains.

Another great branch of trade in which Private Ownership and private freedom is manifestly antagonistic to the public welfare is the Drink Traffic. Here we have a commodity, essentially a drug, its use readily developing a vice, deleterious at its best, complex in composition, and particularly susceptible to adulteration and the enhancement of its attraction by poisonous ingredients and indeed to every sort of mischievous secret manipulation. Probably nothing is more rarely found pure and honest than beer or whisky; whisky begins to be blended and doctored before it leaves the distillery. And we allow the production and distribution of this drug of alcoholic drink to be from first to last a source of private profit. We so contrive it that we put money prizes upon the propaganda of drink. Is it any wonder that drink is not only made by adulteration far more evil than it naturally is, but that it is forced upon the public in every possible way?

"He tempts them to drink," I have heard a clergyman say of his village publican. But what else did he think the publican was there for?—to preach total abstinence? Naturally, inevitably, the whole of the Trade is a propaganda—not of drunkenness, but of habitual heavy drinking. The more successful propagandists, the great brewers and distillers grow rich just in the proportion that people consume beer and spirits; they gain honour and peerages in the measure of their success.

It is very interesting to the Socialist to trace the long struggle of the temperance movement against its initial ideas of freedom, and to see how inevitably the most reluctant and unlikely people have been forced to recognize Private Ownership in this trade and for profit as the ultimate evil. I am delighted to have to hand an excellent little tract by "A Ratepayer": National Efficiency and the Drink Traffic. It has a preface by Mr. Haldane, and it is as satisfactory a demonstration of the absolute necessity of thoroughgoing Socialism in this particular field as any Socialist could wish. One encounters the Bishop of Chester, for example, in its pages talking the purest Socialism, and making the most luminous admissions of the impossibility of continued private control, in phrases that need but a few verbal changes to apply equally to milk, to meat, to bread, to housing, to book selling[7]....

[7] For a clear and admirable account of the Socialist attitude to the temperance question, see the tract on Municipal Drink Traffic published by the Fabian Society; price one penny.

VII

Land and housing, railways, food, drink, coal, in each of these great general interests there is a separate strong case for the substitution of collective control for the Private Ownership methods of the present time. There is a great and growing number of people like "A Ratepayer" and Mr. Haldane, who do not call themselves Socialists but who are yet strongly tinged with Socialist conceptions; who are convinced—some in the case of the land, some in the case of the drink trade or the milk, that Private Ownership and working for profit must cease. But they will not admit a general principle, they argue each case on its merits.

The Socialist maintains that, albeit the details of each problem must be studied apart, there does underlie all these cases and the whole economic situation at the present time, one general fact, that through our whole social system from top to base we find things under the influence of a misleading idea that must be changed, and which, until it is changed, will continue to work out in waste, unserviceableness, cramped lives and suffering and death. Each man is for himself, that is this misleading idea, seeking, perforce, ends discordant with the general welfare; who serves the community without exacting pay, goes under; who exacts pay without service prospers and continues; success is not to do well, it is to have and to get; failure is not to do ill, it is to lose and not have; and under these conditions how can we expect anything but dislocated, unsatisfying service at every turn?

The contemporary anti Socialist moralist and the social satirist would appeal to the Owner's sense of duty; he would declare in a platitudinous tone that property had its duties as well as its rights, and so forth. The Socialist, however, looks a little deeper, and puts the thing differently. He brings both rights and duties to a keener scrutiny. What underlies all these social disorders, he alleges, is one simple thing, a misconception of property; an unreasonable exaggeration, an accumulated, inherited exaggeration, of the idea of property. He says the idea of private property, which is just and reasonable in relation to intimate personal things, to clothes, appliances, books, one's home or apartments, the garden one loves or the horse one rides, has become unreasonably exaggerated until it obsesses the world; that the freedom we have given men to claim and own and hold the land upon which we must live, the fuel we burn, the supplies of food and metal we require, the railways and ships upon which our business goes, and to fix what prices they like to exact for all these services, leads to the impoverishment and practical enslavement of the mass of mankind.

And so he comes to his second main generalization, which I may perhaps set out in these words:—

The idea of the private ownership of things and the rights of owners is enormously and mischievously exaggerated in the contemporary world. The conception of private property has been extended to land, to material, to the values and resources accumulated by past generations, to a vast variety of things that are properly the inheritance of the whole race. As a result of this, there is much obstruction and waste of human energy and a huge loss of opportunity and freedom for the mass of mankind; progress is retarded, there is a vast amount of avoidable wretchedness, cruelty and injustice.

The Socialist holds that the community as a whole should be inalienably the owner and administrator of the land, of raw materials, of values and resources accumulated from the past, and that private property must be of a terminable nature, reverting to the community, and subject to the general welfare.

This is the second of the twin generalizations upon which the edifice of modern Socialism rests. Like the first, and like the practical side of all sound religious teaching, it is a specific application of one general rule of conduct, and that is the subordination of the individual motive to the happiness and welfare of the species.

VIII

But now the reader unaccustomed to Socialist discussion will begin to see the crude form of the answer to the question raised by the previous chapter; he will see the resources from which the enlargement of human life we there contemplated is to be derived, and realize the economic methods to be pursued. Collective ownership is the necessary corollary of collective responsibility. There are to be no private land owners, no private bankers and lenders of money, no private insurance adventurers, no private railway owners nor shipping owners, no private mine owners, oil kings, silver kings, coal and wheat forestallers or the like. All this realm of property is to be resumed by the State, is to be State owned and State managed, and the vast revenues that are now devoted to private ends will go steadily to feed, maintain and educate a new and better generation, to promote research and advance science, to build new houses, develop fresh resources, plant, plan, beautify and reconstruct the world.

CHAPTER V

THE SPIRIT OF GAIN AND THE SPIRIT OF SERVICE

I

We have stated now how the constructive plan of Socialism aims to replace the accepted ideas about two almost fundamental human relations by broader and less fiercely egotistical conceptions; how it denies a man "property" rights over his wife and children, leaving, however, all his other relations with them intact, how it would insure and protect their welfare, and how it asserts that a vast range of inanimate things also which are now held as private property must be regarded as the inalienable possession of the whole community. This change in the circle of ideas (as the Herbartians put it) is the essence of the Socialist project.

It means no little change. It means a general change in the spirit of living; it means a change from the spirit of gain (which now necessarily rules our lives) to the spirit of service.

I have tried to show in the preceding chapter that Socialism seeks to make life less squalid and cruel, less degrading and dwarfing for the children that are born into it, and I have tried also to make clear that realization of, and revolt against, the bad management and waste and muddle which result from our present economic system. I want now to point out that Socialism seeks to ennoble the intimate personal life, by checking and discouraging passions that at present run rampant, and by giving wider scope for passions that are now thwarted and subdued. The Socialist declares that life is now needlessly dishonest, base and mean, because our present social organization, such as it is, makes an altogether too powerful appeal to some of the very meanest elements in our nature.

Not perhaps to the lowest. There can be no disputing that our present civilization does discourage much of the innate bestiality of man; that it helps people to a measure of continence, cleanliness and mutual toleration; that it does much to suppress brute violence, the spirit of lawlessness, cruelty and wanton destruction. But on the other hand it does also check and cripple generosity and frank truthfulness, any disinterested creative passion, the love of beauty, the passion for truth and research, and it stimulates avarice, parsimony, overreaching, usury, falsehood and secrecy, by making money getting its criterion of intercourse.

Whether we like it or not, we who live in this world to day find we must either devote a considerable amount of our attention to getting and keeping money, and shape our activities—or, if you will, distort them—with a constant reference to that process, or we must accept futility. Whatever powers men want to exercise, whatever service they wish to do, it is a preliminary condition for most of them that they must, by earning something or selling something, achieve opportunity. If they cannot turn their gift into some saleable thing or get some propertied man to "patronize" them, they cannot exercise these gifts. The gift for getting is the supreme gift—all others bow before it.

Now this is not a thing that comes naturally out of the quality of man; it is the result of a blind and complex social growth, of this set of ideas working against that, and of these influences modifying those. The idea of property has run wild and become a choking universal weed. It is not the natural master passion of a wholesome man to want constantly to own. People talk of Socialism as being a proposal "against human nature," and they would have us believe that this life of anxiety, of parsimony and speculation, of mercenary considerations and forced toil we all lead, is the complete and final expression of the social possibilities of the human soul. But, indeed, it is only quite abnormal people, people of a narrow, limited, specialized intelligence, Rockefellers, Morgans and the like, people neither great nor beautiful, mere financial monomaniacs, who can keep themselves devoted to and concentrated upon gain. To the majority of capable good human stuff, buying and selling, saving and investing, insuring oneself and managing property, is a mass of uncongenial, irrational and tiresome procedure, conflicting with the general trend of instinct and the finer interests of life. The great mass of men and women, indeed, find the whole process so against nature, that in spite of all the miseries of poverty, all the slavery of the economic disadvantage, they cannot urge themselves to this irksome cunning game of besting the world, they remain poor. Most, in a sort of despair, make no effort; many resort to that floundering endeavour to get by accident, gambling; many achieve a precarious and unsatisfactory gathering of possessions, a few houses, a claim on a field, a few hundred pounds in some investment as incalculable as a kite in a gale; just a small minority have and get—for the most part either inheritors of riches or energetic people who, through a real dulness toward the better and nobler aspects of life, can give themselves almost entirely to grabbing and accumulation. To such as these, all common men who are not Socialists do in effect conspire to give the world.

The Anti Socialist argues that out of this evil of encouraged and stimulated avarice comes good, and that this peculiar meanly greedy type that predominates in the individualist world to day, the Rockefeller Harriman type, "creates" great businesses, exploits the possibilities of nature, gives mankind railways, power, commodities. As a matter of fact, a modern intelligent community is quite capable of doing all these things infinitely better for itself, and the beneficent influence of commerce may easily become, and does easily become, the basis of a cant. Exploitation by private persons is no doubt a necessary condition to economic development in an illiterate community of low intelligence, just as flint implements marked a necessary phase in the social development of mankind; but to day the avaricious getter, like some obsolescent organ in the body, consumes strength and threatens health. And to day he is far more mischievous than ever he was before, because of the weakened hold of the old religious organization upon his imagination. For the most part the great fortunes of the modern world have been built up by proceedings either not socially beneficial, or in some cases positively harmful. Consider some of the commoner methods of growing rich. There is first the selling of rubbish for money, exemplified by the great patent medicine fortunes and the fortunes achieved by the debasement of journalism, the sale of prize competition magazines and the like; next there is forestalling, the making of "corners" in such commodities as corn, nitrates, borax and the like; then there is the capture of what Americans call "franchises," securing at low terms by expedients that usually will not bear examination, the right to run some profitable public service for private profit which would be better done in public hands—the various private enterprises for urban traffic, for example; then there are the various more or less complex financial operations, watering stock, "reconstructing," "shaking out" the ordinary shareholder, which transfer the savings of the common struggling person to the financial magnate. All the activities in this list are more or less anti social, yet it is by practising them that the great successes of recent years have been achieved. Fortunes of a second rank have no doubt been made by building up manufactures and industries of various types by persons who have known how to buy labour cheap, organize it well and sell its produce dear, but even in these cases the social advantage of the new product is often largely discounted by the labour conditions. It is impossible, indeed, directly one faces current facts, to keep up the argument of the public good achieved by men under the incentive of gain and the necessity of that incentive to progress and economic development.

Now not only is it true that the subordination of our affairs to this spirit of gain placed our world in the hands of a peculiar, acquisitive, uncreative, wary type of person, and that the mass of people hate serving the spirit of gain and are forced to do so through the obsession of the whole community by this idea of Private Ownership, but it is also true that even now the real driving force that gets the world along is not that spirit at all, but the spirit of service. Even to day it would be impossible for the world to get along if the mass of its population was really specialized for gain. A world of Rockefellers, Morgans and Rothschilds would perish miserably after a vigorous campaign of mutual skinning; it is only because the common run of men is better than these profit hunters that any real and human things are achieved.

Let us go into this aspect of the question a little more fully, because it is one that appears to be least clearly grasped by those who discuss Socialism to day.

II

This fact must be insisted upon, that most of the work of the world and all the good work is done to day for some other motive than gain; that profit seeking not only is not the moving power of the world but that it cannot be, that it runs counter to the doing of effectual work in every department of life.

It is hard to know how to set about proving a fact that is to the writer's perception so universally obvious. One can only appeal to the intelligent reader to use his own personal observation upon the people about him. Everywhere he will see the property owner doing nothing, the profit seeker busy with unproductive efforts, with the writing of advertisements, the misrepresentation of goods, the concoction of a plausible prospectus and the extraction of profits from the toil of others, while the real necessary work of the world—I don't mean the labour and toil only, but the intelligent direction, the real planning and designing and inquiry, the management and the evolution of ideas and methods, is in the enormous majority of cases done by salaried individuals working either for a fixed wage and the hope of increments having no proportional relation to the work done, or for a wage varying within definite limits. All the engineering design, all architecture, all our public services,—the exquisite work of our museum control, for example,—all the big wholesale and retail businesses, almost all big industrial concerns, mines, estates, all these things are really in the hands of salaried or quasi salaried persons now—just as they would be under Socialism. They are only possible now because all these managers, officials, employees are as a class unreasonably honest and loyal, are interested in their work and anxious to do it well, and do not seek profits in every transaction they handle. Give them even a small measure of security and they are content with interesting work; they are glad to set aside the urgent perpetual search for personal gain that Individualists have persuaded themselves is the ruling motive of mankind, they are glad to set these aside altogether and, as the phrase goes, "get something done." And this is true all up and down the social scale. A bricklayer is no good unless he can be interested in laying bricks. One knows whenever a domestic servant becomes mercenary, when she ceases to take, as people say, "a pride in her work," and thinks only of "tips" and getting, she becomes impossible. Does a signalman every time he pulls over a lever, or a groom galloping a horse, think of his wages,—or want to?

I will confess I find it hard to write with any patience and civility of this argument that humanity will not work except for greed or need of money and only in proportion to the getting. It is so patently absurd. I suppose the reasonable Anti Socialist will hardly maintain it seriously with that crudity. He will qualify. He will say that although it may be true that good work is always done for the interest of the doing or in the spirit of service, yet in order to get and keep people at work, and to keep the standard high through periods of indolence and distraction, there must be the dread of dismissal and the stimulating eye of the owner. That certainly puts the case a good deal less basely and much more plausibly.

There is, perhaps, this much truth in that, that most people do need a certain stimulus to exertion and a certain standard of achievement to do their best, but to say that this is provided by private ownership and can only be provided by private ownership is an altogether different thing. Is the British Telephone Service, for example, kept as efficient as it is—which isn't very much, by the bye, in the way of efficiency—by the protests of the shareholders or of the subscribers? Does the grocer's errand boy loiter any less than his brother who carries the Post Office telegrams? In the matter of the public milk supply, again, would not an intelligently critical public anxious for its milk good and early be a far more formidable master than a speculative proprietor in the back room of a creamery? And when one comes to large business organizations managed by officials and owned by dispersed shareholders, the contrast is all to the advantage of the community.

No! the only proper virtues in work, the virtues that must be relied upon, and developed and rewarded in the civilized State we Socialists are seeking to bring about, are the spirit of service and the passion for doing well, the honourable competition not to get but to do. By sweating and debasing urgency, we get meagrely done what we might get handsomely done by the Good Will of emancipated mankind. For all who really make, who really do, the imperative of gain is the inconvenience, the enemy. Every artist, every scientific investigator, every organizer, every good workman, knows that. Every good architect knows that this is so and can tell of time after time when he has sacrificed manifest profit and taken a loss to get a thing done as he wanted it done, right and well; every good doctor, too, has turned from profit and high fees to the moving and interesting case, to the demands of knowledge and the public health; every teacher worth his or her salt can witness to the perpetual struggle between business advantage and right teaching; every writer has faced the alternative of his æsthetic duty and the search for beauty on one hand and the "saleable" on the other. All this is as true of ordinary making as of special creative work. Every plumber capable of his business hates to have to paint his leadwork; every carpenter knows the disgust of turning out unfinished "cheap" work, however well it pays him; every tolerable cook can feel shame for an unsatisfying dish, and none the less shame because by making it materials are saved and economies achieved.

And yet, with all these facts clear as day before any observant person, we are content to live on in an economic system that raises every man who subordinates these wholesome prides and desires to watchful, incessant getting, over the heads of every other type of character; that in effect gives all the power and influence in our State to successful getters; that subordinates art, direction, wisdom and labour to these inferior narrow men, these men who clutch and keep.

Our social system, based on Private Ownership, encourages and glorifies this spirit of gain, and cripples and thwarts the spirit of service. You need but have your eyes once opened to its influence, and thereafter you will never cease to see how the needs and imperatives of property taint the honour and dignity of human life. Just where life should flower most freely into splendour, this chill, malign obsession most nips and cripples. The law that makes getting and keeping an imperative necessity poisons and destroys the freedom of men and women in love, in art and in every concern in which spiritual or physical beauty should be the inspiring and determining factor. Behind all the handsome professions of romantic natures the gaunt facts of monetary necessity remain the rulers of life. Every youth who must sell his art and capacity for gain, every girl who must sell herself for money, is one more sacrifice to the Minotaur of Private Ownership—before the Theseus of Socialism comes.

Opponents of Socialism, ignoring all these things and inventing with that profusion which is so remarkable a trait of the anti Socialist campaign, are wont to declare that we, whose first and last thought is the honour and betterment of life, seek to destroy all beauty and freedom in love, accuse us of aiming at some "human stud farm." The reader will measure the justice of that by the next chapter, but here I would say that just as the private ownership of all that is necessary to humanity, except the air and sunlight and a few things that it has been difficult to appropriate, debases work and all the common services of life, so also it taints and thwarts the emotions, and degrades the intimate physical and emotional existence of an innumerable multitude of people.

All this amounts to a huge impoverishment of life, a loss of beauty and discrimination of rich and subtle values. Human existence to day is a mere tantalizing intimation of what it might be. It is frostbitten and dwarfed from palace to slum. It is not only that a great mass of our population is deprived of space, beauty and pleasure, but that a large proportion of such space, beauty and pleasure as there are in the world must necessarily have a meretricious taint and be in the nature of things bought and made for pay.

III

If there is one profession more than another in which devotion is implied and assumed, it is that of the doctor. It happens that on the morning when this chapter was drafted, I came upon the paragraph that follows; it seemed to me to supply just one striking concrete instance of how life is degraded by our present system, and to offer me a convenient text for a word or so more upon this question between gain and service. It is a little vague in its reference to Mr. Tompkins "of Birmingham," and I should not be surprised if it were a considerable exaggeration of what really happened. But it is true enough to life in this, that it is a common practice, a necessity with doctors in poor neighbourhoods to insist inexorably upon a fee before attendance.

"A case of medical inhumanity is reported from Birmingham. A poor man named Tompkins was taken seriously ill early on Christmas morning, and although snow was falling and the atmosphere was terribly raw, his wife left the house in search of a doctor. The nearest practitioner declined to leave the house without being paid his fee; a second imposed the same condition, and the woman then went to the police station. As the horse ambulance was out, they could not help her, and she tried other doctors. In all the poor woman called on eight, and the only one who did not decline to get up without his fee was down with influenza. Eventually a local chemist was persuaded to see the man, and he ordered his removal to the hospital."

That is the story. You note the charge of "inhumanity" in the very first line, and in much subsequent press comment there was the same note. Apparently every one expects a doctor to be ready at any point in the day or night to attend anybody for nothing. Most Socialists are disposed to agree with the spirit of that expectation. A practising doctor should be in lifelong perpetual war against pain and disease, just as a campaigning soldier is continually alert and serving. But existing conditions will not permit that. Existing conditions require the doctor to get his fee at any cost; if he goes about doing work for nothing, they punish him with shabbiness and incapacitating need, they forbid his marriage or doom his wife and children to poverty and unhappiness. A doctor must make money whatever else he does or does not do; he must secure his fees. He is a private adventurer, competing in a crowded market for gain, and keeping his energies perforce for those who can pay best for them. To expect him to behave like a public servant whose income and outlook are secure, or like a priest whose church will never let him want or starve, is ridiculous. If you put him on a footing with the greengrocer and coal merchant, you must expect him to behave like a tradesman. Why should the press blame the poor doctor of a poor neighbourhood because a moneyless man goes short of medical attendance, when it does not for one moment blame Mr. J. D. Rockefeller because a poor man goes short of oil, or the Duke of Devonshire because tramps need lodgings in Eastbourne? One never reads this sort of paragraph:—

"A case of commercial inhumanity is reported from Birmingham. A poor man named Tompkins was seriously hungry early on Christmas morning, and although snow was falling and the atmosphere was terribly raw, his wife left the house in search of food. The nearest grocer declined to supply provisions without being paid his price; a second imposed the same condition, and the woman then went to the police station. As that is not a soup kitchen, they could not help her, and she tried other grocers and bread shops. In all the poor woman called on eight, and the only one who did not decline to supply food without payment was for some reason bankrupt and out of stock. Eventually a local overseer was persuaded to see the man, and he ordered his removal to the workhouse, where, after considerable hardship, he was partly appeased with skilly."

I, myself, have known an overworked, financially worried doctor at his bedroom window call out, "Have you brought the fee?" and have pitied and understood his ugly alternatives. "Once I began that sort of thing," he explained to me a little apologetically, "they'd none of them pay—none."

The Socialist's remedy for this squalid state of affairs is plain and simple. Medicine is a public service, an honourable devotion; it should no more be a matter of profit making than the food supply service or the house supply service—or salvation. It should be a part of the organization of a civilized State to have a Public Health service of well paid, highly educated men distributed over the country and closely correlated with public research departments and a reserve of specialists, who would be as ready and eager to face dangers and to sacrifice themselves for honour and social necessity as soldiers or sailors. I believe every honourable man in the medical profession under forty now would rather it were so. It is, indeed, a transition from private enterprise to public organization that is already beginning. We have the first intimation of the change in the appearance of the medical officer of health, underpaid, overworked and powerless though he is at the present time. It cannot be long before the manifest absurdity of our present conditions begins a process of socialization of the medical profession entirely analogous to that which has changed three fourths of the teachers in Great Britain from private adventurers to public servants in the last forty years.

And that is the aim of Socialism all along the line; to convert one public service after another from a chaotic profit scramble of proprietors amidst a mass of sweated employees into a secure and disciplined service, in which every man will work for honour, promotion, achievement and the commonweal.

I write a "secure and disciplined service," and I intend by that not simply an exterior but an interior discipline. Let us have done with this unnatural theory that men may submit unreservedly to the guidance of "self interest." Self interest never took a man or a community to any other end than damnation. For all services there is necessary a code of honour and devotion which a man must set up for himself and obey, to which he must subordinate a number of his impulses. The must is seconded by an internal imperative. Men and women want to have a code of honour. In the army, for example, there is among the officers particularly, a tradition of courage, cleanliness and good form, more imperative than any law; in the little band of men who have given the world all that we mean by science, the little host of volunteers and underpaid workers who have achieved the triumphs of research, there is a tradition of self abnegation and of an immense, painstaking, self forgetful veracity. These traditions work. They add something to the worth of every man who comes under them.

Every writer, again, knows clearly the difference between gain seeking and doing good work, and few there are who have not at times done something, as they say, "to please themselves." Then in the studio, for all the non moral protests of Bohemia, there is a tradition, an admirable tradition, of disregard for mercenary imperatives, a scorn of shams and plagiarism that triumphs again and again over economic laws. The public services of the coming civilization will demand, and will develop, a far completer discipline and tradition of honour. Against the development and persistence of all such honourable codes now, against every attempt at personal nobility, at a new chivalry, at sincere artistry, our present individualist system wages pitiless warfare, says in effect, "Fools you are! Look at Rockefeller! Look at Pierpont Morgan! Get money! All your sacrifices only go to their enrichment.

You cannot serve humanity however much you seek to do so. They block your way, enormously receptive of all you give. All the increment of human achievement goes to them—they own it a priori.... Get money! Money is freedom to do, to keep, to rule. Do you care nothing for your wives and children? Are you content to breed servants and dependants for the children of these men? Make things beautiful, make things abundant, make life glorious! Fools! if you work and sacrifice yourselves and do not get, they will possess. Your sons shall be the loan monger's employees, your daughters handmaidens to the millionaire. Or, if you cannot face that, go childless, and let your life work gild the palace of the millionaire's still more acquisitive descendants!"

Who can ignore the base scramble for money under these alternatives?

IV

Let me here insert a very brief paragraph to point out one particular thing, and that is that Socialism does not propose to "abolish competition"—as many hasty and foolish antagonists declare. If the reader has gone through what has preceded this he will know that this is not so. Socialism trusts to competition, looks to competition for the service and improvement of the world. And in order that competition between man and man may have free play, Socialism seeks to abolish one particular form of competition, the competition to get and hold property—even to marry property, that degrades our present world. But it would leave men free to compete for fame, for service, for salaries, for position and authority, for leisure, for love and honour.

V

And now let me take up certain difficulties the student of Socialism encounters. He comes thus far perhaps with the Socialist argument, and then his imagination gets to work trying to picture a world in which a moiety of the population, perhaps even the larger moiety, is employed by the State, and in which the whole population is educated by the State and insured of a decent and comfortable care and subsistence during youth and old age. He then begins to think of how all this vast organization is to be managed, and with that his real difficulties begin.

Now I for one am prepared to take these difficulties very seriously, as the latter part of this book will show. I will even go so far as to say that, to my mind, the contemporary Socialist controversialist meets all this system of objections far too cavalierly. These difficulties are real difficulties for the convinced Socialist as for the inquirer; they open up problems that have still to be solved before the equipment of Socialism is complete. "How will you Socialists get the right men in the right place for the work that has to be done? How will you arrange promotion? How will you determine" (I put the argument in its crudest form) "who is to engage in historical research in the Bodleian, and who is to go out seaward in November and catch mackerel?" Such "posers"—they have a thousand variants—convey the spirit of the living resistance to Socialism; they explain why every rational man is not an enraptured Socialist at the present time.

Throughout the rest of this book I hope that the reader will be able to see growing together in this aspect and then in that, in this and that suggestion, the complex solution of this complex system of difficulties. My object in raising them now is not to dispose of them, but to give them the fullest recognition—and to ask the student to read on. In all these matters the world is imperfect now, and it will still be imperfect under Socialism—though, I firmly believe, with an infinitely lesser and altogether nobler imperfection.

But I do want to point out here that though these are reasonable and, to all undogmatic men, most helpful criticisms of the Socialist design, they are no sort of justification for things as they are. All the difficulties that the ordinary exposition of Socialism seems to leave unsolved are at least equally not solved now. Only rarely does the right man seem to struggle to his place of adequate opportunity. Men and women get their chance in various ways; some of implacable temper and versatile gifts thrust themselves to the position they need for the exercise of their powers; others display an astonishing facility in securing honours and occasions they can then only waste; others, outside their specific gift, are the creatures of luck or the victims of modesty, tactlessness or incapacity. Most of the large businesses of the world now are in the hands of private proprietors and managed either directly by an owner or by directors or managers acting for directors. The quality of promotion or the recognition of capacity varies very much in these great concerns, but they are on the whole probably inferior to the public services. Even where the administration is keenest it must be remembered it is not seeking the men who work the machine best, but the men who can work it cheapest and with the maximum of profit. It is pure romancing to represent the ordinary business magnate as being in perpetual search for capacity among the members of his staff. He wants them to get along and not make trouble.

Among the smaller businesses that still, I suppose, constitute the bulk of the world's economic body, capacity is enormously hampered. I was once an apprentice in a chemist's shop, and also once in a draper's—two of my brothers have been shop assistants, and so I am still able to talk understandingly with clerks and employees, and I know that in all that world all sorts of minor considerations obstruct the very beginnings of efficient selection. Every shop is riddled with jealousies, "sucking up to the gov'nor" is the universal crime, and among the women in many callings promotion is too often tainted by still baser suspicions. No doubt in a badly criticized public service there is such a thing as "sucking up to" the head of the department, but at its worst it is not nearly so bad as things may be in a small private concern under a petty autocrat.

In America it is said that the public services are inferior in personal quality to the staffs of the great private business organizations. My own impression is that, considering the salaries paid, they are, so far as Federal concerns go, immeasurably superior. In State and municipal affairs, American conditions offer no satisfactory criterion; the Americans are, for reasons I have discussed elsewhere,[8] a "State blind" people concentrated upon private getting; they have been negligent of public concerns, and the public appointments have been left to the peculiarly ruffianly type of politician their unfortunate Constitution and their individualist traditions have evolved. In England, too, public servants are systematically undersalaried, so that the big businesses have merely to pay reasonably well to secure the pick of the national capacity. Moreover, it must be remembered by the reader that the public services do not advertise, and that the private businesses do; so that while there is the fullest ventilation of any defects in our military or naval organization, there is a very considerable check upon the discussion of individualist incapacity. An editor will rush into print with the flimsiest imputations upon the breech of a new field gun or the housing of the militia at Aldershot, but he thinks twice before he proclaims that the preserved fruits that pay his proprietor a tribute of some hundreds a year are an unwholesome embalmment of decay. On the whole it is probable that in spite of scandalously bad pay and of the embarrassment of party considerations, the British Navy, Post Office, and Civil Service generally, and the educational work and much of the transit and building work of the London County Council and of many of the greater English and Scotch municipalities, are as well managed as any private businesses in the world.

[8] *The Future in America, Ch. IX. (Chapman & Hall, 1906.)*

On the other hand, one must admit there are political and social conditions that can carry the quality of the State service almost as low as the lowest type of private enterprise. It is little marvel that under the typical eighteenth century monarchy, when the way to ship, regiment and the apostolic succession alike lay through the ante chamber of the king's mistress, there was begotten that absolute repudiation of State Control to which Herbert Spencer was destined at last to give the complete expression, that irrational, passionate belief that whatever else is right the State is necessarily incompetent and wrong....

The gist of this matter seems to be that where you have honourable political institutions, free speech and a general high level of intelligence and education, you will have an efficient criticism of men and their work and powers, and you will get a wholesome system of public promotion and many right men in the right place. The higher the collective intelligence, that is to say, the higher is the collective possibility. Under Socialist institutions which will give education and a sense of personal security to every one, this necessity of criticism is likely to be most freely, frankly and disinterestedly provided. But it is well to keep in mind the entire dependence of Socialism upon a high level of intelligence, education and freedom. Socialist institutions, as I understand them, are only possible in a civilized State, in a State in which the whole population can read, write, discuss, participate and in a considerable measure understand. Education must precede the Socialist State. Socialism, modern Socialism that is to say, such as I am now concerned with, is essentially an exposition of and training in certain general ideas; it is impossible in an illiterate community, a basely selfish community, or in a community without the capacity to use the machinery and the apparatus of civilization. At the best, and it is a poor best, a stupid, illiterate population can but mock Socialism with a sort of bureaucratic tyranny; for a barbaric population too large and various for the folk meeting, there is nothing but monarchy and the ownership of the king; for a savage tribe, tradition and the undocumented will of the strongest males. Socialism, I will admit, presupposes intelligence, and demands as fundamental necessities schools, organized science, literature and a sense of the State.

CHAPTER VI

WOULD SOCIALISM DESTROY THE HOME?

I

For reasons that will become clearer when we tell something of the early history and development of Socialism, the Socialist propositions with regard to the family lie open to certain grave misconceptions. People are told—and told quite honestly and believingly—that Socialism will destroy the home, will substitute a sort of human stud farm for that warm and intimate nest of human life, will bring up our children in incubators and crèches and—Institutions generally.

But before we come to what modern Socialists do desire in these matters, it may be well to consider something of the present reality of the home people are so concerned about. The reader must not idealize. He must not shut his eyes to facts, dream, as Lord Hugh Cecil and Lord Robert Cecil—those admirable champions of a bad cause—probably do, of a beautiful world of homes, orderly, virtuous, each a little human fastness, each with its porch and creeper, each with its books and harmonium, its hymn singing on Sunday night, its dear mother who makes such wonderful cakes, its strong and happy father—and then say, "These wicked Socialists want to destroy all this." Because, in the first place, such homes are being destroyed and made impossible now by the very causes against which Socialism fights, and because in this world at the present time very few homes are at all like this ideal. In reality every poor home is haunted by the spectre of irregular employment and undermined by untrustworthy insurance, it must shelter in insanitary dwellings and its children eat adulterated food because none other can be got. And that, I am sorry to say, it is only too easy to prove, by a second appeal to a document of which I have already made use.

One hears at times still of the austere, virtuous, kindly, poor Scotch home, one has a vision of the "Cottar's Saturday night." "Perish all other dreams," one cries, "rather than that such goodness and simplicity should end." But now let us look at the average poor Scotch home, and compare it with our dream.

Here is the reality.

These entries come from the recently published Edinburgh Charity Organization Society's report upon the homes of about fourteen hundred school children, that is to say, about eight hundred Scotch homes. Remember they are sample homes. They are, as I have already suggested by quoting authorities for London and York—and as any district visitor will recognize—little worse and little better than the bulk of poor people's homes in Scotland and England at the present time. I am just going to copy down—not a selection, mind—but a series of consecutive entries taken haphazard from this implacable list. My last quotation was from cases 1, 2, 3 and so on; I've now thrust my fingers among the pages and come upon numbers 191 and 192, etc. Here they are, one after the other, just as they come in the list:—

"191. A widow and child lodging with a married son. Three grown up people and three children occupy one room and bed closet. The widow leads a wandering life, and is intemperate. The house is thoroughly bad and insanitary. The child is pallid and delicate looking, and receives little attention, for the mother is usually out working. He plays in the streets. Five children are dead. Boy has glands and is fleabitten. Evidence from Police, School Officer and Employer.

"192. A miserable home. Father dead. Mother and eldest son careless and indifferent. Of the five children, the two eldest are grown up. The elder girl is working, and she is of a better type and might do well under better circumstances; she looks overworked. The mother is supposed to char; she gets parish relief, and one child earns out of school hours. Four children are dead. The children at school are dirty and ragged. The mother could get work if she did not drink. The children at school get free dinners and clothing, and the family is favourably reported on by the Church. The second child impetigo; neck glands; body dirty. The third, glands; dirty and fleabitten. Housing: six in two small rooms. Evidence from Parish Sister, Parish Council, School Charity, Police, Teacher, Children's Employment and School Officer.

"193. A widow, apparently respectable and well doing, but may drink. She must in any case have a struggle to maintain her family, though she has much help from Parish, Church, etc. She works out. The children at school are fed, and altogether a large amount of charity must be received, as two Churches have interested themselves in the matter. Three children dead. Housing: three in two tiny rooms. Evidence from Church, Parish Council, School Charity, Police, Parish Sister, Teacher, Insurance and Factor.

"194. The father drinks, and, to a certain extent, the mother; but the home is tidy and clean, and the rent is regularly paid. Indeed, there is no sign of poverty. There is a daughter who has got into trouble. Only two children out of nine are alive. The father comes from the country and seems intelligent enough, but he appears to have degenerated. They go to a mission, it is believed for what they can get from it. Housing: four in two rooms. Evidence from Club, Church, Factor and Police.

"195. The husband is intemperate. The mother is quiet, but it is feared that she drinks also. She seems to have lost control of her little boy of seven. The parents married very young, and the first child was born before the marriage. The man's work is not regular, and probably things are not improving with him. Still, the house is fairly comfortable, and they pay club money regularly, and have a good police report. One child has died. Housing: five in two rooms. Evidence from Parish Sister, Police, Club, Employer, School mistress and Factor.

"196. A filthy, dirty house. The most elementary notions of cleanliness seem disregarded. The father's earnings are not large, and the house is insanitary, but more might be made of things if there were sobriety and thrift. There does not, however, appear to be great drunkenness, and five small children must be difficult to bring up on the money coming in. There are two women in the house. The eldest child dirty and fleabitten. Housing: seven in two rooms. Evidence from Police, Club, Employer, School mistress and School Officer.

"197. The parents are thoroughly drunken and dissolute. They have sunk almost to the lowest depths of social degradation. There is no furniture in the house, and the five children are neglected and starved. One boy earns a trifle out of school hours. All accounts agree as to the character of the father and mother, though they have not been in the hands of the police. Second child has rickets, bronchitis, slight glands and is bow legged. Two children have died. Housing: seven in two rooms. Evidence from Police, Parish Sister, Employer and School mistress.

"198. This house is fairly comfortable, and there is no evidence of drink, but the surroundings have a bad and depressing effect on the parents. The children are sent to school very untidy and dirty, and are certainly underfed. The father's wages are very small, and only one boy is working; there are six altogether. The mother chars occasionally. Food and clothing is given to school children. The man is in a saving club. The eldest child fleabitten; body unwashed. The second, glands; fleabitten and dirty; cretinoid; much undergrown. Two have died. Housing: seven in two rooms. Evidence from School Charity, Factor, Police and School mistress.

"199. The house was fairly comfortable and the man appeared to be intelligent and the wife hard working, but the police reports are very bad; there are several convictions against the former. He has consequently been idle, and the burden of the family has rested on the wife. There are six children, two of them are working and earning a little, but a large amount of charity from school, church and private generosity keeps the family going. The children are fearfully verminous. There is a suggestion that some baby farming is done, so many are about. Eldest child anæmic; glands; head badly crusted; lice very bad. Second child, numerous glands; head covered with crusts; lice very bad. Four have died. Housing: eight in two rooms. Evidence from Police, Teacher, Church, Parish Sister and Factor.

"200. The home is wretched and practically without furniture. The parents were married at ages 17 and 18. One child died, and their mode of life has been reckless, if not worse. The present means of subsistence cannot be ascertained, as the man is idle; however, he recently joined the Salvation Army and signed the pledge. The child at school is helped with food and clothes. The girl very badly bitten; lice and fleas, hair nits. Housing: four in one room. Evidence from Church, School Charity, Co operative, Employer, Parish Sister, Police and School mistress."

Total of children still living, 39.

Total of children dead, 27.

Need I go on? They are all after this fashion, eight hundred of them.

And if you turn from the congested town to the wholesome, simple country, here is the sort of home you have. This passage is a cutting from the Daily News of Jan. 1, 1907; and its assertions have never been contradicted. It fills one with only the mildest enthusiasm for the return of our degenerate townsmen "back to the land." I came upon it as I read that morning's paper after drafting this chapter.

"Our attention has been called to a sordid Herefordshire tragedy recently revealed at an inquest on a child aged one year and nine months, who died in Weobly Workhouse of pneumonia. She entered the institution emaciated to half the proper weight of her age and with a broken arm—till then undiscovered—that the doctors found to be of about three weeks' standing. Her mother was shown to be in an advanced stage of consumption; one child had died at the age of seven months, and seven now remain. The father, whose work consists in tending eighty nine head of cattle and ten pigs, is in receipt of eleven shillings a week, three pints of skim milk a day, and a cottage that has been condemned by the sanitary inspector and described as having no bedroom windows. We are not surprised to learn that the coroner, before taking the verdict, asked the house surgeon, who gave evidence, whether he could say that death 'was accelerated by anything.' Our wonder is that the reply was in the negative. The cottage is in the possession of the farmer who employs the man, but his landlord is said to be liable for repairs. That landlord is a clergyman of the Church of England, a J.P., a preserver of game, and owner of three or four thousand acres of land."

And here, again, is the Times, by no means a Socialist organ, generalizing from official statements:—

"Houses unfit for human habitation, rooms destitute of light and ventilation, overcrowding in rural cottages, contaminated water supplies, accumulations of every description of filth and refuse, a total absence of drainage, a reign of unbelievable dirt in milk shops and slaughter houses, a total neglect of bye laws, and an inadequate supervision by officials who are frequently incompetent; such, in a general way, is the picture that is commonly presented in the reports of inquiries in certain rural districts made by medical officers of the Local Government Board."

And even of such homes as this there is an insufficiency. In 1891 95, more than a quarter of the deaths in London occurred in workhouses and other charitable institutions.[9] Now suppose the modern Socialist did want to destroy the home; suppose that some Socialists have in the past really wanted to do so, remember that that is the reality they wanted to destroy.

[9] Studies Scientific and Social, Vol. II., Ch. XXIV.; by Dr. Alfred Russel Wallace. (Macmillan & Co., 1900.)

But does the modern Socialist want to destroy the home? Rather, I hold, he wants to save it from a destruction that is even now going on, to—I won't say restore it, because I have very grave doubts if the world has ever yet held a high percentage of good homes, but raise it to the level of its better realizations of happiness and security. And it is not only I say this, but all my fellow Socialists say it too. Read, for example, that admirable paper, "Economic and Social Justice," in Dr. Alfred Russel Wallace's Studies Scientific and Social, and you will have the clearest statement of the attitude of a representative modern Socialist to this question.

II

The reader must get quite out of his head the idea that the present system maintains the home and social purity.

In London at the present time there are thousands of prostitutes; in Paris, in Berlin, in every great city of Europe or America, thousands; in the whole of Christendom there cannot be less than a million of these ultimate instances of our civilization. They are the logical extremity of a civilization based on cash payments. Each of these women represents a smashed and ruined home and wasted possibilities of honour, service and love, each one is so much sheer waste. For the food they consume, their clothing, their lodging, they render back nothing to the community as a whole, and only a gross, dishonouring satisfaction to their casual employers. And don't imagine they are inferior women, that there has been any selection of the unfit in their sterilization; they are, one may see for oneself, well above the average in physical vigour, in spirit and beauty. Few of them have come freely to their trade, the most unnatural in the world; few of them have anything but shame and loathing for their life; and most of them must needs face their calling fortified by drink and drugs. For virtuous people do not begin to understand the things they endure. But it pays to be a prostitute, it does not pay to be a mother and a home maker, and the gist of the present system of individual property is that a thing must pay to exist.... So much for one aspect of our present system of a "world of homes."

Consider next the great army of employed men and women, shop assistants, clerks, and so forth, living in, milliners, typists, teachers, servants who have practically no prospect whatever of marrying and experiencing those domestic blisses the Socialist is supposed to want to rob them of. They are involuntary monks and nuns, celibate not from any high or religious motive, but through economic hardship. Consider all that amount of pent up, thwarted or perverted emotional possibility, the sheer irrational waste of life implied....

We have glanced at the reality of the family among the poor; what is it among the rich? Does the wealthy mother of the upper middle class or upper class really sit among her teeming children, teaching them in an atmosphere of love and domestic exaltation? As a matter of fact she is a conspicuously devoted woman if she gives them an hour a day—the rest of the time they spend with nurse or governess, and when they are ten or eleven off they go to board at the preparatory school. Whenever I find among my press cuttings some particularly scathing denunciation of Socialists as home destroyers, as people who want to snatch the tender child from the weeping mother to immure it in some terrible wholesale institution, I am apt to walk out into my garden, from which three boarding schools for little children of the prosperous classes are visible, and rub my eyes and renew that sight and marvel at my kind....

Consider now, with these things in mind, the real drift of the first main Socialist proposition, and compare its tendency with these contemporary conditions. Socialism regards parentage under proper safeguards and good auspices as "not only a duty but a service" to the State; that is to say it proposes to pay for good parentage—in other words to endow the home. Socialism comes not to destroy but to save.

And how will the endowment be done? Very probably it will be found that the most convenient and best method of doing this will be to subsidize the mother—who is, or should be, the principal person concerned in this affair—for her children; to assist her, not as a charity, but as a right in the period before the birth of her anticipated child, and afterwards to provide her with support for that child so long as it is kept clean in a tolerable home, in good health, well taught and properly clad. It will say to the sound mothering woman, Not type writing, nor shirt sewing, nor charing is your business— these children are. Neglect them, ill treat them, prove incompetent, and your mother right will cease and we shall take them away from you and do what we can for them; love them, serve them and, through them, the State, and you will serve yourself. Is that destroying the home? Is it not rather the rescue of the home from economic destruction?

Certain restrictions, it is true, upon our present way of doing things would follow almost necessarily from the adoption of these methods. It is manifest that no intelligent State would willingly endow the homes of hopelessly diseased parents, of imbecile fathers or mothers, of obstinately criminal persons or people incapable of education. It is evident, too, that the State would not tolerate chance fatherhood, that it would insist very emphatically upon marriage and the purity of the home, much more emphatically than we do now. Such a case as the one numbered 197, a beautiful instance of the sweet, old fashioned, homely, simple life of the poor we Socialists are supposed to be vainly endeavouring to undermine—would certainly be dealt with in a drastic and conclusive spirit....

III

So far Socialism goes toward regenerating the family and sustaining the home. But let there be no ambiguity on one point. It will be manifest that while it would reinvigorate and confirm the home, it does quite decidedly tend to destroy what has hitherto been the most typical form of the family throughout the world, that is to say the family which is in effect the private property of the father, the patriarchal family. The tradition of the family in which we are still living, we must remember, has developed from a former state in which man owned the wife or child as completely as he owned horse or hut. He was the family's irresponsible owner. Socialism seeks to make him and his wife its jointly responsible heads. Until quite recently the husband might beat his wife and put all sorts of physical constraint upon her; he might starve her or turn her out of doors; her property was his; her earnings were his; her children were his. Under certain circumstances it was generally recognized he might kill her. To day we live in a world that has faltered from the rigours of this position, but which still clings to its sentimental consequences. The wife now a days is a sort of pampered and protected half property. If she leaves her husband for another man, it is regarded not as a public offence on her part, but as a sort of mitigated theft on the part of the latter, entitling the former to damages. Politically she doesn't exist; the husband sees to all that. But on the other hand he mustn't drive her by physical force, but only by the moral pressure of disagreeable behaviour. Nor has he the same large powers of violence over her children that once he had. He may beat—within limits. He may dictate their education so far as his religious eccentricities go, and be generous or meagre with the supplies. He may use his "authority" as a vague power far on into their adult life, if he is a forcible character. But it is at its best a shorn splendour he retains. He has ceased to be an autocrat and become a constitutional monarch; the State, sustained by the growing reasonableness of the world, intervenes more and more between him and the wife and children who were once powerless in his hands.

The Socialist would end that old legal predominance altogether. The woman, he declares, must be as important and responsible a citizen in the State as the man. She must cease to be in any sense or degree private property. The man must desist from tyrannizing in the nursery and do his proper work in the world. So far, therefore, as the family is a name for a private property in a group of related human beings vesting in one of them, the Head of the Family, Socialism repudiates it altogether as unjust and uncivilized; but so far as the family is a grouping of children with their parents, with the support and consent and approval of the whole community, Socialism advocates it, would make it for the first time, so far as a very large moiety of our population is concerned, a possible and efficient thing.

Moreover, as the present writer has pointed out elsewhere,[10] this putting of the home upon a public basis destroys its autonomy. Just as the Socialist and all who have the cause of civilization at heart would substitute for the inefficient, wasteful, irresponsible, unqualified "private adventure school" that did such infinite injury to middle class education in Great Britain during the Victorian period a public school, publicly and richly endowed and responsible and controlled, so the Socialist would put an end to the uncivilized go as you please of the private adventure family. "Socialism in fact is the State family. The old family of the private individual must vanish before it just as the old water works of private enterprise or the old gas company."[11] To any one not idiotic nor blind with a passionate desire to lie about Socialism, the meaning of this passage is perfectly plain. Socialism seeks to broaden the basis of the family and to make the once irresponsible parent responsible to the State for its welfare. Socialism creates parental responsibility.

[10] *Socialism and the Family. (A. C. Fifield. 6d.)*

[11] *Socialism and the Family.*

IV

And here we may give a few words to certain questions that are in reality outside the scope of Socialists altogether, special questions involving the most subtle ethical and psychological decisions. Upon them Socialists are as widely divergent as people who are not Socialists, and Socialism as a whole presents nothing but an open mind. They are questions that would be equally open to discussion in relation to an Individualist State or to any sort of State. Certain religious organizations have given clear and imperative answers to some or all of these questions, and so far as the reader is a member of such an organization, he may rest assured that Socialism, as an authoritative whole, has nothing to say for or against his convictions. This cannot be made too plain by Socialists, nor too frequently repeated by them. A very large part of the so called arguments against them arise out of deliberate misrepresentations and misconceptions of some alleged Socialist position in these indifferent matters.

I refer more particularly to the numerous problems in private morality and social organization arising from sexual conduct. May a man love one woman only in his life, or more, and may a woman love only one man? Should marriage be an irrevocable life union or not? Is sterile physical love possible, permissible, moral, honourable or intolerable? Upon all these matters individual Socialists, like most other people, have their doubts and convictions, but it is no more just to saddle all Socialism with their private utterances and actions upon these issues than it would be to declare that the Roman Catholic Communion is hostile to beauty because worshippers coming and going have knocked the noses off the figures on the bronze doors of the Church of San Zeno at Verona, or that Christianity involves the cultivation of private vermin, because of the condition of Saint Thomas à Beckett's hair shirt.[12] To argue in that way is to give up one's birthright as a reasonable being.

[12] *"The haircloth encased the whole body down to the knees; the hair drawers, as well as the rest of the dress, being covered on the outside with white linen so as to escape observation; and the whole so fastened together as to admit of being readily taken off for his daily scourgings, of which yesterday's portion was still apparent in the stripes on his body. Such austerity had hitherto been unknown to English saints, and the marvel was increased by the sight—to our notions so revolting— of the innumerable vermin with which the haircloth abounded—boiling over with them, as one account describes it, like water in a simmering cauldron. At the dreadful sight all the enthusiasm of the previous night revived with double ardour. They looked at each other in silent wonder, then exclaimed, 'See, see what a true monk he was, and we knew it not!' and burst into alternate fits of weeping and laughter, between the sorrow of having lost such a head, and the joy of having found such a saint." (Historical Memorials of Canterbury, by the Rev. Arthur Penrhyn Stanley, D.D.)*

Upon certain points modern Socialism is emphatic; women and children must not be dealt with as private property, women must be citizens equally with men, children must not be casually born, their parents must be known and worthy; that is to say there must be deliberation in begetting children, marriage under conditions. And there Socialism stops.

Socialism has not even worked out what are the reasonable conditions of a State marriage contract, and it would be ridiculous to pretend it had. This is not a defect in Socialism particularly, but a defect in human knowledge. At countless points in the tangle of questions involved, the facts are not clearly known. Socialism does not present any theory whatever about the duration of marriage, whether, as among the Roman Catholics, it should be absolutely for life, or, as some hold, for ever; or, as among the various divorce permitting Protestant bodies, until this or that eventuality; or even, as Mr. George Meredith suggested some years ago, for a term of ten years. In these matters Socialism does not decide, and it is quite reasonable to argue that Socialism need not decide. Socialism maintains an attitude of neutrality. And the practical effect of an attitude of neutrality is to leave these things as they are at present. The State is not urgently concerned with these questions. So long as a marriage contract provides for the health and sanity of the contracting parties, and for their proper behaviour so far as their offspring is concerned, and for so long as their offspring need it, the demands of the community, as the guardian of the children, are satisfied. That certainly would be the minimum marriage, the State marriage, and I, for my own part, would exact nothing more in the legal contract. But a number of more representative Socialists than I are for a legally compulsory life marriage. Some—but they are mostly of the older, less definite, Social Democratic teaching—are for a looser tie. Let us clearly understand that we are here talking of the legal marriage only—the State's share. We are not talking of what people will do, but of how much they are to be made to do. A vast amount of stupid confusion arises from forgetting that. What was needed more than that minimum I have specified would be provided, I believe—it always has been provided hitherto, even to excess—by custom, religion, social influence, public opinion.

For it may not be altogether superfluous to remind the reader how little of our present moral code is ruled by law. We have in England, it is true, certain laws prescribing the conditions of the marriage contract, penalties of a quite ferocious kind to prevent bigamy, and a few quite trivial disabilities put upon those illegitimately born. But there is no legal compulsion upon any one to marry now, and far less legal restriction upon irregular and careless parentage than would be put in any scientifically organized Socialism. Do let us get it out of our heads that monogamy is enforced by law at the present time. It is not. You are only forbidden to enter into normal marriage with more than one person. If a man of means chooses to have as many concubines as King Solomon and live with them all openly, the law (I am speaking of Great Britain) will do nothing to prevent him. If he chooses to go through any sort of nuptial ceremony, provided it does not simulate a legal marriage, with some or all of them he may. And to any one who evades the legal marriage bond, there is a vast range of betrayal and baseness as open as anything can be. "Free Love" is open to any one who chooses to practise it to day. The real controlling force in these matters is social influence, public opinion, a sort of conscience and feeling for the judgment of others that is part of the normal human equipment. And the same motives and considerations that keep people's lives pure and discreet now, will be all the more freely in operation under Socialism, when money will count for less and reputation for more than they do now. Modern Socialism is a project to change the organization of living and the circle of human ideas; but it is no sort of scheme to attempt the impossible, to change human nature and to destroy the social sensitiveness of man.

I do not deny the intense human interest of these open questions, the imperative need there is to get the truth, whether one considers it to be one's own truth or the universal truth, upon them. But my point is that they are to be discussed apart from Socialist theory, and that anyhow they have nothing to do with Socialist politics. It is no doubt interesting to discuss the benefits of vaccination and the justice and policy of its public compulsion, to debate whether one should eat meat or confine oneself to a vegetable dietary, whether the overhead or the slot system is preferable for tramway traction, whether steamboats are needed on the Thames in winter, and whether it is wiser to use metal or paper for money; but none of these things have anything to do with the principles of Socialism. Nor need we decide whether Whistler, Raphael or Carpaccio has left us the most satisfying beauty, or which was the greater musician, Wagner, Scarlatti or Beethoven, nor pronounce on the Bacon Shakespeare controversy in any prescribed way, because we accept Socialism.

Coming to graver matters there are ardent theologians who would create an absolute antagonism between Socialism and Christianity, who would tie up Socialism with some extraordinary doctrine of Predestination, or deny the possibility of a Christian being a Socialist or a Socialist being a Christian. But these are matters on different planes. In a sense Socialism is a religion; to me it is a religion, in the sense, that is, that it gives a work to do that is not self seeking, that it determines one in a thousand indecisions, that it supplies that imperative craving of so many human souls, a devotion. But I do not see why a believer in any of the accepted creeds of Christianity, from the Apostles' Creed upward, should not also whole heartedly give himself to this great work of social reconstruction. To believe in a real and personal Heaven is surely not to deny earth with its tragedy, its sorrows, its splendid possibilities. It is simply to believe a little more concretely than I do, that is all. To assert the brotherhood of man under God seems to me to lead logically to a repudiation of the severities of Private Ownership—that is to Socialism. When the rich young man was told to give up his property to follow Christ, when the disciples were told to leave father and mother, it seems to me ridiculous to present Christianity as opposed to the self abnegation of the two main generalizations of Socialism—that relating to property in things, and that relating to property in persons. It is true that the Church of Rome has taken the deplorable step of forbidding Socialism (or at least Socialismus) to its adherents; but there is no need for Socialists to commit a reciprocal stupidity. Let us Socialists at any rate keep our intellectual partitions up. The Church that now quarrels with Socialism once quarrelled with astronomy and geology, and astronomers and geologists went on with their own business. Both religion and astronomy are still alive and in the same world together. And the Vatican observatory, by the bye, is honourably distinguished for its excellent stellar photographs. Perhaps, after all, the Church does not mean by Socialismus Socialism as it is understood in English; perhaps it simply means the dogmatically anti Christian Socialism of the Continental type.

I am not advocating indifference to any interest I have here set aside as irrelevant to Socialism. Men have discussed and will, I hope, continue to discuss such questions as I have instanced with passionate zeal; but Socialism need not be entangled by their decisions. We can go on our road to Socialism, we can get to Socialism, to the Civilized State, whichever answer is given to any of these questions, great or small.

CHAPTER VII

WOULD MODERN SOCIALISM ABOLISH ALL PROPERTY?

I

Having in the previous chapter cleared up a considerable mass of misconception and possibility of misrepresentation about the attitude of Socialism to the home, let us now devote a little more attention to the current theory of property and say just exactly where Modern Socialism stands in that matter.

The plain fact of the case is that the Socialist, whether he wanted to or no, would no more be able to abolish personal property altogether than he would be able to abolish the human liver. The extension of one's personality to things outside oneself is indeed as natural and instinctive a thing as eating. But because the liver is necessary and inevitable, there is no reason why it should be enlarged to uncomfortable proportions, and because eating is an unconquerable instinct there is no excuse for repletion. The position of the modern Socialist is that the contemporary idea of personal property is enormously exaggerated and improperly extended to things that ought not to be "private"; not that it is not a socially most useful and desirable idea within its legitimate range.

There can be no doubt that many of those older writers who were "Socialists before Socialism," Plato, for instance, and Sir Thomas More, did very roundly abolish private property altogether. They were extreme Communists, and so were many of the earlier Socialists; in More's Utopia, doors might not be fastened, they stood open; one hadn't even a private room. These earlier writers wished to insist upon the need of self abnegation in the ideal State, and to startle and confound, they insisted overmuch. The early Christians, one gathers, were almost completely communistic, and that interesting experiment in Christian Socialism (of a rather unorthodox type of Christianity), the American Oneida community, was successfully communistic in every respect for many years. But the modern Socialist is not a communist; the modern Socialist, making his scheme of social reconstruction for the whole world and for every type of character, recognizes the entire impracticability of such dreams, recognizing, too, it may be, the sacrifice of human personality and distinction such ideals involve.

The word "property," one must remember, is a slightly evasive word. Absolute property hardly exists—absolute, that is to say, in the sense of unlimited right of disposal; almost all property is incomplete and relative. A man, under our present laws, has no absolute property even in his own life; he is restrained from suicide and punished if he attempt it. He may not go offensively filthy nor indecently clad; there are limits to his free use of his body. The owner of a house, of land, of a factory is subject to all sorts of limitations, building regulations for example, and so is the owner of horse or dog. Nor again is any property exempt from taxation. Even now property is a limited thing, and it is well to bear that much in mind. It can be defined as something one may do "what one likes with," subject only to this or that specific restriction, and at any time, it would seem, the State is at least legally entitled to increase the quantity and modify the nature of the restriction. The extremest private property is limited to a certain sanity and humanity in its use.

In that sense every adult now a days has private property in his or her own person, in clothes, in such personal implements as hand tools, as a bicycle, as a cricket bat or golf sticks. In quite the same sense would he have it under Socialism so far as these selfsame things go. The sense of property in such things is almost instinctive; my little boys of five and three have the keenest sense of mine and (almost, if not quite so vividly) thine in the matter of toys and garments. The disposition of modern Socialism is certainly no more to override these natural tendencies than it is to fly in the face of human nature in regard to the home. The disposition of modern Socialism is indeed far more in the direction of confirming and insuring this natural property. And again modern Socialism has no designs upon the money in a man's pocket. It is quite true that the earlier and extreme Socialist theorists did in their communism find no use for money, but I do not think there are any representative Socialists now who do not agree that the State must pay and receive in money, that money is indispensable to human freedom. The featurelessness of money, its universal convertibility, gives human beings a latitude of choice and self expression in its spending that is inconceivable without its use.

All such property Socialism will ungrudgingly sustain, and it will equally sustain property in books and objects of æsthetic satisfaction, in furnishing, in the apartments or dwelling house a man or woman occupies and in their household implements. It will sustain far more property than the average working class man has to day. Nor will it prevent savings or accumulations, if men do not choose to expend their earnings—nor need it interfere with lending. How far it will permit or countenance usury is another question altogether. There will no doubt remain, after all the work a day needs of the world have been met by a scientific public organization of the general property in Nature, a great number of businesses and enterprises and new and doubtful experiments outside the range of legitimate State activity. In these, interested and prosperous people will embark their surplus money as shareholders in a limited liability company, making partnership profits or losses in an entirely proper manner. But whether there should be debentures and mortgages or preference shares, or suchlike manipulatory distinctions, or interest in any shape or form, I am inclined to doubt. A money lender should share risk as well as profit—that is surely the moral law in lending that forbids usury; he should not be allowed to bleed a failing business with his inexorable percentage and so eat up the ordinary shareholder or partner any more than the landlord should be allowed to eat up the failing tenant for rent. That was once the teaching of Christianity, and I do not know enough of the history or spiritual development of the Catholic Church to tell when she became what she now appears to be—the champion of the rent exacting landlord and the usurer against Socialism. It is the present teaching of Socialism. If usury obtains at all under the Socialist State, if inexorable repayments are to be made in certain cases, it will, I conceive, be a State monopoly. The State will be the sole banker for every hoard and every enterprise, just as it will be the universal landlord and the universal fire and accident and old age insurance office. In money matters as in public service and administration, it will stand for the species, the permanent thing behind every individual accident and adventure.

Posthumous property, that is to say the power to bequeath and the right to inherit things, will also persist in a mitigated state under Socialism. There is no reason whatever why it should not do so. There is a strong natural sentiment in favour of the institution of heirlooms, for example; one feels a son might well own—though he should certainly not sell—the intimate things his father desires to leave him. The pride of descent is an honourable one, the love for one's blood, and I hope that a thousand years from now some descendant will still treasure an obsolete weapon here, a picture there, or a piece of faint and faded needlework from our days and the days before our own. One may hate inherited privileges and still respect a family tree.

Widows and widowers again have clearly a kind of natural property in the goods they have shared with the dead; in the home, in the garden close, in the musical instruments and books and pleasant home like things. Now, in nine cases out of ten, we do in effect bundle the widow out; she remains nominally owner of the former home, but she has to let it furnished or sell it, to go and live in a boarding house or an exiguous flat.

Even perhaps a proportion of accumulated money may reasonably go to friend or kin. It is a question of public utility; Socialism has done with absolute propositions in all such things, and views these problems now as questions of detail, matters for fine discriminations. We want to be quit of pedantry. All that property which is an enlargement of personality, the modern Socialist seeks to preserve; it is that exaggerated property that gives power over the food and needs of one's fellow creatures, property and inheritance in land, in industrial machinery, in the homes of others and in the usurer's grip upon others, that he seeks to destroy. The more doctrinaire Socialists will tell you they do not object to property for use and consumption, but only to property in "the means of production," but I do not choose to resort to over precise definitions. The general intention is clear enough, the particular instance requires particular application. But it is just because we modern Socialists want every one to have play for choice and individual expression in all these realities of property that we object to this monstrous property of a comparatively small body of individuals expropriating the world.

I am inclined to think—but here I speak beyond the text of contemporary Socialist literature—that in certain directions Socialism, while destroying property, will introduce a compensatory element by creating rights. For example, Socialism will certainly destroy all private property in land and in natural material and accumulated industrial resources; it will be the universal landlord and the universal capitalist, but that does not mean that we shall all be the State's tenants at will. There can be little doubt that the Socialist State will recognize the rights of the improving occupier and the beneficial hirer. It is manifestly in accordance both with justice and public policy that a man who takes a piece of land and creates a value on it—by making a vineyard, let us say—is entitled to security of tenure, is to be dispossessed only in exceptional circumstances and with ample atonement. If a man who takes an agricultural or horticultural holding comes to feel that there he will toil and there later he will rest upon his labours, I do not think a rational Socialism will war against this passion for the vine and fig tree. If it absolutely refuses the idea of freehold, it will certainly not repudiate leasehold. I think the State may prove a far more generous and sentimental landlord in many things than any private person.

In another correlated direction, too, Socialism is quite reconcilable with a finer quality of property than our landowner ridden Britain allows to any but the smallest minority. I mean property in the house one occupies.... If I may indulge in a quite unauthorized speculation, I am inclined to think there may be two collateral methods of home building in the future. For many people always there will need to be houses to which they may come and go for longer and shorter tenancies and which they will in no manner own. Now a days such people are housed in the exploits of the jerry builder— all England is unsightly with their meagre pretentious villas and miserable cottages and tenement houses. Such homes in the Socialist future will certainly be supplied by the local authority, but they will be fair, decent houses by good architects, fitted to be clean and lit, airy and convenient, the homes of civilized people, sightly things altogether in a generous and orderly world. But in addition there will be the prosperous private person with a taste that way, building himself a home as a lease holder under the public landlord. For him, too, there will be a considerable measure of property, a measure of property that might even extend to a right, if not of bequest, then at any rate of indicating a preference among his possible successors in the occupying tenancy....

Then there is a whole field of proprietary sensations in relation to official duties and responsibility. Men who have done good work in any field are not to be lightly torn from it. A medical officer of health who has done well in his district, a teacher who has taught a generation of a town, a man who has made a public garden, have a moral lien upon their work for all their lives. They do not get it under our present conditions. I know that it will be quite easy to say all this is a question of administration and detail. It is. But it is, nevertheless, important to state it clearly here, to make it evident that the coming of Socialism involves no destruction of this sort of identification of a man with the thing he does; this identification that is so natural and desirable—that this living and legitimate sense of property will if anything be encouraged and its claims strengthened under Socialism. To day that particularly living sort of property sense is often altogether disregarded. Every day one hears of men who have worked up departments in businesses, men who have created values for employers, men who have put their lives into an industrial machine, being flung aside because their usefulness is over, or out of personal pique, or to make way for favourites, for the employer's son or cousin or what not, without any sort of appeal or compensation. Ownership is autocracy; at the best it is latent injustice in all such matters of employment.

Then again, consider the case of the artist and the inventor who are too often forced by poverty now to sell their early inventions for the barest immediate subsistence. Speculators secure these initial efforts—sometimes to find them worthless, sometimes to discover in them the sources of enormous wealth. In no matter is it more difficult to estimate value than in the case of creative work; few geniuses are immediately recognized, and the history of art, literature and invention is full of Chattertons and Savages who perished before recognition came, and of Dickenses who sold themselves unwisely. Consider the immense social benefit if the creator even now possessed an inalienable right to share in the appreciation of his work. Under Socialism it would for all his life be his—and the world's, and controllable by him. He would be free to add, to modify, to repeat.

In all these respects modern Socialism tends to create and confirm property and rights, the property of the user, the rights of the creator. It is quite other property it tends to destroy; the property, the claim, of the creditor, the mortgagee, the landlord, and usurer, the forestaller, gambling speculator, monopolizer and absentee.... In very truth Socialism would destroy no property at all, but only that sham property that, like some wizard cast illusion, robs us all.

III

And now we are discussing the Socialist attitude towards property, it may be well to consider a little group of objections that are often made in anti Socialist tracts. I refer more particularly to a certain hard case, the hard case of the Savings of the Virtuous Small Man.

The reader, if he is at all familiar with this branch of controversial literature, probably knows how that distressing case is put. One is presented with a poor man of inconceivable industry, goodness and virtue; he has worked, he has saved; at last, for the security of his old age, he holds a few shares in a business, a "bit of land" or—perhaps through a building society—house property. Would we— the Anti Socialist chokes with emotion—so alter the world as to rob him of that? ... The Anti Socialist gathers himself together with an effort and goes on to a still more touching thought ... the widow![13]

[13] "The ethical case for slavery in the Southern States of America," my friend Mr. Graham Wallas reminds me, "was largely argued on the instance of the widow 'with a few strong slaves.'"

Well, I think there are assurances in the previous section to disabuse the reader's mind a little in this matter. This solicitude for the Saving Small Man and for the widow and orphan seems to me one of the least honest of all the anti Socialist arguments. The man "who has saved a few pounds," the poor widow woman and her children clinging to some scrap of freehold are thrust forward to defend the harvest of the landlord and the financier. Let us look at the facts of the case and see how this present economic system of ours really does treat the "stocking" of the poor.

In the first place it does not guarantee to the small investor any security for his little hoard at all. He comes into the world of investment ill informed, credulous or only unintelligently suspicious—and he is as a class continually and systematically deprived of his little accumulations. One great financial operation after another in the modern world, as any well informed person can witness, eats up the small investor. Some huge, vastly respectable looking enterprise is floated with a capital of so many scores or hundreds of thousands, divided into so many thousands of ordinary shares, so many five or six per cent. preference, so much debentures. It begins its career with a flourish of prosperity, the ordinary shares for a few years pay seven, eight, ten per cent. The Virtuous Small Man provides for his widow and his old age by buying this estimable security. Its price clambers to a premium, and so it passes slowly and steadily from its first speculative holder into the hands of the investing public.

Then comes a slow, quiet, downward movement, a check at the interim dividend, a rapid contraction. Consider such a case as that of the great British Electric Traction Company which began with ordinary shares at ten, which clambered above twenty one (21 7/8), which is now (October 1907) fluctuating about two. Its six per cent, preference shares have moved between fourteen and five and a half. Its ordinary shares represent a total capital of £1,333,010, and its preference £1,614,370; so that here in this one concern we have a phantom appearance and disappearance of over two million pounds' worth of value and a real disappearance of perhaps half that amount. It requires only a very slight knowledge of the world to convince one that the bulk of that sum was contributed by the modest investments of mediocre and small people out of touch with the real conditions of the world of finance.

These little investors, it is said, are the bitter champions of private finance against the municipalities and Socialists. One wonders why.

One could find a score of parallels and worse instances representing in the end many scores of millions of pounds taken from the investing public in the last few years. I will, however, content myself with one sober quotation from the New York Journal of Commerce, which the reader will admit is not likely to be a willing witness for Socialism. Commenting on the testimony of the principal witness, Mr. Harriman, of the Illinois Central Railroad, before the Inter State Commerce Commission (March 1907), it says:—

"On his own admission he was one of a 'combine' of four who got possession of the Chicago and Alton Railroad, and immediately issued bonds for $40,000,000, out of the proceeds of which they paid themselves a dividend of 30 per cent, on the stock they held, besides taking the bonds at 65 and subsequently selling them at 90 or more, some of them to life insurance companies with which Mr. Harriman had some kind of relation. There were no earnings or surplus out of which the dividend could be paid, but the books of the company were juggled by transferring some $12,000,000 expended for betterments to capital account as a sort of bookkeeping basis for the performance.

"Besides this, the Chicago and Alton Railroad was transformed into a 'railway,' and a capitalization of a little under $40,000,000 was swollen to nearly $123,000,000 to cover an actual expenditure in improvements of $22,500,000. In the process there was an injection of about $60,600,000 of 'water' into the stock held by the four, some of which was sold to the Union Pacific, of which Mr. Harriman was president, and more was 'unloaded' upon the Rock Island. Mr. Harriman refused to tell how much he made out of that operation.

"It shows how some of our enormous fortunes are made, as well as what motives and purposes sometimes prevail in the use of the power entrusted to the directors and officers of corporations. It is a simple and elementary principle that all values are created by the productive activity of capital, labour and ability in industrial operations of one kind and another. No wealth comes out of nothing, but all must be produced and distributed, and what one gets by indirection another loses or fails to get. The personal profit of these speculative operations in which the capital, credit and power of corporations are used by those entrusted with their direction come out of the general body of stockholders whose interests are sacrificed, or out of the public investors who are lured and deceived, or out of shippers who are overtaxed for the service for which railroads are chartered, or out of all these in varying proportions. In other words they are the fruits of robbery."

So that you see it is not only untrue that Socialism would rob a poor man of his virtuously acquired "bit of property," but the direct contrary is the truth, that the present system, non Socialism, is now constantly butchering thrift! Simple people believe the great financiers win and lose money to each other. They are not—to put it plainly—such fools. They use the public, and the public goes on being used, as a perpetual source of freshly accumulated wealth. I know one case of a man of fifty who serves in a shop, a most industrious, competent man, who has been saving and investing money all his life in what he had every reason to believe were safe and sober businesses; he has been denying himself pleasures, cramping his life to put by about a third of his wages every year since he was two and twenty, and to day he has not got his keep for a couple of years, and his only security against disablement and old age is his subscription to a Friendly Society, a society which I have a very strong suspicion is no better off than most other Friendly Societies—and that is by no means well off, and by no means confident of the future.

It is possible to argue that the small man ought to take more pains about his investments, but, as a matter of fact, investing money securely and profitably is a special occupation of extraordinary complexity, and the common man with a few hundred pounds has no more chance in that market than he would have under water in Sydney Harbour amidst a shoal of sharks. It may be said that he is greedy, wants too much interest, but that is nonsense. One of the crudest gulfs into which small savings have gone in the case of the British public has been the trap of Consols, which pay at the present price less than three per cent. Servants and working men with Post Office Savings' Bank accounts were urged, tempted and assisted to invest in this solemn security—even when it stood at 114. Those who did so have now (November 1907) lost almost a third of their money.

It is scarcely too much to say that a very large proportion of our modern great properties, tramway systems, railways, gas works, bread companies, have been created for their present owners the debenture holders and mortgagers, the great capitalists, by the unintentional altruism of that voluntary martyr, the Saving Small Man.

Of course the habitual saver can insure with an insurance company for his old age and against all sorts of misadventures, and because of the Government interference with "private enterprise" in that sort of business, be reasonably secure; but under Socialism he would be able to do that with absolute security in the State Insurance Office—if the universal old age pension did not satisfy him. That, however, is beside our present discussion. I am writing now only of the sort of property that Socialism would destroy, and to show how little benefit or safety it brings to the small owner now. The unthinking rich prate "thrift" to the poor, and grow richer by a half judicious, half unconscious absorption of the resultant savings; that, in brief, is the grim humour of our present financial method.

It is not only in relation to investments that this absorption of small parcels of savings goes on. In every town the intelligent and sympathetic observer may see, vivid before the eyes of all who are not blind by use and wont, the slow subsidence of petty accumulations, The lodging house and the small retail shop are, as it were, social "destructors"; all over the country they are converting hopeful, enterprising, ill advised people with a few score or hundreds of pounds, slowly, inevitably into broken hearted failures. It is, to my mind, the crudest aspect of our economic struggle. In the little High Street of Sandgate, over which my house looks, I should say between a quarter and a third of the shops are such downward channels from decency to despair; they are sanctioned, inevitable citizen breakers. Now it is a couple of old servants opening a "fancy" shop or a tobacco shop, now it is a young couple plunging into the haberdashery, now it is a new butcher or a new fishmonger or a grocer. This perpetual procession of bankruptcies has made me lately shun that pleasant looking street, that in my unthinking days I walked through cheerfully enough. The doomed victims have a way of coming to the doors at first and looking out politely and hopefully. There is a rich and lucrative business done by certain wholesale firms in starting the small dealer in almost every branch of retail trade; they fit up his shop, stock him, take his one or two hundred pounds and give him credit for forty or fifty. The rest of his story is an impossible struggle to pay rent and get that debt down. Things go on for a time quite bravely. I go furtively and examine the goods in the window, with a dim hope that this time something really will come off; I learn reluctantly from my wife that they are no better than any one else's, and rather dearer than those of the one or two solid and persistent shops that do the steady business of the place. Perhaps I see the new people going to church once or twice very respectably, as I set out for a Sunday walk, and if they are a young couple the husband usually wears a silk hat. Presently the stock in the window begins to deteriorate in quantity and quality, and then I know that credit is tightening. The proprietor no longer comes to the door, and his first bright confidence is gone. He regards one now through the darkling panes with a gloomy animosity. He suspects one all too truly of dealing with the "Stores." ... Then suddenly he has gone; the savings are gone, and the shop—like a hungry maw—waits for a new victim. There is the simple common tragedy of the little shop; the landlord of the house has his money all right, the ground landlord has, of course, every penny of his money, the kindly wholesalers are well out of it, and the young couple or the old people, as the case may be, are looking for work or the nearest casual ward—just as though there was no such virtue as thrift in the world.

The particular function of the British lodging house—though the science of economics is silent on this point—is to use up the last strength of the trusty old servant and the plucky widow. These people will invest from two or three hundred to a thousand pounds in order to gain a bare subsistence by toiling for boarders and lodgers. It is their idea of a safe investment. They can see it all the time. All over England this process goes on. The curious inquirer may see every phase for himself by simply looking for rooms among the apartment houses of such a region as Camden Town, London; he will realize more and more surely as he goes about that none of these people gain money, none of them ever recover the capital they sink, they are happy if they die before their inevitable financial extinction. It is so habitual with people to think of classes as stable, of a butcher or a baker as a man who keeps a shop of a certain sort at a certain level throughout a long and indeterminate life, that it may seem incredible to many readers that those two typically thrifty classes, the lodging letting householder and the small retailer, are maintained by a steady supply of failing individuals; the fact remains that it is so. Their little savings are no good to them, investments and business beginnings mock them alike: steadily, relentlessly our competitive system eats them up.

It is said that no class of people in the community is more hostile to Socialism and Socialistic legislation than these small owners and petty investors, these small ratepayers. They do not understand. Rent they consider in the nature of things like hunger and thirst; the economic process that dooms the weak enterprise to ruin is beyond the scope of their intelligence; but the rate collector who calls and calls again for money, for more money, to educate "other people's children," to "keep paupers in luxury," to "waste upon roads and light and trams," seems the agent of an unendurable wrong. So the poor creatures go out pallidly angry to vote down that hated thing municipal enterprise, and to make still more scope for that big finance that crushes them in the wine press of its exploitation. It is a wretched and tragic antagonism, for which every intelligent Socialist must needs have sympathy, which he must meet with patience—and lucid explanations. If the public authority took rent there would be no need of rates; that is the more obvious proposition. But the ampler one is the cruelty, the absurdity and the social injury of the constant consumption of unprotected savings which is an essential part of our present system.

It is a doctrinaire and old fashioned Socialism that quarrels with the little hoard; the quarrel of modern Socialism is with the landowner and the great capitalist who devour it.

IV

While we are discussing the true attitude of modern Socialism to property, it will be well to explain quite clearly the secular change of opinion that is going on in the Socialist ranks in regard to the process of expropriation. Even in the case of those sorts of property that Socialism repudiates, property in land, natural productions, inherited business capital and the like, Socialism has become humanized and rational from its first extreme and harsh positions.

The earlier Socialism was fierce and unjust to owners. "Property is Robbery," said Proudhon, and right down to the nineties Socialism kept too much of the spirit of that proposition. The property owner was to be promptly and entirely deprived of his goods, and to think himself lucky he was not lynched forthwith as an abominable rascal. The first Basis of the Fabian Society, framed so lately as 1884, seems to repudiate "compensation," even a partial compensation of property owners, though in its practical proposals the Fabian Society has always admitted compensatory arrangements. The exact words of the Basis are "without compensation though not without such relief to expropriated individuals as may seem fit to the community." The wording is pretty evidently the result of a compromise between modern views and older teachings. If the Fabian Society were rewriting its Basis now I doubt if any section would insist even upon that eviscerated "without compensation."

Now property is not robbery. It may be a mistake, it may be unjust and socially disadvantageous to recognize private property in these great common interests, but every one concerned, and the majority of the property owners certainly, held and hold in good faith, and do their best by the light they have. We live to day in a vast tradition of relationships in which the rightfulness of that kind of private property is assumed, and suddenly, instantly, to deny and abolish it would be—I write this as a convinced and thorough Socialist—quite the most dreadful catastrophe human society could experience. For what sort of provisional government should we have in that confusion?

Expropriation must be a gradual process, a process of economic and political readjustment, accompanied at every step by an explanatory educational advance. There is no reason why a cultivated property owner should not welcome and hasten its coming. Modern Socialism is prepared to compensate him, not perhaps "fully" but reasonably, for his renunciations and to avail itself of his help, to relieve him of his administrative duties, his excess of responsibility for estate and business. It does not grudge him a compensating annuity nor terminating rights of user. It has no intention of obliterating him nor the things he cares for. It wants not only to socialize his possessions, but to socialize his achievement in culture and all that leisure has taught him of the possibilities of life. It wants all men to become as fine as he. Its enemy is not the rich man but the aggressive rich man, the usurer, the sweater, the giant plunderer, who are developing the latent evil of riches. It repudiates altogether the conception of a bitter class war between those who Have and those who Have Not.

But this new tolerant spirit in method involves no weakening of the ultimate conception. Modern Socialism sets itself absolutely against the creation of new private property out of land, or rights or concessions not yet assigned. All new great monopolistic enterprises in transit, building and cultivation, for example, must from the first be under public ownership. And the chief work of social statesmanship, the secular process of government, must be the steady, orderly resumption by the community, without violence and without delay, of the land, of the apparatus of transit, of communication, of food distribution and of all the great common services of mankind, and the care and training of a new generation in their collective use and in more civilized conceptions of living.

CHAPTER VIII

THE MIDDLE CLASS MAN, THE BUSINESS MAN, AND SOCIALISM

I

Let me insert here a few remarks upon a question that arises naturally out of the preceding discussion, and that is the future of that miscellaneous section of the community known as the middle class. It is one that I happen to know with a peculiar intimacy.

For a century or more the grinding out of the middle class has been going on. I began to find it interesting—altogether too interesting indeed, when I was still only a little boy. My father was one of that multitude of small shopkeepers which has been caught between the "Stores" and such like big distributors above and the rising rates below, and from the knickerbocker stage onward I was acutely aware of the question hanging over us. "This isn't going on," was the proposition. "This shop in which our capital is invested will never return it. Nobody seems to understand what is happening, and there is nobody to advise or help us. What are we going to do?"

Except that people are beginning to understand a little now what it all means, exactly the same question hangs over many hundreds of thousands of households to day, not only over the hundreds of small shopkeepers, but of small professional men, of people living upon small parcels of investments, of clerks who find themselves growing old and their value depreciated by the competition of a new, better educated generation, of private school masters, of boarding and lodging house keepers and the like. They are all vaguely aware of something more than personal failure, of a drift and process which is against all their kind, of the need of "doing something" for themselves and their children, something different from just sticking to the shop or the "situation"— and they don't know what to do! What ought they to do?

Well, first, before one answers that, let us ask what it is exactly that is grinding the middle class in this way. Is it a process we can stop? Can we direct the millstones? If we can, ought we to do so? And if we cannot, or decide that it isn't worth while, then what can we do to mitigate this cruelty of slowly impoverishing and taxing out of existence a class that was once the backbone of the community? It is not mere humanity dictates this much, it is a question that affects the State as a whole. It must be extremely bad for the spirit of the nation and for our national future that its middle mass should be in a state of increasing financial worry and stress, irritated, depressed, and broken in courage. One effect is manifest in our British politics now. Each fresh election turns upon expenditure more evidently than the last, and the promise to reduce taxation or lower the rates overrides more and more certainly any other consideration. What are Empire or Education to men who feel themselves drifting helplessly into debt? What chance has any constructive scheme with an electorate of men who are being slowly submerged in an economic bog?

The process that has brought the middle class into these troubles is a complex one, but the essential thing about it seems to be this, that there is a change of scale going on in most human affairs, a substitution of big organizations for detached individual effort almost everywhere. A hundred and fifty years ago or so the only very rich people in the community were a handful of great landowners and a few bankers; the rest of the world's business was being done by small prosperous independent men. The labourers were often very poor and wretched, ill clad, bootless, badly housed and short of food, but there was nevertheless a great deal of middle class comfort and prosperity. The country was covered with flourishing farmers, every country town was a little world in itself, with busy tradespeople and professional men; manufacturing was still done mainly by small people employing a few hands, master and apprentice working together; in every town you found a private school or so, an independent doctor and the like, doing well in a mediocre, comfortable fashion. All the carrying trade was in the hands of small independent carriers; the shipping was held by hundreds of small shipowners. And London itself was only a larger country town. It was, in effect, a middle class world ruled over by aristocrats; the millstones had as yet scarcely stirred.

Then machinery came into the lives of men, and steam power, and there began that change of scale which is going on still to day, making an ever widening separation of master and man and an ever enlarging organization of industry and social method. Its most striking manifestation was at first the substitution of organized manufacture in factories for the half domestic hand industrialism of the earlier period; the growth of the fortunes of some of the merchants and manufacturers to dimensions comparable with the wealth of the great landowners, and the sinking of the rest of their class towards the status of wage earners. The development of joint stock enterprise arose concurrently with this to create a new sort of partnership capable of handling far greater concerns than any single wealthy person, as wealth was measured by the old scale, could do. There followed a great development of transit, culminating for a time in the coming of the railways and steamships, which abolished the isolation of the old towns and brought men at the remotest quarters of the earth into business competition. Big towns of the modern type, with half a million inhabitants or more, grew up rapidly all over Europe and America. For the European big towns are as modern as New York, and the East End and south side of London scarcely older than Chicago. Shopkeeping, like manufactures, began to concentrate in large establishments, and big wholesale distribution to replace individual buying and selling. As the need for public education under the changing conditions of life grew more and more urgent, the individual enterprise of this school master and that gave place to the organized effort of such giant societies as (in Britain) the old National School Society and the British School Society, and at last to State education. And one after another the old prosperous middle class callings fell under the stress of the new development.

The process still goes on, and there can be little doubt of the ultimate issue. The old small manufacturers are either ruined or driven into sweating and the slums; the old coaching innkeeper and common carrier have been impoverished or altogether superseded by the railways and big carrier companies; the once flourishing shopkeeper lives to day on the mere remnants of the trade that great distributing stores or the branches of great companies have left him. Tea companies, provision dealing companies, tobacconist companies, make the position of the old established private shop unstable and the chances of the new beginner hopeless. Railways and tramways take the custom more and more effectually past the door of the small draper and outfitter to the well stocked establishments at the centre of things; telephone and telegraph assist that shopping at the centre more and more. The small "middle class" school master finds himself beaten by revived endowed schools and by new public endowments; the small doctor, the local dentist, find Harley Street always nearer to them and practitioners in motor cars from the great centres playing havoc with their practices. And while the small men are more and more distressed, the great organizations of trade, of production, of public science, continue to grow and coalesce, until at last they grow into national or even world trusts, or into publicly owned monopolies. In America slaughtering and selling meat has grown into a trust, steel and iron are trustified, mineral oil is all gathered into a few hands. All through the trades and professions and sciences and all over the world the big eats up the small, the new enlarged scale replaces the old.

And this is equally true, though it is only now beginning to be recognized, of the securities of that other section of the middle class, the section which lives upon invested money. There, too, big eats little. There, too, the small man is more and more manifestly at the mercy of the large organization. It was a pleasant illusion of the Victorian time that one put one's hundred pounds or thousand pounds "into something," beside the rich man's tens of thousands, and drew one's secure and satisfying dividends. The intelligent reader of Mr. Lawson's Frenzied Finance or of the bankruptcy proceedings of Mr. Hooley realizes this idyll is scarcely true to nature. Through the seas and shallows of investment flow great tides and depressions, on which the big fortunes ride to harbour while the little accumulations, capsized and swamped, quiver down to the bottom. It becomes more and more true that the small man saves his money for the rich man's pocket. Only by drastic State intervention is a certain measure of safety secured for insurance, and in America recently we have had the spectacle of the people's insurance money used as a till by the rich financiers.

And when the middle class man turns in his desperation from the advance of the big competitor who is consuming him, as a big codfish eats its little brother, to the State, he meets a tax paper; he sees as the State's most immediate aspect the rate collector and inexorable demands. The burthen of taxation certainly falls upon him, and it falls upon him because he is collectively the weakest class that possesses any property to be taxed. Below him are classes either too poor to tax or too politically effective to stand taxation. Above him is the class which owns a large part of the property in the world; but it also owns the newspapers and periodicals that are necessary for an adequate discussion of social justice, and it finds it cheaper to pay a voluntary tax to the hoardings at election time than to take over the small man's burdens. He rolls about between these two parties, antagonized first to one and then the other, and altogether helpless and ineffectual. So the millstones grind, and so it would seem they will continue to grind until there is nothing between them; until organized property in the hands of the few on the one hand and the proletariat on the other grind face to face. So, at least, Karl Marx taught in Das Kapital.

But when one says the middle class will disappear, one means that it will disappear as a class. Its individuals and its children will survive, and the whole process is not nearly so fatalistic as the Marxists would have us believe. The new great organizations that are replacing the little private enterprises of the world before machinery are not all private property. There are alternatives in the matter of handling a great business. To the exact nature of these alternatives the middle class mind needs to direct itself if it is to exert any control whatever over its future. Take the case of the butcher. It is manifestly written on the scroll of destiny that the little private slaughter house, the little independent butcher's shop, buying and selling locally, must disappear. The meat will all be slaughtered at some great, conveniently organized centre, and distributed thence to shops that will necessarily be mere agencies for distributing meat. Now, this great slaughtering and distributing business may either be owned by one or a group of owners working it for profit—in which case it will be necessary for the State to employ an unremunerative army of inspectors to see that the business is kept decently clean and honest—or it may be run by the public authority. In the former case the present day butcher or his son will be a slaughterman or shopkeeper employed by the private owners; in the latter case by the public authority. This is equally true of a milk seller, of a small manufacturer, of a builder, of a hundred and one other trades. They are bound to be incorporated in a larger organization; they are bound to become salaried men where formerly they were independent men, and it is no good struggling against that. It is doubtful, indeed, whether from the standpoint of welfare it would be worth the middle class man's while to struggle against that. But in the case of very many great public services—meat, milk, bread, transit, housing and land administration, education and research, and the public health—it is still an open question whether the big organization is to be publicly owned, publicly controlled, and constantly refreshed by public scrutiny and comment, or whether it is to be privately owned, and conducted solely for the profit of a small group of very rich owners. The alternatives are Plutocracy or Socialism, and between these the middle class man remains weakly undecided and ineffectual, lending no weight to and getting small consideration therefore from either side. He remains so because he has not grasped the real nature of his problem, because he clings in the face of overwhelming fate to the belief that in some way the wheels of change may be arrested and his present method of living preserved.

I think, if he could shake himself free from that impossible conservatism he would realize that his interests lie with the interests of the intelligent working class man—that is to say, in the direction of Socialism rather than in the direction of capitalistic competition; that the best use he can make of such educational and social advantages as still remain for him is to become the willing leader instead of the panic fierce antagonist of the Socialist movement. His place, I hold, is to forward the development of that State and municipal machinery the Socialist foreshadows, and to secure for himself and his sons and daughters an adequate position and voice in the administration. Instead of struggling to diminish that burthen of public expenditure which educates and houses, conveys and protects him and his children, he ought rather to increase it joyfully, while at the same time working manfully to transfer its pressure to the broad shoulders of those very rich people who have hitherto evaded their legitimate share of it. The other course is to continue his present policy of obstinate resistance to the extension of public property and public services. In which case these things will necessarily become that basis of monopolistic property on which the coming plutocracy will establish itself. The middle class man will be taxed and competed out of independence just the same, and he will become a salaried officer just the same, but with a different sort of master and under different social conditions according as one or other of these alternatives prevails.

Which is the better master—the democratic State or a "combine" of millionaires? Which will give the best social atmosphere for one's children to breathe—a Plutocracy or a Socialism? That is the real question to which the middle class man should address himself.

No doubt to many minds a Plutocracy presents many attractions. In the works of Thomas Love Peacock, and still more clearly in the works of Mr. W. H. Mallock, you will find an agreeable rendering of that conception. The bulk of the people will be organized out of sight in a state of industrious and productive congestion, and a wealthy, leisurely, and refined minority will live in spacious homes, with excellent museums, libraries, and all the equipments of culture; will go to town, concentrate in Paris, London, and Rome, and travel about the world. It is to these large, luxurious, powerful lives that the idealist naturally turns. Their motor cars, their aeroplanes, their steam yachts will awaken terror and respect in every corner of the globe. Their handsome doings will fill the papers. They will patronize the arts and literature, while at the same time mellowing them by eliminating that too urgent insistence upon contemporary fact which makes so much of what is done to day harsh and displeasing. The middle class tradition will be continued by a class of stewards, tenants, managers, and foremen, secretaries and the like, respected and respectful. The writer, the artist, will lead lives of comfortable dependence, a link between class and class, the lowest of the rich man's guests, the highest of his servants. As for the masses, they will be fed with a sort of careless vigour and considerable economy from the Chicago stockyards, and by agricultural produce trusts, big breweries, fresh water companies, and the like; they will be organized industrially and carefully controlled. Their spiritual needs will be provided for by churches endowed by the wealthy, their physical distresses alleviated by the hope of getting charitable aid, their lives made bright and adventurous by the crumbs of sport that fall from the rich man's table. They will crowd to see the motor car races, the aeroplane competitions. It will be a world rich in contrasts and not without its gleam of pure adventure. Every bright young fellow of capacity will have the hope of catching the eye of some powerful personage, of being advanced to some high position of trust, of even ending his days as a partner, a subordinate assistant plutocrat. Or he may win a quite agreeable position by literary or artistic merit. A pretty girl, a clever woman of the middle class would have before her even more brilliant and romantic possibilities.

There can be no denying the promises of colour and eventfulness a Plutocracy holds out, and though they do not attract me, I can quite understand their appeal to the more ductile and appreciative mind of Mr. Mallock. But there are countervailing considerations. There is, it is said, a tendency in Plutocracies either to become unprogressive, unenterprising and stagnantly autocratic, or to develop states of stress and discontent, and so drift towards Cæsarism. The latter was the fate of the Roman Republic, and may perhaps be the destiny of the budding young Plutocracy of America. But the developing British Plutocracy, like the Carthaginian, will be largely Semitic in blood, and like the Carthaginian may resist these insurgent tendencies.

So much for the Plutocratic possibility. If the middle class man on any account does not like that outlook, he can turn in the other direction; and then he will find fine promises indeed, but much more uncertainty than towards Plutocracy. Plutocracies the world has seen before, but a democratic civilization organized upon the lines laid down by modern Socialists would be a new beginning in the world's history. It is not a thing that will come about by itself; it will have to be the outcome of a sustained moral and intellectual effort in the community. If there is not that effort, if things go on as they are going now, the coming of a Plutocracy is inevitable. That effort, I am convinced, cannot be successfully made by the lower class man alone; from him, unaided and unguided, there is nothing to be expected but wild convulsive attempts at social upheaval, which, whether they succeed (as the French Revolution did) or fail (as did the insurrectionary outbreaks of the Republic in Rome), lead ultimately to a Napoleon or a Cæsar. But our contemporary civilization is unprecedented in the fact that the whole population now reads, and that intelligence and free discussion saturate the whole mass. Only time can show what possibilities of understanding, leadership, and political action lie in our new generation of the better educated middle class. Will it presently begin to define a line for itself? Will it remain disorganized and passive, or will it become intelligent and decisive between these millstones of the organized property and the organizing State, between Plutocracy and Socialism, whose opposition is the supreme social and political fact in the world at the present time?

II

Perhaps, also, it may be helpful here to insert a view of the contemporary possibilities of Socialism from a rather different angle, a view that follows on to the matter of the previous section, but appeals to a different section of the Middle Class. It is a quotation from the Magazine of Commerce for September 1907, and leads to an explanation by the present writer.

"The recent return of Mr. Grayson, a Socialist, as member of Parliament for the Colne Valley, has brought prominently before the public mind the question of Socialism. Mr. Pete Curran's success at Jarrow a month or so ago, and the large number of Labour members returned at the last General Election, caused more or less desultory comment on Socialism as a possible feature of practical politics in the remote future; but Mr. Grayson can certainly claim that his achievement at Colne Valley brought the question of Socialism in to the very forefront at one bound. It is difficult to ignore Socialism, to dismiss it as a mere fad and fancy of a few hare brained enthusiasts, after Mr. Grayson's success. The verdict of Colne Valley may be the verdict of many another constituency where so called working class electors are numerically predominant. When we consider that the manual worker represents the majority of the electorate of the country, this contingency does not appear to be so very remote, provided that the leaders of Socialism can organize their resources and canvass the working men on a wide and carefully planned scale. In this respect the Colne Valley result may very well give them the lead and stimulus they have been waiting for. It must be borne in mind, too, that the forward section of the Labour Party is avowedly Socialist in its sympathies, and a definite start may therefore be said to have been made towards capturing the machinery of Government in the Cause of Socialism.

"How will Socialism affect the business world? This is a question which many thoughtful business men must have already put to themselves. For reply we must go to the leaders of Socialism, and discover what their policy actually is. The common impression that Socialism spells barefaced confiscation is too superficial to be seriously adduced as an argument against Socialism. The leaders of the Cause include some of the cleverest men of the day—men who have a more rational basis for their policy than that of simply robbing Peter to pay Paul. The suggestion that Socialism means a compulsory 'share out' may be rightly dismissed as an idle scare. The most bitter opponent of Socialism must at least admit that there is a stronger argument to be met than that implied by the parrot cry of 'spoliation.' Socialism has, at any rate, so far advanced as to be allowed the ordinary courtesies of debate. We may oppose it tooth and nail, but we must confront argument with argument and not with abuse.

"Despite much excellent literature which is read widely by cultured people, very little is known by the general public of the principles which modern British Socialists have adopted as their guiding rules. Few business men care to study the subject. We have therefore addressed a letter to the chief leaders of the Cause, with the purpose of ascertaining the effect which Socialism would have on our business habits. Our object was to discover how far Socialism might disturb or improve business; whether it would altogether subvert present methods, or whether it could be applied without injury to these methods. To put the matter very plainly, we wished to learn whether we should carry on our business much as we do now, giving free play to individual effort and individual fortune building.

"The reply of Mr. Wells is as follows:—

"'MY DEAR SIR,

"'I wish very much I could reply at adequate length to your very admirably framed question. The constant stream of abuse and of almost imbecile misrepresentations of Socialism in the Press has no doubt served to distort the idea of our movement in the minds of a large proportion of busy men, and filled them with an unfounded dread of social insecurity. If it were possible to allay that by an epigrammatic programme, "Socialism in a Nutshell," so to speak, I would do my best. But the economic and trading system of a modern State is not only a vast and complex tangle of organizations, but at present an uncharted tangle, and necessarily the methods of transition from the limited individualism of our present condition to the scientifically organized State, which is the Socialist ideal, must be gradual, tentative and various.

"'To build up a body of social and economic science, to develop a class of trained administrators, to rearrange local government areas, to educate the whole community in the "sense of the State" are necessary parts of the Socialist scheme. You must try and induce your readers to recognize that when Socialism finds such supporters as Sir Oliver Lodge and Professor Karl Pearson, as William Morris (who revolutionized the furniture trade), as Granville Barker (who is revolutionizing the London stage), as Mr. George Cadbury and Mr. Fels (whose names are not unknown in the world of advertisement), as Mr. Allan (of the Allan Line), as Mr. George Bernard Shaw and Mrs. Shaw, Mr. and Mrs. Sidney Webb and Sir Sidney Olivier (the present Governor of Jamaica)—all of them fairly comfortable and independent people, practically acquainted with the business of investment and affairs generally and quite alive to the present relations of property to the civilized life—the suggestion that it is a raid of the ignorant "Have nots" on the possessions of the wise and good "Haves" cannot be a very intelligent one nor addressed to very intelligent people. Essentially Socialism is the scientifically organized State as distinguished from the haphazard, wasteful, blundering, child sweating State of the eighteenth century. It is the systematization of present tendency. Necessarily its methods of transition will be progressively scientific and humane.

"'So far as your specific questions go, I do not think there could possibly be anything in the nature of "compulsory profit sharing" if a Socialist Government came into office. There is at present a compulsory profit sharing in the form of an income tax, but that tax does not appeal to the Socialist as a particularly scientific one. The advent of a strongly Socialist Government would mean no immediate revolutionary changes at all. There would be, no doubt, a vigorous acceleration of the educational movement to increase the economic value and productivity of the average citizen of the next generation, and legislation upon the lines laid down by the principle of the "minimum wage" to check the waste of our national resources by destructive employment. Also a systematic shifting of the burthen of taxation from enterprise to rent would begin. But nothing convulsive would occur.'"

"'The means of transit and communication of the country (both internal and external), and especially the railways and canals (which are now rapidly falling into inefficiency through the exhaustion of their capital upon excessive dividends in the past), would probably be transferred from competitive private to organized public control—a transfer that would certainly be enormously stimulating to business generally. There would be no "robbery," the former shareholders would become stock or annuity holders. Nor would there be any financial convulsion due to the raising of the "enormous sum" necessary to effect this purchase. The country would simply create stock, while at the same time taking over assets to balance the new liability.

"'A Socialist Government would certainly also acquire the coal mines and the coal trade, and relieve industry from the inconveniences due to the manipulation of the supply of this vitally important factor, and it would accelerate the obvious tendency of the present time to bring the milk trade, the drink trade, slaughtering, local traffic, lighting and power supply into public hands. But none of this is the destruction of property, but only its organization and standardization. Such a State organization of public services is, I submit, enough to keep a Socialist Government busy for some few years, and makes not only for social progress, but social stability.

"'And does an honest and capable business man stand to lose or gain by the coming of such a Socialist Government? I submit that, on the whole, he stands to gain. Let me put down the essential points in his outlook as I conceive them.

"'Under a Socialist Government such as is quite possible in England at the present time:—

"'He will be restricted from methods of production and sale that are socially mischievous.

"'He will pay higher wages.

"'He will pay a larger proportion of his rate rent outgoings to the State and Municipality, and less to the landlord. Ultimately he will pay it all to the State or Municipality, and as a voter help to determine how it shall be spent, and the landlord will become a Government stock holder. Practically he will get his rent returned to him in public services.

"'He will speedily begin to get better educated, better fed and better trained workers, so that he will get money value for the higher wages he pays.

"'He will get a regular, safe, cheap supply of power and material. He will get cheaper and more efficient internal and external transit.

"'He will be under an organized scientific State, which will naturally pursue a vigorous scientific collective policy in support of the national trade.

"'He will be less of an adventurer and more of a citizen....'"

So I wrote to the Magazine of Commerce, and that for the energetic man who is conducting a real and socially useful business is the outlook. Socialism is not the coming of chaos and repudiation, it is the coming of order and justice. For confusion and accident and waste, the Socialist seeks to substitute design and collective economy. That too is the individual aim of every good business man who is not a mere advertising cheat or financial adventurer. To the sound minded, clear headed man of affairs, Socialism appeals just as it appeals to the scientific man, to the engineer, to the artist, because it is the same reality, the large scale aspect of the same constructive motive, that stirs in himself.

III

Let me finally quote the chairman of one of the most enterprising and enlightened business organizations of our time to show that in claiming the better type of business man for modern Socialism I am making no vain boast. Sir John Brunner may not call himself a Socialist, but this is very probably due to the fact that he gets his ideas of Socialism from the misquotations of its interested adversaries. This that follows from the Manchester Guardian is pure Socialism.

Speaking at the annual meeting of Brunner, Mond and Co., Ltd., in Liverpool (1907), the chairman, Sir John Brunner, M.P., made a remarkable pronouncement on the subject of the collective ownership of canals. He said:—

"I have been one of a Royal Commission visiting the North of France, Belgium, and Northern Germany, and our duty has been to examine what those three countries have done in the improvement of their canals and their waterways. We have been very deeply impressed by what we have seen, and I can tell you to day, speaking as a man of business to men of business, that the fact that in these three countries there is communal effort—that is to say, that the State in money and in credit for the benefit of the national trade—has brought to those three countries enormous, almost incalculable, benefits; and I think that any man, any intelligent man, who studies this matter as I have studied it for a great many years, will come the conclusion, as I have come very clearly and decidedly, that the old policy which we have adopted for generations of leaving all public works to private enterprise—the old policy, so called, of laissez faire—is played out completely, and I am of opinion, very firmly, that, if we mean to hold our own in matters of trade, we must learn to follow the example that has been set us not only by France, Belgium, and Germany, but by the United States and by every one of the Colonies of our Empire. Everywhere do you find that trade is helped by the effort of the community, by the force of the State, and I shall be very heartily pleased if those who hear me will think the matter over and decide for themselves whether or not we as business people—pre-eminently the business people of the world—are to maintain the old policy of leaving everything to private enterprise, or whether we are to act together for the good of all in this important matter of the national trade."

CHAPTER IX

SOME COMMON OBJECTIONS TO SOCIALISM

I

In the preceding eight chapters I have sought to give as plain and full an account of the great generalizations of Socialism as I can, and to make it clear exactly what these generalizations convey, and how far they go in this direction and that. Before we go on to a brief historical and anticipatory account of the actual Socialist movement, it may be worth while to take up and consider compactly the chief objections that are urged against the general propositions of Socialism in popular discussion.

Now a very large proportion of these arise out of the commonest vice of the human mind, its disposition to see everything as "yes" or "no," as "black" or "white," its impatience, its incapacity for a fine discrimination of intermediate shades.[14] The queer old scholastic logic still prevails remarkably in our modern world; you find Mr. Mallock, for example, going about arranging his syllogisms, extracting his opponent's "self contradictions," and disposing of Socialism with stupendous self satisfaction in all the magazines. He disposes of Socialism quite in the spirit of the young mediæval scholar returning home to prove beyond dispute that "my cat has ten tails" and, given a yard's start, that a tortoise can always keep ahead of a running man. The essential fallacy is always to declare that either a thing is A or it is not A; either a thing is green or it is not green; either a thing is heavy or it is not heavy. Unthinking people, and some who ought to know better, fall into that trap. They dismiss from their minds the fact that there is a tinge of green in nearly every object in the world, and that there is no such thing as pure green, unless it be just one line or so in the long series of the spectrum; they forget that the lightest thing has weight and that the heaviest thing can be lifted. The rest of the process is simple and has no relation whatever to the realities of life. They agree to some hard and fast impossible definition of Socialism, permit the exponent to extract absurdities therefrom as a conjurer gets rabbits from a hat, and retire with a conviction that on the whole it is well to have had this disturbing matter settled once for all.

[14] See "Scepticism of the Instrument," the Appendix to A Modern Utopia. (Chapman & Hall.)

For example, the Anti Socialist declares that Socialism "abolishes property." He makes believe there is a hard absolute thing called "property" which must either be or not be, which is now, and which will not be under Socialism. To any person with a philosophical education this is a ridiculous mental process, but it seems perfectly rational to an untrained mind—and that is the usual case with the Anti Socialist. Having achieved this initial absurdity, he then asks in a tone of bitter protest whether a man may not sleep in his own bed, and is he to do nothing if he finds a coal heaver already in possession when he retires? This is the method of Mr. G. R. Sims, that delightful writer, who from altitudes of exhaustive misunderstanding tells the working man that under Socialism he will have—I forget his exact formula, but it is a sort of refrain—no money of his own, no home of his own, no wife of his own, no hair of his own! It is effective nonsense in its way—but nonsense nevertheless. In my preceding chapters I hope I have made it clear that "property" even to day is a very qualified and uncertain thing, a natural vague instinct capable of perversion and morbid exaggeration and needing control, and that Socialism seeks simply to give it a sharper, juster and rationally limited form in relation to the common weal.

Or again, the opponent has it that Socialism "abolishes the family"—and with it, of course, "every sacred and tender association," etc., etc. To that also I have given a chapter.

I do not think much Anti Socialism is dishonest in these matters. The tricks of deliberate falsification, forgery and falsehood that discredit a few Conservative candidates and speakers in the north of England and smirch the reputations of one or two London papers, are due to a quite exceptional streak of baseness in what is on the whole a straightforward opposition to Socialism. Anti Socialism, as its name implies, is no alternative doctrine; it is a mental resistance, not a mental force. For the most part one is dealing with sheer intellectual incapacity; with people, muddle headed perhaps, but quite well meaning, who are really unable to grasp the quantitative element in things. They think with a simple flat certitude that if, for example, a doctor says quinine is good for a case it means that he wishes to put every ounce of quinine that can be procured into his patient, to focus all the quinine in the world upon him; or that if a woman says she likes dancing, that thereby she declares her intention to dance until she drops. They are dear lumpish souls who like things "straightforward" as they say—all or nothing. They think qualifications or any quantitative treatment "quibbling," to be loudly scorned, bawled down and set aside.

In controversy the temptations for a hot and generous temperament, eager for victory, to misstate and overstate the antagonist's position are enormous, and the sensible Socialist must allow for them unless he is to find discussion intolerable. The reader of the preceding chapters should know exactly how Socialism stands to the family relations, the things it urges, the things it regards with impartiality or patient toleration, the things it leaves alone. The preceding chapters merely summarize a literature that has been accessible for years. Yet it is extraordinary how few antagonists of Socialism seem able even to approach these questions in a rational manner. One admirably typical critic of a pamphlet in which I propounded exactly the same opinions as are here set out in the third chapter, found great comfort in the expression "brood mares." He took hold of my phrase, "State family," and ran wild with it. He declared it to be my intention that women were no longer to be wives but "brood mares" for the State. Nothing would convince him that this was a glaring untruth. His mind was essentially equestrian; "human stud farm" was another of his expressions.[15] Ridicule and argument failed to touch him; I believe he would have gone to the stake to justify his faith that Socialists want to put woman in the Government haras. His thick headedness had, indeed, a touch of the heroic.

[15] What makes the expression particularly inappropriate in my case is the fact that in my Mankind in the Making there is a clearly reasoned chapter (Ch. II.) which has never been answered, in which I discuss and, I think, conclusively dispose of Mr. Francis Galton's ideas of Eugenics and deliberate stirpiculture.

Then a certain Father Phelan of St. Louis, no doubt in a state of mental exaltation as honest as it was indiscriminating, told the world through the columns of an American magazine that I wanted to tear the babe from the mother's breast and thrust it into an "Institution." He said worse things than that—but I set them aside as pulpit eloquence. Some readers, no doubt, knew better and laughed, but many were quite sincerely shocked, and resolved after that to give Socialism a very wide berth indeed. Honi soit qui mal y pense; the revolting ideas that disgusted them were not mine, they came from some hot dark reservoir of evil thoughts that years of chastity and discipline seem to have left intact in Father Phelan's soul.

The error in all these cases is the error of overstatement, of getting into a condition of confused intellectual excitement, and because a critic declares your window curtains too blue, saying, therefore, and usually with passion, that he wants the whole universe, sky and sea included, painted bright orange. The inquirer into the question of Socialism will find that an almost incurable disease of these controversies. Again and again he will meet with it. If after that critic's little proposition about your window curtains he chances to say that on the whole he thinks an orange sky would be unpleasant, the common practice is to accuse him of not "sticking to his guns."

My friends, Mr. G. K. Chesterton and Mr. Max Beerbohm, those brilliant ornaments of our age, when they chance to write about Socialism, confess this universal failing—albeit in a very different quality and measure. They are not, it is true, distressed by that unwashed coal heaver who haunts the now private bed of the common Anti Socialist, nor have they any horrid vision of the fathers of the community being approved by a select committee of the County Council—no doubt wrapped in horse cloths and led out by their grooms—such as troubles the spurred and quivering soul of that equestrian—I forget his name—the "brood mare" gentleman who denounced me in the Pall Mall Gazette; but their souls fly out in a passion of protest against the hints of discipline and order the advancement of Socialism reveals. Mr. G. K. Chesterton mocks valiantly and passionately, I know, against an oppressive and obstinately recurrent anticipation of himself in Socialist hands, hair clipped, meals of a strictly hygienic description at regular hours, a fine for laughing—not that he would want to laugh—and austere exercises in several of the more metallic virtues daily. Mr. Max Beerbohm's conception is rather in the nature of a nightmare, a hopeless, horrid, frozen flight from the pursuit of Mr. Sidney Webb and myself, both of us short, inelegant men indeed, but for all that terribly resolute, indefatigable, incessant, to capture him, to drag him off to a mechanical Utopia and there to take his thumb mark and his name, number him distinctly in indelible ink, dress him in an unbecoming uniform, and let him loose (under inspection) in a world of neat round lakes of blue lime water and vistas of white sanitary tiling....

The method of reasoning in all these cases is the same; it is to assume that whatever the Socialist postulates as desirable is wanted without limit or qualification, to imagine whatever proposal is chosen for the controversy is to be carried out by uncontrolled monomaniacs, and so to make a picture of the Socialist dream. This picture is presented to the simple minded person in doubt with "This is Socialism. Surely! SURELY! you don't want this!"

And occasionally the poor, simple minded person really is overcome by these imagined terrors. He turns back to our dingy realities again, to the good old grimy world he knows, thanking God beyond measure that he will never live to see the hateful day when one baby out of every four ceases to die in our manufacturing towns, when lives of sordid care are banished altogether from the earth, and when the "sense of humour" and the cult of Mark Tapley which flourishes so among these things will be in danger of perishing from disuse....

But the reader sees now what Socialism is in its essentials, the tempered magnificence of the constructive scheme to which it asks him to devote his life. It is a laborious, immense project to make the world a world of social justice, of opportunity and full living, to abolish waste, to abolish the lavish unpremeditated cruelty of our present social order. Do not let the wit or perversity of the adversary or, what is often a far worse influence, the zeal and overstatement of the headlong advocate, do not let the manifest personal deficiencies of this spokesman or that, distract you from the living heart in Socialism, its broad generosity of conception, its immense claim in kinship and direction upon your Good Will.

II

For the convenience of those readers who are in the position of inquirers, I had designed at this point a section which was to contain a list of the chief objections to Socialism—other than mere misrepresentations—which are current now a days. I had meant at first to answer each one fully and gravely, to clear them all up exhaustively and finally before proceeding. But I find now upon jotting them down, that they are for the most part already anticipated by the preceding chapters, and so I will note them here, very compactly indeed, and make but the briefest comment upon each.

There is first the assertion, which effectually bars a great number of people from further inquiry into Socialist teaching, that Socialism is contrary to Christianity. I would urge that this is the absolute inversion of the truth. Christianity involves, I am convinced, a practical Socialism if it is honestly carried out. This is not only my conviction, but the reader, if he is a Nonconformist, can find it set out at length by Dr. Clifford in a Fabian tract, Socialism and the Teaching of Christ; and, if a Churchman, by the Rev. Stewart Headlam in another, Christian Socialism. He will find a longer and fuller discussion of this question in the Rev. R. J. Campbell's Christianity and Social Order. In the list of members of such a Socialist Society as the Fabian Society will be found the names of clergy of the principal Christian denominations, excepting only the Roman Catholic Church. It is said, indeed, that a good Catholic of the Roman Communion cannot also be any sort of Socialist. Even this very general persuasion may not be correct. I believe the papal prohibition was originally aimed entirely at a specific form of Socialism, the Socialism of Marx, Engels and Bebel, which is, I must admit, unfortunately strongly anti Christian in tone, as is the Socialism of the British Social Democratic Federation to this day. It is true that many leaders of the Socialist party have also been Secularists, and that they have mingled their theological prejudices with their political work. This is the case not only in Germany and America, but in Great Britain, where Mr. Robert Blatchford of the Clarion, for example, has also carried on a campaign against doctrinal Christianity. But this association of Secularism and Socialism is only the inevitable throwing together of two sets of ideas because they have this in common, that they run counter to generally received opinions; there is no other connection. Many prominent Secularists, like Charles Bradlaugh and Mr. J. M. Robertson, are as emphatically anti Socialist as the Pope. Secularists and Socialists get thrown together and classed together just as early Christians and criminals and rebels against the Emperor were no doubt thrown together in the Roman gaols. They had this much in common, that they were in conflict with what most people considered to be right. It is a confusion that needs constant explaining away. It is to me a most lamentable association of two entirely separate thought processes, one constructive socially and the other destructive intellectually, and I have already, in Chapter VI., § 4, done my best to disavow it.

Socialism is pure Materialism, it seeks only physical well being,—just as much as nursing lepers for pity and the love of God is pure materialism that seeks only physical well being.

Socialism advocates Free Love. This objection I have also disposed of in Chapter VI., §§ 2 and 4.

Socialism renders love impossible, and reduces humanity to the condition of a stud farm. This, too, has been already dealt with; see Chapter III., §§ 2 and 5, and Chapter VI., §§ 2, 3, and 4. These two objections generally occur together in the same anti Socialist speech or tract.

Socialism would destroy parental responsibility. This absurd perversion is altogether disposed of in Chapter VI., § 3. It is a direct inversion of current Socialist teaching.

III

Socialism would open the way to vast public corruption. This is flatly opposed to the experience of America, where local administration has been as little Socialistic and as corrupt as anywhere in the world. Obviously in order that a public official should be bribed, there must be some wealthy person outside the system to bribe him and with an interest in bribing him. When you have a weak administration with feeble powers and resources and strong unscrupulous private corporations seeking to override the law and public welfare, the possibilities of bribing are at the highest point. In a community given over to the pursuit of gain, powerful private enterprises will resort to corruption to get and protract franchises, to evade penalties, to postpone expropriation, and they will do it systematically and successfully. And even where there is partial public enterprise and a competition among contractors, there will certainly be, at least, attempts at corruption to get contracts. But where the whole process is in public hands, where can the bribery creep in; who is going to find the money for the bribes, and why?

It is urged that in another direction there is likely to be a corruption of public life due to the organized voting of the employés in this branch of the public service or that, seeking some advantage for their own service. This is Lord Avebury's bogey.[16] Frankly, such voting by services is highly probable. The tramway men or the milk service men may think they are getting too long hours or too low pay in comparison with the teachers or men on the ocean liners, and the thing may affect elections. That is only human nature, and the point to bear in mind is that this sort of thing goes on to day, and goes on with a vigour out of all proportion to the mild possibilities of a Socialist régime. The landowners of Great Britain, for example, are organized in the most formidable manner against the general interests of the community, and constantly subordinate the interests of the common weal to their conception of justice to their class; the big railways are equally potent, and so are the legal profession and the brewers. But to day these political interventions of great organized services athwart the path of statesmanship are sustained by enormous financial resources. The State employés under Socialism will be in the position of employing one another and paying one another; the teacher, for example, will be educating the sons of the tramway men up to the requirements of the public paymaster, and travelling in the trams to and from his work; there will be close mutual observation and criticism, therefore, and a strong community of spirit, and that will put very definite limits indeed upon the possibly evil influence of class and service interests in politics.

[16] On Municipal and National Trading, by Lord Avebury. (Macmillan & Co., 1907.)

Socialism would destroy Incentive and Efficiency. This is dealt with in Chapter V. on the Spirit of Gain and the Spirit of Service.

Socialism is economically unsound. The student of Socialism who studies—and every student of Socialism should study very carefully—the literature directed against Socialism, will encounter a number of rather confused and frequently very confusing arguments running upon "business" or "economic" lines. In nearly all of these the root error is a misconception of the nature and aim of Socialist claims. Sometimes this misconception is stated and manifest, often it is subtly implied, and then it presents the greatest difficulties to the inexpert dialectician. I find, for instance, Mr. W. H. Lever, in an article on Socialism and Business in the Magazine of Commerce for October 1907, assuming that there will be no increase in the total wealth of the community under Socialism, whereas, as my fourth chapter shows, Socialist proposals in the matter of property aim directly at the cessation of the waste occasioned by competition through the duplication and multiplication of material and organizations (see for example the quotation from Elihu, p. 69), and at the removal of the obstructive claims of private ownership (see p. 65) from the path of production. If Socialism does not increase the total wealth of the community, Socialism is impossible.

Having made this assumption, however, Mr. Lever next assumes that all contemporary business is productive of honest, needed commodities, and that its public utility and its profitable conduct measure one another. But this ignores the manifest fact that success in business now a days is far more often won by the mere salesmanship of mediocre or inferior or short weight goods than it is by producing exceptional value, and the Kentish railways, for example, are a standing contrast of the conflict between public service and private profit seeking. But having committed himself to these two entirely unsound assumptions, it is easy for Mr. Lever to show that since Socialism will give no more wealth, and since what he calls Labour, Capital and the Employer (i.e. Labour, Plant and Management) are necessary to production and must be maintained out of the total product, there will be little more, practically, for the Labourer under Socialist conditions than under the existing régime. Going on further to assume that the Owner is always enterprising and intelligent and public spirited, and the State stupid (which is a quite unjustifiable assumption), he shows their share may even be less. But the whole case for the Socialist proposals, the student must bear in mind, rests upon the recognition that private management of our collective concerns means chaotic and socially wasteful management—however efficient it may be in individual cases for competitive purposes—and that the systematic abolition of the parasitic Owner from our economic process implies the replacement of confusion by order and an immense increase in the efficiency of that economic process. Socialism is economy. If the student of Socialism does not bear this in mind, if once he allows the assumption to creep in that Socialism is not so much a proposal to change, concentrate and organize the economic process, as one to distribute the existing wealth of the country in some new manner, he will find there is a bad case for Socialism.

It is an amusing and I think a fair comment on the arguments of Mr. Lever that a year or so ago he was actually concerned—no doubt in the interests of the public as well as his own—in organizing the production and distribution of soap so as to economize the waste and avoid the public disservice due to the extreme competition of the soap dealers. He wanted to do in the soap industry just exactly what Socialism wants to do in the case of all public services, that is to say he wanted to give it the economic advantages of a Great Combine. In some directions the saving to the soap interest would have been immense; all the vast expenditure upon newspaper advertisements, for example, all the waste upon competing travellers would have been saved. Whether the public would have benefited greatly or not is beside the present question; Mr. Lever and other great soap proprietors would certainly have benefited enormously. They would have benefited by working as a collective interest instead of as independent private owners. But in this little experiment in what was really a sort of voluntary Socialism for particular ends, Mr. Lever reckoned without another great system of private adventurers, the halfpenny newspaper proprietors, who had hitherto been drawing large sums from soap advertisement, and who had in fact been so far parasitic on the public soap supply. One group of these papers at once began a campaign against the "Soap Trust," a campaign almost as noisy and untruthful as the anti Socialist campaign. They accused Mr. Lever of nearly every sort of cheating that can be done by a soap seller, and anticipated every sort of oppression a private monopolist can practise. In the end they paid unprecedented damages for libel, but they stopped Mr. Lever's intelligent and desirable endeavours to replace the waste and disorder of our existing soap supply by a simple and more efficient organization. Mr. Lever cannot have forgotten these facts; they were surely in the back of his mind when he wrote his "Socialism and Business" paper, and it is a curious instance of the unconscious limitations one may encounter in a mind of exceptional ability that he could not bring them forward and apply them to the problem in hand.

Socialism is unbusinesslike. See Chapter VIII., §§ 2 and 3.

IV

Socialism would destroy freedom. This is a more considerable difficulty. To begin with it may be necessary to remind the reader that absolute freedom is an impossibility. As I have written in my Modern Utopia:—

"The idea of individual liberty is one that has grown in importance and grows with every development of modern thought. To the classical Utopists freedom was relatively trivial. Clearly they considered virtue and happiness as entirely separable from liberty, and as being altogether more important things. But the modern view, with its deepening insistence upon individuality and upon the significance of its uniqueness, steadily intensifies the value of freedom, until at last we begin to see liberty as the very substance of life, that indeed it is life, and that only the dead things, the choiceless things live in absolute obedience to law. To have free play for one's individuality is, in the modern view, the subjective triumph of existence, as survival in creative work and offspring is its objective triumph. But for all men, since man is a social creature, the play of will must fall short of absolute freedom. Perfect human liberty is possible only to a despot who is absolutely and universally obeyed. Then to will would be to command and achieve, and within the limits of natural law we could at any moment do exactly as it pleased us to do. All other liberty is a compromise between our own freedom of will and the wills of those with whom we come in contact. In an organized state each one of us has a more or less elaborate code of what he may do to others and to himself, and what others may do to him. He limits others by his rights and is limited by the rights of others, and by considerations affecting the welfare of the community as a whole.

"Individual liberty in a community is not, as mathematicians would say, always of the same sign. To ignore this is the essential fallacy of the cult called Individualism. But in truth, a general prohibition in a State may increase the sum of liberty, and a general permission may diminish it. It does not follow, as these people would have us believe, that a man is more free where there is least law, and more restricted where there is most law. A socialism or a communism is not necessarily a slavery, and there is no freedom under anarchy....

"It follows, therefore, in a modern Utopia, which finds the final hope of the world in the evolving interplay of unique individualities, that the State will have effectually chipped away just all those spendthrift liberties that waste liberty, and not one liberty more, and so have attained the maximum general freedom."...

That is the gist of the Socialist's answer to this accusation. He asks what freedom is there to day for the vast majority of mankind? They are free to do nothing but work for a bare subsistence all their lives, they may not go freely about the earth even, but are prosecuted for trespassing upon the health giving breast of our universal mother. Consider the clerks and girls who hurry to their work of a morning across Brooklyn Bridge in New York, or Hungerford Bridge in London; go and see them, study their faces. They are free, with a freedom Socialism would destroy. Consider the poor painted girls who pursue bread with nameless indignities through our streets at night. They are free by the current standard. And the poor half starved wretches struggling with the impossible stint of oakum in a casual ward, they too are free! The nimble footman is free, the crushed porter between the trucks is free, the woman in the mill, the child in the mine. Ask them! They will tell you how free they are. They have happened to choose these ways of living—that is all. No doubt the piquancy of the life attracts them in many such cases.

Let us be frank; a form of Socialism might conceivably exist without much freedom, with hardly more freedom than that of a British worker to day. A State Socialism tyrannized over by officials who might be almost as bad at times as uncontrolled small employers, is so far possible that in Germany it is practically half existent now. A bureaucratic Socialism might conceivably be a state of affairs scarcely less detestable than our own. I will not deny there is a clear necessity of certain addenda to the wider formulæ of Socialism if we are to be safeguarded effectually from the official. We need free speech, free discussion, free publication, as essentials for a wholesome Socialist State. How they may be maintained I shall discuss in a later chapter. But these admissions do not justify the present system. Socialism, though it failed to give us freedom, would not destroy anything that we have in this way. We want freedom now, and we have it not. We speak of freedom of speech, but to day, in innumerable positions, Socialist employés who declared their opinions openly would be dismissed. Then again in religious questions there is an immense amount of intolerance and suppression of social and religious discussion to day, especially in our English villages. As for freedom of action, most of us, from fourteen to the grave, are chased from even the leisure to require freedom by the necessity of earning a living....

Socialism, as I have stated it thus far, and as it is commonly stated, would give economic liberty to men and women alike, it would save them from the cruel urgency of need, and so far it would enormously enlarge freedom, but it does not guarantee them political or intellectual liberty. That I frankly admit, and accept as one of the incompletenesses of contemporary Socialism. I conceive, therefore, as I shall explain at length in a later chapter, that it is necessary to supplement such Socialism as is currently received by certain new propositions. But to admit that Socialism does not guarantee freedom, is not to admit that Socialism will destroy it. It is possible, given certain conditions, for men to be nearly absolutely free in speech, in movement, in conduct; enormously free, that is, as compared with our present conditions, in a Socialist State established upon the two great propositions I have formulated in Chapters III. and IV. So that the statement that Socialism will destroy freedom is a baseless one of no value as a general argument against the Socialist idea.

V

Socialism would reduce life to one monotonous dead level! This in a world in which the majority of people live in cheap cottages, villa residences and tenement houses, read halfpenny newspapers and wear ready made clothes!

Socialism would destroy Art, Invention and Literature. I do not know why this objection is made, unless it be that the objectors suppose that artists will not create, inventors will not think, and no one write or sing except to please a wealthy patron. Without his opulent smile, where would they be? Well, do not let us be ungrateful; the arts owe much to patronage. Go to Venice, go to Florence, and you will find a glorious harvest of pictures and architecture, sown and reaped by a mercantile plutocracy. But then in Rome, in Athens, you will find an equal accumulation made under very different conditions. Reach a certain phase of civilization, a certain leisure and wealth, and art will out, however the wealth may be distributed. In certain sumptuous directions art flourishes now, and would certainly flourish less in a Socialist State; in the gear of ostentatious luxury, in private furniture of all sorts, in palace building, in the exquisite confections of costly feminine adornment, in the luxurious binding of books, in the cooking of larks, in the distinguished portraiture of undistinguished persons, in the various refinements of prostitution, in the subtle accommodations of mystic theology, in jewellery. It is quite conceivable that in such departments Socialism will discourage and limit æsthetic and intellectual effort. But no mercantile plutocracy could ever have produced a Gothic cathedral, a folk lore, a gracious natural type of cottage or beautiful clothing for the common people, and no mercantile plutocracy will ever tolerate a literature of power. If the coming of Socialism destroys arts, it will also create arts; the architecture of private palaces will give place to an architecture of beautiful common homes, cottages and colleges, and to a splendid development of public buildings, the Sargents of Socialism will paint famous people instead of millionaires' wives, poetry and popular romantic literature will revive. For my own part I have no doubt where the balance of advantage lies.

It seems reasonable to look to the literary and artistic people themselves for a little guidance in this matter. Well, we had in the nineteenth century an absolute revolt of artists against Individualism. The proportion of open and declared Socialists among the great writers, artists, playwrights, critics, of the Victorian period was out of all proportion to the number of Socialists in the general population. Wilde in his Soul of Man under Socialism, Ruskin in many volumes of imperishable prose, Morris in all his later life, have witnessed to the unending protest of the artistic spirit against the rule of gain. Some of these writers are not, perhaps, to be regarded as orthodox Socialists in the modern sense, but their disgust with and contempt for Individualist competition is entirely in the vein of our teaching.

Even this Individualistic country of ours, after the shameful shock of the Great Exhibition of 1851, decided that it could no longer leave art to private enterprise, and organized that systematic government Art Teaching that has, in spite of its many defects, revolutionized the æsthetic quality of this country. And so far as research and invention go, one may very reasonably appeal to such an authority on the other side, as the late Mr. Beit, of Wernher Beit & Co. The outcome of his experience as an individualist financier was to convince him that the only way to raise the standard of technical science in England, and therewith of economic enterprise, was by the endowment of public teaching, and the huge "London Charlottenburg" rises—out of his conviction. Even Messrs. Rockefeller and Carnegie admit the failure of Individualism in this matter by pouring money into public universities and public libraries. All these heads of the commercial process confess by such acts just exactly what this objection of the inexperienced denies, that is to say the power of the State to develop art, invention and knowledge; the necessity that this duty should be done if not by, then at any rate through, the State.

Socialism may very seriously change the direction of intellectual and æsthetic endeavour; that one admits. But there is no reason whatever for supposing it will not, and there are countless reasons for supposing that it will, enormously increase the opportunities and encouragements for æsthetic and intellectual endeavour.

VI

Socialism would arrest the survival of the Fittest. Here is an objection from quite a new quarter. It is the stock objection of the science student. Hitherto we have considered religious and æsthetic difficulties, but this is the difficulty of the mind that realizes clearly the nature of the biological process, the secular change in every species under the influence of its environment, and is most concerned with that. Species, it is said, change—and the student of the elements of science is too apt to conclude that this change is always ascent in the scale of being—by the killing off of the individuals out of harmony with the circumstances under which the species is living. This is not quite true. The truer statement is that species change because, allowing for chance and individual exceptions, only those individuals survive to reproduce themselves who are fairly well adjusted to the conditions of life; so that in each generation there is only a small proportion of births out of harmony with these conditions. This sounds very like the previous proposition, but it differs in this that the accent is shifted from the "killing" to the suppression of births, that is the really important fact. In any case, then, the believer in evolution holds that the qualities encouraged by the environment increase in the species and the qualities discouraged diminish. The qualities that have survival value are not always what we human beings consider admirable—that is a consideration many science students fail to grasp. The remarkable habits of all the degenerating crustacea, for example, the appetite of the vulture, the unpleasing personality of the common hyæna, all that less charming side of Mother Nature that her scandalized children may read of in Cobbold's Human Parasites, are the result of survival under the pressure of environment, just as much as the human eye or the wing of an eagle. Let the objector therefore ask himself what sort of "fittest" are surviving now.

The plain answer is that under our present conditions the Breeding Getter wins, the man who can hold and keep and reproduce his kind. People with the instinct of owning stronger than any other instinct float out upon the top of our seething mass, and flourish there. Aggressive, intensely acquisitive, reproductive people—the ignoble sort of Jew is the very type of it—are the people who will prevail in a social system based on private property and mercantile competition. No creative power, no nobility, no courage can battle against them. And below—in the slums and factories, what will be going on? The survival of a race of stunted toilers, with great resisting power to infection, contagion and fatigue, omnivorous as rats....

Don't imagine that the high infantile death rate of our manufacturing centres spares the fine big children. It does not. Here is the effectual answer to that. It is taken from the Report of the Education Committee of the London County Council for the year 1905, and it is part of an account of an inquiry conducted by the headmaster of one school in a poor neighbourhood.

"The object of the inquiry was to discover the causes of variation in the physical condition of children within the limits of this single school. Each of the 405 boys was carefully weighed and measured without boots, a note was made of the condition of the teeth, and a general estimate of the personal cleanliness and sufficiency of clothing as a basis for determining the home conditions of neglect or otherwise from external evidence. The teacher of each class added an estimate of mental capacity." (Here follow tabular arrangements of results, and height and weight charts.)

"... It may be noted in the heights and weights for each age that the curve is not a continuous line of growth, but that at some ages it springs nearer to, and at others sinks further from, the normal. The greatest effect upon the life capital of the population is produced by the infantile mortality, which in some years actually kills off during the first year one in five of all children born; the question naturally arises what is its effect upon the survivors—do the weakly ones get killed off and only the strong muddle through, or does the adverse environment which slaughters one in five have a maiming effect upon those left?... When the infantile mortality for the parish in which the school is situate was charted above the physique curve, an absolute correspondence is to be observed. The children born in a year when infantile mortality is low show an increased physique, rising nearest to the normal in the extraordinary good year 1892; and those born in the years of high mortality show a decreased physique.... It appears certain, therefore, that in years of high infantile mortality the conditions, to which one in five or six of the children born are sacrificed, have a maiming effect upon the other four or five."

The fine big children are born in periods of low infantile mortality, that is the essential point.

So that anyhow, since the fittest under present conditions is manifestly the ratlike, the survival of the fittest that is going on now is one that it is highly desirable to stop as soon as possible, and so far Socialism will arrest the survival of the fittest. But that does not mean that it will stop the development of the species altogether. It will merely shift the incident of selection and rejection to a new set of qualities. I think I have already hinted (Chapter VI., § 2) that a State that undertakes to sustain all the children born into it will do its best to secure good births. That implies a distinct bar to the marriage and reproduction of the halt and the blind, the bearers of transmissible diseases and the like. And women being economically independent will have a far freer choice in wedlock than they have now. Now they must in practice marry men who can more or less keep them, they must subordinate every other consideration to that. Under Socialism they will certainly look less to a man's means and acquisitive gifts, and more to the finer qualities of his personality. They will prefer prominent men, able men, fine, vigorous and attractive persons. There will, indeed, be far more freedom of choice on either side than under the sordid conditions of the present time. I submit that such a free choice is far more likely to produce a secular increase in the beauty, the intellectual and physical activity and the capacity of the race, than our present haphazard mercenariness.

The science student will be interested to read in this connection The Ethic of Free Thought (A. & C. Black, 1888), Socialism in Theory and Practice (1884), and The Chances of Death, and other Studies in Evolution (Arnold, 1897), by Karl Pearson. Professor Pearson is not in all respects to be taken as an authoritative exponent of Modern Socialism, and he is associated with no Socialist organization, but his treatment of the biological aspect is that of a specialist and a master.

VII

Socialism is against Human Nature. This objection I have left until last because, firstly, it is absolutely true, and secondly, it leads naturally to the newer ideas that have already peeped out once or twice in my earlier chapters and which will now ride up to a predominance in what follows, and particularly the idea that an educational process and a moral discipline are not only a necessary part, but the most fundamental part of any complete Socialist scheme. Socialism is against Human Nature. That is true, and it is equally true of everything else; capitalism is against human nature, competition is against human nature, cruelty, kindness, religion and doubt, monogamy, polygamy, celibacy, decency, indecency, piety and sin are all against human nature. The present system in particular is against human nature, or what is the policeman for, the soldier, the debt collector, the judge, the hangman? What means the glass along my neighbour's wall? Human nature is against human nature. For human nature is in a perpetual conflict; it is the Ishmael of the universe, against everything, and with everything against it; and within, no more and no less than a perpetual battleground of passion, desire, cowardice, indolence and good will. So that our initial proposition as it stands at the head of this section, is, as an argument against Socialism, just worth nothing at all.

None the less valuable is it as a reminder of the essential constructive task of which the two primary generalizations of Socialism we have so far been developing are but the outward and visible forms. There is no untutored naturalness in Socialism, no uneducated blind force on our side. Socialism is made of struggling Good Will, made out of a conflict of wills. I have tried to let it become apparent that while I do firmly believe not only in the splendour and nobility of the Socialist dream but in its ultimate practicality, I do also recognize quite clearly that with people just as they are now, with their prejudices, their ignorances, their misapprehensions, their unchecked vanities and greeds and jealousies, their crude and misguided instincts, their irrational traditions, no Socialist State can exist, no better State can exist, than the one we have now with all its squalor and cruelty. Every change in human institutions must happen concurrently with a change of ideas. Upon this plastic, uncertain, teachable thing Human Nature, within us and without, we have, if we really contemplate Socialism as our achievement, to impose guiding ideas and guiding habits, we have to co ordinate all the Good Will that is active or latent in our world in one constructive plan. To day the spirit of humanity is lost to itself, divided, dispersed and hidden in little narrow distorted circles of thought. These divided, misshapen circles of thought are not "human nature," but human nature has fallen into these forms and has to be released. Our fundamental business is to develop the human spirit. It is in the enlargement and enrichment of the average circle of thought that the essential work and method of Socialism is to be found.

CHAPTER X

SOCIALISM A DEVELOPING DOCTRINE

I

So far we have been discussing the broad elementary propositions of Modern Socialism. As we have dealt with them, they amount to little more than a sketch of the foundation for a great scheme of social reconstruction. It would be a poor service to Socialism to pretend that this scheme is complete. From this point onward one enters upon a series of less unanimous utterances and more questionable suggestions. Concerning much of what follows, Socialism has as yet not elaborated its teaching. It has to do so, it is doing so, but huge labours lie before its servants. Before it can achieve any full measure of realization, it has to overcome problems at present but half solved, problems at present scarcely touched, the dark unsettling suggestion of problems that still await formulation. The Anti Socialist is freely welcome to all these admissions. No doubt they will afford grounds for some cheap transitory triumph. They affect our great generalizations not at all; they detract nothing from the fact that Socialism presents the most inspiring, creative scheme that ever came into the chaos of human affairs. The fact that it is not cut and dried, that it lives and grows, that every honest adherent adds not only to its forces but to its thought and spirit, is itself inspiration.

The new adherent to Socialism in particular must bear this in mind, that Socialism is no garment made and finished that we can reasonably ask the world to wear forthwith. It is not that its essentials remain in doubt, it is not that it does not stand for things supremely true, but that its proper method and its proper expedients have still to be established. Over and above the propaganda of its main constructive ideas and the political work for their more obvious and practical application, an immense amount of intellectual work remains to be done for Socialism. The battle for Socialism is to be fought not simply at the polls and in the market place, but at the writing desk and in the study. To many questions, the attitude of Socialism to day is one of confessed inquiring imperfection.[17] It would indeed be very remarkable if a proposition for changes so vast and comprehensive as Socialism advances was in any different state at this present time.

[17] The student will find very clear, informing, and suggestive reading in Kirkup's History of Socialism (A. & C. Black, 1906). It is a fine, impartial account of these developments, which may well be used as a corrective (or confirmation) of this book.

It is so recently as 1833 that the world first heard the word Socialism.[18] It appeared then, with the vaguest implications and the most fluctuating definition, as a general term for a disconnected series of protests against the extreme theories of Individualism and Individualist Political Economy; against the cruel, race destroying industrial spirit that then dominated the world. Of these protests the sociological suggestions and experiments of Robert Owen were most prominent in the English community, and he it is, more than any other single person, whom we must regard as the father of Socialism. But in France ideas essentially similar were appearing about such movements and personalities as those of Saint Simon, Proudhon and Fourier. They were part of a vast system of questionings and repudiations, political doubts, social doubts, hesitating inquiries and experiments.

[18] It was probably first used in the Poor Man's Guardian in that year. See The Life of Francis Place, by Graham Wallas, p. 353.

It is only to be expected that early Socialism should now appear as not only an extremely imperfect but a very inconsistent system of proposals. Its value lay not so much in its plans as in its hopeful and confident denials. It had hold of one great truth; it moved one great amendment to the conception of practical equality the French Revolution had formulated, and that was its clear indication of the evil of unrestricted private property and of the necessary antagonism of the interests of the individual to the common weal, of "Wealth against Commonwealth," that went with that. While most men had to go propertyless in a world that was privately owned, the assertion of equality was an empty lie. For the rest, primordial Socialism was entirely sketchy and experimental. It was wild as the talk of school boys. It disregarded the most obvious needs. It did not provide for any principle of government, or for the maintenance of collective thought and social determination, it offered no safeguards and guarantees for even the most elementary privacies and freedoms; it was extraordinarily non constructive. It was extreme in its proposed abolition of the home, and it flatly ignored the huge process of transition needed for a change so profound and universal.

The early Socialism was immediately millennial. It had no patience. The idea was to be made into a definite project forthwith; Fourier drew up his compact scheme, arranged how many people should live in each phalange and so forth, and all that remained to do, he thought, was to sow phalanges as one scatters poppy seed. With him it was to be Socialism by contagion, with many of his still hastier contemporaries it was to be Socialism by proclamation. All the evils of society were to crumble to ruins like the Walls of Jericho at the first onset of the Great Idea.

Our present generation is less buoyant perhaps, but wiser. However young you may be as a reformer, you know you must face certain facts those early Socialists ignored. Whatever sort of community you dream of, you realize that it has to be made of the sort of people you meet every day or of the children growing up under their influence. The damping words of the old philosopher to the ardent Social reformer of seventeen were really the quintessence of our criticism of revolutionary Socialism: "Will your aunts join us, my dear? No! Well—is the grocer on our side? And the family solicitor? We shall have to provide for them all, you know, unless you suggest a lethal chamber."

For a generation Socialism, in the exaltation of its self discovery, failed to measure these primary obstacles, failed to recognize the real necessity, the quality of the task of making these people understand. To this day the majority of Socialists still fail to grasp completely the Herbartian truth, the fact that every human soul moves within its circle of ideas, resisting enlargement, incapable indeed if once it is adult of any extensive enlargement, and that all effectual human progress can be achieved only through such enlargement. Only ideas cognate to a circle of ideas are assimilated or assimilable; ideas too alien, though you shout them in the ear, thrust them in the face, remain foreign and incomprehensible.

The early Socialists, arriving at last at their Great Idea, after toilsome questionings, after debates, disputations, studies, trials, saw, and instantly couldn't understand those others who did not see; they failed altogether to realize the leaps they had made, the brilliant omissions they had achieved, the difficulties they had evaded to get to this magnificent conception. I suppose such impatience is as natural and understandable as it is unfortunate. None of us escape it. Much of this early Socialism is as unreal as mathematics, has much the same relation to truth as the abstract absolute process of calculation has to concrete individual things; much of it more than justifies altogether that "black or white" method of criticism of which I wrote in the preceding chapter. They were as downright and unconsidering, as little capable of the reasoned middle attitude. Proudhon, perceiving that the world was obsessed by a misconception of the scope of property whereby the many were enslaved to the few, went off at a tangent to the announcement that "Property is Robbery," an exaggeration that, as I have already shown, still haunts Socialist discussion. The ultimate factor of all human affairs, the psychological factor, was disregarded. Like the classic mathematical problem, early Socialism was always "neglecting the weight of the elephant"—or some other—from the practical point of view— equally essential factor. This was, perhaps, an unavoidable stage. It is probable that by no other means than such exaggeration and partial statement could Socialism have got itself begun. The world of 1830 was fatally wrong in its ideas of property; early Socialism rose up and gave those ideas a flat, extreme, outrageous contradiction. After that analysis and discussion became possible.

The early Socialist literature teems with rash, suggestive schemes. It has the fertility, the confusion, the hopefulness, the promise of glowing youth. It is a quarry of ideas, a mine of crude expedients, a fountain of emotions. The abolition of money, the substitution of Labour Notes, the possibility, justice and advantage of equalizing upon a time basis the remuneration of the worker, the relation of the new community to the old family, a hundred such topics were ventilated—were not so much ventilated as tossed about in an impassioned gale.

Much of this earlier Socialist literature was like Cabet's book, actually Utopian in form; a still larger proportion was Utopian in spirit; its appeal was imaginative, and it aimed to be a plan of a new state as definite and detailed as the plan for the building of a house. It has been the fashion with a number of later Socialist writers and speakers, mind struck with that blessed word "evolution," confusing "scientific," a popular epithet to which they aspired, with "unimaginative," to sneer at the Utopian method, to make a sort of ideal of a leaden practicality, but it does not follow because the

Utopias produced and the experiments attempted were in many aspects unreasonable and absurd that the method itself is an unsound one. At a certain phase of every creative effort you must cease to study the thing that is, and plan the thing that is not. The early Socialisms were only premature plans and hasty working models that failed to work.

And it must be remembered when we consider Socialism's early extravagancies, that any idea or system of ideas which challenges the existing system is necessarily, in relation to that system, outcast. Mediocre men go soberly on the highroads, but saints and scoundrels meet in the gaols. If A and B rebel against the Government, they are apt, although they rebel for widely different reasons, to be classed together; they are apt indeed to be thrown together and tempted to sink even quite essential differences in making common cause against the enemy. So that from its very beginning Socialism was mixed up—to this day it remains mixed up—with other movements of revolt and criticism, with which it has no very natural connection. There is, for example, the unfortunate entanglement between the Socialist theory and that repudiation of any but subjective sexual limitations which is called "free love," and there is that still more unfortunate association of its rebellion against orthodox economic theories, with rebellion against this or that system of religious teaching. Several of the early Socialist communities, again, rebelled against ordinary clothing, and their women made short hair and bloomers the outward and visible associations of the communistic idea. In Holyoake's History of Co operation it is stated that one early experiment was known to its neighbours as "the grass eating Atheists of Ham Common." I have done my very best (in Chapter VIII., § 2) to clear the exposition of Socialism from these entanglements, but it is well to recognize that these are no corruptions of its teaching, but an inevitable birth infection that has still to be completely overcome.

II

The comprehensively constructive spirit of modern Socialism is very much to seek in these childhood phases that came before Marx. These early projects were for the most part developed by literary men (and by one philosophic business man, Owen) to whose circle of ideas the conception of State organization and administration was foreign. They took peace and order for granted—they left out the school master, the judge and the policeman, as the amateur architect of the anecdote left out the staircase. They set out to contrive a better industrial organization, or a better social atmosphere within the present scheme of things. They wished to reform what they understood, and what was outside their circle of ideas they took for granted, as they took the sky and sea. Not only was their literature Utopian literature, about little islands of things begun over again from the beginning, but their activities tended in the direction of Utopian experiments equally limited and isolated. Here again a just critic will differ from many contemporary Socialists in their depreciation of this sort of work. Owen's experiments in socialized production were of enormous educational and scientific value. They were, to use a mining expert's term, "hand specimens" of human welfare of the utmost value to promoters. They made factory legislation possible; they initiated the now immense co operative movement; they stirred commonplace imaginations as only achievement can stir them; they set going a process of amelioration in industrial conditions that will never, I believe, cease again until the Socialist state is attained.

But apart from Owen and the general advertisement given to Socialist ideas, it must be admitted that a great majority of Socialist communities have, by every material standard, failed rather than succeeded. Some went visibly insolvent and to pieces, others were changed by prosperity. Some were wrecked by the sudden lapse of the treasurer into an extreme individualism. Essentially Socialism is a project for the species, but these communities made it a system of relationships within a little group; to the world without they had necessarily to turn a competitive face, to buy and sell and advertise on the lines of the system as it is. If they failed, they failed; if they succeeded they presently found themselves landlords, employers, no more and no less than a corporate individualism. I have described elsewhere[19] the fate of the celebrated Oneida community of New York State, and how it is now converted into an aggressive, wealthy, fighting corporation of the most modern type, employing immigrant labour.

[19] *The Future in America. (Chapman & Hall, 1906.)*

Professed and conscious Socialism in its earliest stages, then, was an altogether extreme proposition, it was at once imperfect and over emphatic, and it was confused with many quite irrelevant and inconsistent novelties with regard to diet, dress, medicine and religion. Its first manifest, acknowledged and labelled fruits were a series of futile "communities"—Noyes' History of American Socialisms gives their simple history of births and of fatal infantile ailments—Brook Farm, Fourierite "Phalanges" and the like. But correlated with these extreme efforts, drawing ideas and inspiration from them, was the great philanthropic movement for the amelioration of industrialism, that was, I insist, for all its absence of a definite Socialist label in many cases, an equally legitimate factor in the making of the great conception of modern Socialism. Socialism may be the child of the French Revolution, but it certainly has one aristocratic Tory grandparent. There can be little dispute of the close connection of Lord Shaftesbury's Factory Acts, that commencement of constructive statesmanship in industrialism, with the work of Owen. The whole Victorian period marks a steady development of social organization out of the cruel economic anarchy of its commencement; the beginnings of public education, adulteration acts and similar checks upon the extremities of private enterprise, the great successful experiments of co operative consumers' associations and the development of what has now become a quasi official representation of labour in the State through the Trade Unions. Two great writers, Carlyle and Ruskin, the latter a professed Socialist, spent their powers in a relentless campaign against the harsh theories of the liberty of property, the gloomy superstitions of political economy that barred the way to any effectual constructive scheme. An enormous work was done throughout the whole Victorian period by Socialists and Socialistic writers, in criticizing and modifying the average circle of ideas, in bringing conceptions that had once seemed weird, outcast and altogether fantastic, more and more within the range of acceptable practicality.

The first early Socialisms were most various and eccentric upon the question of government and control. They had no essential political teaching. Many, but by no means all, were inspired by the democratic idealism of the first French Revolution. They believed in a mystical something that was wiser and better than any individual,—the People, the Common Man. But that was by no means the case with all of them. The Noyes community was a sort of Theocratic autocracy; the Saint Simonian tendency was aristocratic. The English Socialism that in the middle Victorian period developed partly out of the suggestions of Owen's beginnings and partly as an independent fresh outpouring of the struggling Good Will in man, that English Socialism that found a voice in Ruskin and in Maurice and Kingsley and the Christian Socialists, was certainly not democratic. It kept much of what was best in the "public spirit" of contemporary English life, and it implied if it did not postulate a "governing class." Benevolent and even generous in conception, its exponents betray all too often the ties of social habituations, the limited circle of ideas of English upper and upper middle class life, easy and cultivated, well served and distinctly, most unmistakably, authoritative.

While the experimental Utopian Socialisms gave a sort of variegated and conflicting pattern of a reorganized industrialism and (incidentally to that) a new heaven and earth, the benevolent Socialism, Socialistic Liberalism and Socialistic philanthropy of the middle Victorian period, really went very little further in effect than a projected amelioration and moralization of the relations of rich and poor. It needed the impact of an entirely new type of mind before Socialism began to perceive its own significance as an ordered scheme for the entire reconstruction of the world, began to realize the gigantic breadth of its implications.

CHAPTER XI

REVOLUTIONARY SOCIALISM

I

It was Karl Marx who brought the second great influx of suggestion into the intellectual process of Socialism. Before his time there does not seem to have been any clear view of economic relationships as having laws of development, as having interactions that began and went on and led towards new things. But Marx had vision. He had—as Darwin and the evolutionists had, as most men with a scientific training, and many educated men without that advantage now have—a sense of secular change. Instead of being content with the accepted picture of the world as a scene where men went on producing and distributing wealth and growing rich or poor, it might be for endless ages, he made an appeal to history and historical analogies, and for the first time viewed our age of individualist industrial development, not as a possibly permanent condition of humanity, but as something unstable and in motion, as an economic process, that is to say, with a beginning, a middle, and as he saw it, an almost inevitable end.

The last thing men contrive to discern in every question is the familiar obvious, and it came as a great and shattering discovery to the economic and sociological thought of the latter half of the nineteenth century that there was going on not simply a production but an immense concentration of wealth, a differentiation of a special wealthy class of landholder and capitalist, a diminution of small property owners and the development of a great and growing class of landless, nearly propertyless men, the proletariat. Marx showed—he showed so clearly that to day it is recognized by every intelligent man—that given a continuance of our industrial and commercial system, of uncontrolled gain seeking, that is, given a continuance of our present spirit and ideas of property, there must necessarily come a time when the owner and the proletarian will stand face to face, with nothing—if we except a middle class of educated professionals dependent on the wealthy, who are after all no more than the upper stratum of the proletariat—to mask or mitigate their opposition. We shall have two classes, the class conscious worker and the class conscious owner, and they will be at war. And with a broad intellectual sweep he flung the light of this conception upon the whole contemporary history of mankind. Das Kapital was no sketch of Utopias, had no limitation to the conditions or possibilities of this country or that. "Here," he says, in the widest way, "is what is going on all over the world. So long as practically untrammelled private property, such as you conceive it to day, endures, this must go on. The worker gravitates steadily everywhere to a bare subsistence, the rest of the proceeds of his labour swell the power of the owners. So it will go on while gain and getting are the rule of your system, until accumulated tensions between class and class smash this present social organization and inaugurate a new age."

In considering the thought and work of Karl Marx, the reader must bear in mind the epoch in which that work commenced. The intellectual world was then under the sway of an organized mass of ideas known as the Science of Political Economy, a mass of ideas that has now not so much been examined and refuted as slipped away imperceptibly from its hold upon the minds of men. In the beginning, in the hands of Adam Smith—whose richly suggestive book is now all too little read—political economy was a broad minded and sane inquiry into the statecraft of trade based upon current assumptions of private ownership and personal motives, but from him it passed to men of perhaps, in some cases, quite equal intellectual energy but inferior vision and range. The history of Political Economy is indeed one of the most striking instances of the mischief wrought by intellectual minds devoid of vision, in the entire history of human thought. Special definition, technicality, are the stigmata of second rate intellectual men; they cannot work with the universal tool, they cannot appeal to the general mind. They must abstract and separate. On such men fell the giant's robe of Adam Smith, and they wore it after their manner. Their arid atmospheres are intolerant of clouds, an outline that is not harsh is abominable to them. They criticized their master's vagueness and must needs mend it. They sought to give political economy a precision and conviction such a subject will not stand. They took such words as "value," an incurably and necessarily vague word, "rent," the name of the specific relation of landlord and tenant, and "capital," and sought to define them with relentless exactness and use them with inevitable effect. So doing they departed more and more from reality. They developed a literature more abundant, more difficult and less real than all the exercises of the schoolmen put together. To use common words in uncommon meanings is to sow a jungle of misunderstanding. It was only to be expected that the bulk of this economic literature resolves upon analysis into a ponderous, intricate, often astonishingly able and foolish wrangling about terminology.

Now in the early Victorian period in which Marx planned his theorizing, political economy ruled the educated world. Ruskin had still to attack the primary assumptions of that tyrannous and dogmatic edifice. The duller sort of educated people talked of the "immutable laws of political economy" in the blankest ignorance that the basis of everything in this so called science was a plastic human convention. Humane impulses were checked, creative effort tried and condemned by these mystical formulæ. Political economy traded on the splendid achievements of physics and chemistry and pretended to an inexorable authority. Only a man of supreme intelligence and power, a man resolved to give his lifetime to the task, could afford in those days to combat the pretensions of the political economist; to deny that his categories presented scientific truth, and to cast that jargon aside. As for Marx, he saw fit to accept the verbal instruments of his time (albeit he bent them not a little in use), to accommodate himself to their spirit and to split and re classify and re define them at his need. So that he has become already difficult to follow, and his more specialized exponents among Socialists use terms that arouse no echoes in the contemporary mind. The days when Socialism need present its theories in terms of a science whose fundamental propositions it repudiates, are at an end. One hears less and less of "surplus value" now, as one hears less and less of McCulloch's Law of Wages. It may crop up in the inquiries of some intelligent mechanic seeking knowledge among the obsolescent accumulations of a public library, or it may for a moment be touched upon by some veteran teacher. But the time when social and economic science had to choose between debatable and inexpressive technicalities on the one hand or the stigma of empiricism on the other, is altogether past.

The language a man uses, however, is of far less importance than the thing he has to say, and it detracts little from the cardinal importance of Marx that his books will presently demand restatement in contemporary phraseology, and revision in the light of contemporary facts. He opened out Socialism. It is easy to quibble about Marx, and say he didn't see this or that, to produce this eddy in a backwater or that as a triumphant refutation of his general theory. One may quibble about the greatness of Marx as one may quibble about the greatness of Darwin; he remains great and cardinal. He first saw and enabled the world to see capitalistic production as a world process, passing by necessity through certain stages of social development, and unless some change of law and spirit came to modify it, moving towards an inevitable destiny. His followers are too apt to regard that as an absolutely inevitable destiny, but the fault lies not at his door. He saw it as Socialism. It did not appear to him as it does to many that there is a possible alternative to Socialism, that the process may give us, not a triumph for the revolting proletariat, but their defeat, and the establishment of a plutocratic aristocracy culminating in imperialism and ending in social disintegration. From his study, from the studious rotunda of the British Museum Reading room he made his prophecy of the growing class consciousness of the workers, of the inevitable class war, of the revolution and the millennium that was to follow it. He gathered his facts, elaborated his deductions and waited for the dawn.

So far as his broad generalization of economic development goes, events have wonderfully confirmed Marx. The development of Trusts, the concentration of property that America in particular displays, he foretold. Given that men keep to the unmodified ideas of private property and individualism, and it seems absolutely true that so the world must go. And in the American Appeal to Reason, for example, which goes out weekly from Kansas to a quarter of a million of subscribers, one may, if one chooses, see the developing class consciousness of the workers, and the promise—and when strikers take to rifles and explosives as they do in Pennsylvania and Colorado, something more than the promise—of the class war....

But the modern Socialist considers that this generalization is a little too confident and comprehensive; he perceives that a change in custom, law or public opinion may delay, arrest or invert the economic process, and that Socialism may arrive after all not by a social convulsion, but by the gradual and detailed concession of its propositions. The Marxist presents dramatically what after all may come methodically and unromantically, a revolution as orderly and quiet as the precession of the equinoxes. There may be a concentration of capital and a relative impoverishment of the general working mass of people, for example, and yet a general advance in the world's prosperity and a growing sense of social duty in the owners of capital and land may do much to mask this antagonism of class interests and ameliorate its miseries. Moreover, this antagonism itself may in the end find adequate expression through temperate discussion, and the class war come disguised beyond recognition, with hates mitigated by charity and swords beaten into pens, a mere constructive conference between two classes of fairly well intentioned albeit perhaps still biassed men and women.

II

The circle of ideas in which Marx moved was that of a student deeply tinged with the idealism of the renascent French Revolution. His life was the life of a recluse from affairs—an invalid's life; a large part of it was spent round and about the British Museum Reading room, and his conceptions of Socialism and the social process have at once the spacious vistas given by the historical habit and the abstract quality that comes with a divorce from practical experience of human government. Only in England and in the eighties did the expanding propositions of Socialism come under the influence of men essentially administrative. As a consequence Marx, and still more the early Marxists, were and are negligent of the necessities of government and crude in their notions of class action. He saw the economic process with a perfect lucidity, practically he foretold the consolidation of the Trusts, and his statement of the necessary development of an entirely propertyless working class with an intensifying class consciousness is a magnificent generalization. He saw clearly up to that opposition of the many and the few, and then his vision failed because his experience and interests failed. There was to be a class war, and numbers schooled to discipline by industrial organization were to win.

After that the teaching weakens in conviction. The proletariat was to win in the class war; then classes would be abolished, property in the means of production and distribution would be abolished, all men would work reasonably—and the millennium would be with us.

The constructive part of the Marxist programme was too slight. It has no psychology. Contrasted, indeed, with the splendid destructive criticisms that preceded it, it seems indeed trivial. It diagnoses a disease admirably, and then suggests rather an incantation than a plausible remedy. And as a consequence Marxist Socialism appeals only very feebly to the man of public affairs or business or social experience. It does not attract teachers or medical men or engineers. It arouses such men to a sense of social instability but it offers no remedy. They do not believe in the mystical wisdom of the People. They find no satisfactory promise of a millennium in anything Marx foretold.

To the labouring man, however, accustomed to take direction and government as he takes air and sky, these difficulties of the administrative and constructive mind do not occur. His imagination raises no questioning in that picture of the proletariat triumphant after a class war and quietly coming to its own. It does not occur to him for an instant to ask "how?"

Question the common Marxist upon these difficulties and he will relapse magnificently into the doctrine of laissez faire. "That will be all right," he will tell you.

"How?"

"We'll take over the Trusts and run them."...

It is part of the inconveniences attending all powerful new movements of the human mind that the disciple bolts with the teacher, overstates him, underlines him, and it is no more than a tribute to the potency of Marx that he should have paralyzed the critical faculty in a number of very able men. To them Marx is a final form of truth. They talk with bated breath of a "classic Socialism," to which no man may add one jot or one tittle, to which they are as uncritically pledged as extreme Bible Christians are bound to the letter of the "Word."...

The peculiar evil of the Marxist teaching is this, that it carries the conception of a necessary economic development to the pitch of fatalism, it declares with all the solemnity of popular "science" that Socialism must prevail. Such a fatalism is morally bad for the adherent; it releases him from the inspiring sense of uncertain victory, it leads him to believe the stars in their courses will do his job for him. The common Marxist is apt to be sterile of effort, therefore, and intolerant— preaching predestination and salvation without works.

By a circuitous route, indeed, the Marxist reaches a moral position curiously analogous to that of the disciple of Herbert Spencer. Since all improvement will arrive by leaving things alone, the worse things get, the better; for so much the nearer one comes to the final exasperation, to the class war and the Triumph of the Proletariat. This certainty of victory in the nature of things makes the Marxists difficult in politics, pedantic sticklers for the letter of the teaching, obstinate opponents of what they call "Palliatives"—of any instalment system of reform. They wait until they can make the whole journey in one stride, and would, in the meanwhile, have no one set forth upon the way. In America the Marxist fatalism has found a sort of supreme simplification in the gospel of Mr. H. G. Wilshire. The Trusts, one learns, are to consolidate all the industry in the country, own all the property. Then when they own everything, the Nation will take them over. "Let the Nation own the Trusts!" The Nation in the form of a public, reading capitalistic newspapers, inured to capitalistic methods, represented and ruled by capital controlled politicians, will suddenly take over the Trusts and begin a new system....

It would be quite charmingly easy—if it were only in the remotest degree credible.

The Marxist teaching tends to an unreasonable fatalism. Its conception of the world after the class war is over is equally antagonistic to intelligent constructive effort. It faces that Future, utters the word "democracy," and veils its eyes.

The conception of democracy to which the Marxist adheres is that same mystical democracy that was evolved at the first French Revolution; it will sanction no analysis of the popular wisdom. It postulates a sort of spirit hidden as it were in the masses and only revealed by a universal suffrage of all adults—or, according to some Social Democratic Federation authorities who do not believe in women, all adult males—at the ballot box. Even a large proportion of the adults will not do—it must be all. The mysterious spirit that thus peers out and vanishes again at each election is the People, not any particular person, but the quintessence, and it is supposed to be infallible; it is supposed to be not only morally but intellectually omniscient. It will not even countenance the individuality of elected persons, they are to be mere tools, delegates, from this diffused, intangible Oracle, the Ultimate Wisdom....

Well, it may seem ungracious to sneer at the grotesque formulation of an idea profoundly wise, at the hurried, wrong, arithmetical method of rendering that collective spirit a community undoubtedly can and sometimes does possess—I myself am the profoundest believer in democracy, in a democracy awake intellectually, conscious and self disciplined—but so long as this mystic faith in the crowd, this vague, emotional, uncritical way of evading the immense difficulties of organizing just government and a collective will prevails, so long must the Socialist project remain not simply an impracticable but, in an illiterate, badly organized community, even a dangerous suggestion. I as a Socialist am not blind to these possibilities, and it is foolish because a man is in many ways on one's side that one should not call attention to his careless handling of a loaded gun. Social Democracy may conceivably become a force that in the sheer power of untutored faith may destroy government and not replace it. I do not know how far that is not already the case in Russia. I do not know how far this may not ultimately be the case in the United States of America.

The Marxist teaching, great as was its advance on the dispersed chaotic Socialism that preceded it, was defective in other directions as well as in its innocence of any scheme of State organization. About women and children, for example, it was ill informed; its founders do not seem to have been inspired either by educational necessities or philoprogenitive passion. No biologist—indeed no scientific mind at all—seems to have tempered its severely "economic" tendencies. It so over accentuates the economic side of life that at moments one might imagine it dealt solely with some world of purely "productive" immortals, who were never born and never aged, but only warred for ever in a developing industrial process.

Now reproduction and not production is the more central fact of social life. Women and children and education are things in the background of the Marxist proposal—like a man's dog, or his private reading, or his pet rabbits. They are in the foreground of modern Socialism. The Social Democrat's doctrines go little further in this direction than the Liberalism that founded the United States, which ignored women, children and niggers, and made the political unit the adult white man. They were blind to the supreme importance of making the next generation better than the present as the aim and effort of the whole community. Herr Bebel's book, Woman, is an ample statement of the evils of woman's lot under the existing régime, but the few pages upon the Future of Woman with which he concludes are eloquent of the jejune insufficiency of the Marxist outlook in this direction. Marriage, which modern Socialism tends more and more to sustain, was to vanish—at least as a law made bond; women were to count as men so far as the State is concerned....

This disregard of the primary importance of births and upbringing in human affairs and this advocacy of mystical democracy alike contribute to blind the Marxist to the necessity of an educational process and of social discipline and to the more than personal importance of marriage in the Socialist scheme. He can say with a light and confident heart to untrained, ignorant, groping souls: "Destroy the Government; expropriate the rich, establish manhood suffrage, elect delegates strictly pledged—and you will be happy!"

A few modern Marxists stipulate in addition for a Referendum, by which the acts of the elected delegates can be further checked by referring disputed matters to a general vote of all the adults in the community....

IV

My memory, as I write these things of Marxism, carries me to the dusky largeness of a great meeting in Queen's Hall, and I see again the back of Mr. Hyndman's head moving quickly, as he receives and answers questions. It was really one of the strangest and most interesting meetings I have ever attended. It was a great rally of the Social Democratic Federation, and the place—floor, galleries and platform—was thick but by no means overcrowded with dingy, earnest people. There was a great display of red badges and red ties, and many white faces, and I was struck by the presence of girls and women with babies. It was more like the Socialist meetings of the popular novel than any I had ever seen before. In the chair that night was Lady Warwick, that remarkable intruder into the class conflict, a blond lady, rather expensively dressed, so far as I could judge, about whom the atmosphere of class consciousness seemed to thicken. Her fair hair, her floriferous hat, told out against the dim multitudinous values of the gathering unquenchably; there were moments when one might have fancied it was simply a gathering of village tradespeople about the lady patroness, and at the end of the proceedings, after the red flag had been waved, after the "Red Flag" had been sung by a choir and damply echoed by the audience, some one moved a vote of thanks to the Countess in terms of familiar respect that completed the illusion.

Mr. Hyndman's lecture was entitled "In the Rapids of Revolution," and he had been explaining how inevitable the whole process was, how Russia drove ahead, and Germany and France and America, to the foretold crisis and the foretold millennium. But incidentally he also made a spirited exhortation for effort, for agitation, and he taunted England for lagging in the schemes of fate. Some one amidst the dim multitude discovered an inconsistency in that.

Now the questions were being handed in, written on strips of paper, and at last that listener's difficulty cropped up.

"What's this?" said Mr. Hyndman; unfolded the slip and read out: "Why trouble to agitate or work if the Trusts are going to do it all for us?"

The veteran leader of the Social Democratic Federation paused only for a moment.

"Well, we've got to get ready for it, you know," he said, rustling briskly with the folds of the question to follow—and with these words, it seemed to me, that fatalistic Marxism crumbled down to dust.

We have got to get ready for it. Indeed, we have to make it—by education and intention and set resolve. Socialism is to be attained not by fate, but by will.

V

And here, as a sort of Eastern European gloss upon Marxist Socialism, as an extreme and indeed ultimate statement of this marriage of mystical democracy to Socialism, we may say a word of Anarchism. Anarchism carries the administrative laissez faire of Marx to its logical extremity. "If the common, untutored man is right anyhow—why these ballot boxes; why these intermediaries in the shape of law and representative?"

That is the perfectly logical outcome of ignoring administration and reconstruction. The extreme Social Democrat and the extreme Individualist meet in a doctrine of non resistance to the forces of Evolution—which in this connection they deify with a capital letter. Organization, control, design, the disciplined will, these are evil, they declare—the evil of life. So you come at the end of the process, if you are active minded, to the bomb as the instrument of man's release to unimpeded virtue, and if you are pacific in disposition to the Tolstoyan attitude of passive resistance to all rule and property.

Anarchism, then, is as it were a final perversion of the Socialist stream, a last meandering of Socialist thought, released from vitalizing association with an active creative experience. Anarchism comes when the Socialist repudiation of property is dropped into the circles of thought of men habitually ruled and habitually irresponsible, men limited in action and temperamentally adverse to the toil, to the vexatious rebuffs and insufficiencies, the dusty effort, fatigue, and friction of the practical pursuit of a complex ideal. So that it most flourishes eastwardly, where men, it would seem, are least energetic and constructive, and it explodes or dies on American soil.

Anarchism, with its knife and bomb, is a miscarriage of Socialism, an acephalous birth from that fruitful mother. It is an unnatural offspring, opposed in nature to its parent, for always from the beginning the constructive spirit, the ordering and organizing spirit has been strong among Socialists. It was by a fallacy, an oversight, that laissez faire in politics crept into a movement that was before all things an organized denial of laissez faire in economic and social life....

I write this of the Anarchism that is opposed to contemporary Socialism, the political Anarchism. But there is also another sort of Anarchism, which the student of these schools of thought must keep clear in his mind from this, the Anarchism of Tolstoy and that other brand of William Morris, neither of which waves any flag of black, nor counsels violence; they present that conception of untrammelled and spontaneous rightness and goodness which is, indeed, I hazard, the moral ideal of all rightly thinking men. It is worth while to define very clearly the relation of this second sort of Anarchism, the nobler Anarchism, to the toiling constructive Socialism which many of us now make our practical guide in life's activities, to say just where they touch and where they are apart.

Now the ultimate ideal of human intercourse is surely not Socialism at all, but a way of life that is not litigious and not based upon jealously guarded rights, which is free from property, free from jealousy, and "above the law." There, there shall not be "marriage or giving in marriage." The whole mass of Christian teaching points to such an ideal; Paul and Christ turn again and again to the ideal of a world of "just men made perfect," in which right and beauty come by instinct, in which just laws and regulations are unnecessary and unjust ones impossible. "Turn your attention," says my friend, the Rev. Stewart Headlam, in his admirable tract on Christian Socialism—

"Turn your attention to that series of teachings of Christ's which we call parables—comparisons, that is to say, between what Christ saw going on in the every day world around Him and the Kingdom of Heaven. If by the Kingdom of Heaven in these parables is meant a place up in the clouds, or merely a state in which people will be after death, then I challenge you to get any kind of meaning out of them whatever. But if by the Kingdom of Heaven is meant (as it is clear from other parts of Christ's teaching is the case) the righteous society to be established upon earth, then they all have a plain and beautiful meaning; a meaning well summed up in that saying so often quoted against us by the sceptic and the atheist, 'Seek ye first the Kingdom of God and His righteousness, and all these things shall be added unto you;' or, in other words, 'Live,' Christ said, 'all of you together, not each of you by himself; live as members of the righteous society which I have come to found upon earth, and then you will be clothed as beautifully as the Eastern lily and fed as surely as the birds.'"

And the Rev. R. J. Campbell, who comes to Socialism by way of Nonconformity, is equally convincing in support of this assertion that the "Kingdom of Heaven" was and is a terrestrial ideal.

This is not simply the Christian ideal of society, it is the ideal of every right thinking man, of every man with a full sense of beauty. You will find it rendered in two imperishably beautiful Utopias of our own time, both, I glory to write, by Englishmen, the News from Nowhere of William Morris, and Hudson's exquisite Crystal Age. Both these present practically Anarchist States, both assume idealized human beings, beings finer, simpler, nobler than the heated, limited and striving poor souls who thrust and suffer among the stresses of this present life. And the present writer, too—I must mention him here to guard against a confusion in the future—when a little while ago he imagined humanity exalted morally and intellectually by the brush of a comet's tail,[20] was forced by the logic of his premises and even against his first intention to present not a Socialist State but a glorious anarchism as the outcome of that rejuvenescence of the world.

[20] In the Days of the Comet. (Macmillan & Co., 1906.) Anti Socialist speakers and writers are in the habit of quoting passages of a review from the Times Literary Supplement, published during the heat of the "Book War," and promptly controverted, as though they were quotations from this book.

But the business of Socialism lies at a lower level and concerns immediate things; our material is the world as it is, full of unjust laws, bad traditions, bad habits, inherited diseases and weaknesses, germs and poisons, filths and envies. We are not dealing with magnificent creatures such as one sees in ideal paintings and splendid sculpture, so beautiful they may face the world naked and unashamed; we are dealing with hot eared, ill kempt people, who are liable to indigestion, baldness, corpulence and fluctuating tempers; who wear top hats and bowler hats or hats kept on by hat pins (and so with all the other necessary clothing); who are pitiful and weak and vain and touchy almost beyond measure, and very naughty and intemperate; who have, alas! to be bound over to be in any degree faithful and just to one another. To strip such people suddenly of law and restraint would be as dreadful and ugly as stripping the clothes from their poor bodies....

That Anarchist world, I admit, is our dream; we do believe—well, I, at any rate, believe this present world, this planet, will some day bear a race beyond our most exalted and temerarious dreams, a race begotten of our wills and the substance of our bodies, a race, so I have said it, "who will stand upon the earth as one stands upon a footstool, and laugh and reach out their hands amidst the stars," but the way to that is through education and discipline and law. Socialism is the preparation for that higher Anarchism; painfully, laboriously we mean to destroy false ideas of property and self, eliminate unjust laws and poisonous and hateful suggestions and prejudices, create a system of social right dealing and a tradition of right feeling and action. Socialism is the school room of true and noble Anarchism, wherein by training and restraint we shall make free men.

There is a graceful and all too little known fable by Mr. Max Beerbohm, The Happy Hypocrite, which gives, I think, not only the relation of Socialism to philosophic Anarchism, but of all discipline to all idealism. It is the story of a beautiful mask that was worn by a man in love, until he tired even of that much of deceit and, a little desperately, threw it aside—to find his own face beneath changed to the likeness of the self he had desired. So would we veil the greed, the suspicion of the self seeking scramble of to day under institutions and laws that will cry "duty and service" in the ears and eyes of all mankind, keep down the evil so long and so effectually that at last law will be habit, and greed and self seeking cease for ever, from being the ruling impulse of the world. Socialism is the mask that will mould the world to that better Anarchism of good men's dreams....

But these are long views, glimpses beyond the Socialist horizon. The people who would set up Anarchism to day are people without human experience or any tempering of humour, only one shade less impossible than the odd one sided queer beings one meets, ridiculously inaccessible to laughter, who, caricaturing their Nietzsche and misunderstanding their Shaw, invite one to set up consciously with them in the business of being Overmen, to rule a world full of our betters, by fraud and force. It is a foolish teaching saved only from being horrible by being utterly ludicrous. For us the best is faith and humility, truth and service, our utmost glory is to have seen the vision and to have failed—not altogether.... For ourselves and such as we are, let us not "deal in pride," let us be glad to learn a little of this spirit of service, to achieve a little humility, to give ourselves to the making of Socialism and the civilized State without presumption—as children who are glad they may help in a work greater than themselves and the toys that have heretofore engaged them.

CHAPTER XII

ADMINISTRATIVE SOCIALISM

I

Marx gave to Socialism a theory of world wide social development, and rescued it altogether from the eccentric and localized associations of its earliest phases; he brought it so near to reality that it could appear as a force in politics, embodied first as the International Association of Working Men, and then as the Social Democratic movement of the continent of Europe that commands to day over a third of the entire poll of German voters. So much Marx did for Socialism. But if he broadened its application to the world, he narrowed its range to only the economic aspect of life. He arrested for a time the discussion of its biological and moral aspects altogether. He left it an incomplete doctrine of merely economic reconstruction supplemented by mystical democracy, and both its mysticism and incompleteness, while they offered no difficulties to a labouring man ignorant of affairs, rendered it unsubstantial and unattractive to people who had any real knowledge of administration.

It was left chiefly to the little group of English people who founded the Fabian Society to supply a third system of ideas to the amplifying conception of Socialism, to convert Revolutionary Socialism into Administrative Socialism.

This new development was essentially the outcome of the reaction of its broad suggestions of economic reconstruction upon the circle of thought of one or two young officials of genius, and of one or two persons upon the fringe of that politic social stratum of Society, the English "governing class." I make this statement, I may say, in the loosest possible spirit. The reaction is one that was not confined to England, it was to some extent inevitable wherever the new movement in thought became accessible to intelligent administrators and officials. But in the peculiar atmosphere of British public life, with its remarkable blend of individual initiative and a lively sense of the State, this reaction has had the freest development. There was, indeed, Fabianism before the Fabian Society; it would be ingratitude to some of the most fruitful social work of the middle Victorian period to ignore the way in which it has contributed in suggestion and justification to the Socialist synthesis.

The city of Birmingham, for example, developed the most extensive process of municipalization as the mere common sense of local patriotism. But the movement was without formulæ and correlation until the Fabians came.

That unorganized, unpaid public service of public spirited aristocratic and wealthy financial and business people, the "governing class," which dominated the British Empire throughout the nineteenth century, has, through the absence of definite class boundaries in England and the readiness of each class to take its tone from the class above, that "Snobbishness" which is so often heedlessly dismissed as altogether evil, given a unique quality to British thought upon public questions and to British conceptions of Socialism. It has made the British mind as a whole "administrative." As compared with the American mind, for example, the British is State conscious, the American State blind. The American is no doubt intensely patriotic, but the nation and the State to which his patriotism points is something overhead and comprehensive like the sky, like a flag hoisted; something, indeed, that not only does not but must not interfere with his ordinary business occupations. To have public spirit, to be aware of the State as a whole and to have an administrative feeling towards it, is necessarily to be accessible to constructive ideas—that is to say, to Socialistic ideas. In the history of thought in Victorian Great Britain, one sees a constant conflict of this administrative disposition with the individualistic commercialism of the aggressively trading and manufacturing class, the class that in America reigns unchallenged to this day. In the latter country Individualism reigns unchallenged, it is assumed; in the former it has fought an uphill fight against the traditions of Church and State and has never absolutely prevailed. The political economists and Herbert Spencer were its prophets, and they never at any time held the public mind in any invincible grip. Since the eighties that grip has weakened more and more. Socialistic thought and legislation, therefore, was going on in Great Britain through all the Victorian period. Nevertheless, it was the Fabian Society that, in the eighties and through the intellectual impetus of at most four or five personalities, really brought this obstinately administrative spirit in British affairs into relation with Socialism as such.

The dominant intelligence of this group was Mr. Sidney Webb, and as I think of him thus coming after Marx to develop the third phase of Socialism, I am struck by the contrast with the big bearded Socialist leaders of the earlier school and this small, active, unpretending figure with the finely shaped head, the little imperial under the lip, the glasses, the slightly lisping, insinuating voice. He emerged as a Colonial Office clerk of conspicuous energy and capacity, and he was already the leader and "idea factory" of the Fabian Society when he married Miss Beatrice Potter, the daughter of a Conservative Member of Parliament, a girl friend of Herbert Spencer, and already a brilliant student of sociological questions. Both he and she are devotees to social service, living laborious, ordered, austere, incessant lives, making the employment of secretaries their one extravagance, and alternations between research and affairs their change of occupation. A new type of personality altogether they were in the Socialist movement, which had hitherto been richer in eloquence than discipline. And during the past twenty years of the work of the Fabian Society through their influence, one dominant question has prevailed. Assuming the truth of the two main generalizations of Socialism, taking that statement of intention for granted, how is the thing to be done? They put aside the glib assurances of the revolutionary Socialists that everything would be all right when the People came to their own; and so earned for themselves the undying resentment of all those who believe the world is to be effectually mended by a liberal use of chest notes and red flags. They insisted that the administrative and economic methods of the future must be a secular development of existing institutions, and inaugurated a process of study—which has long passed beyond the range of the Fabian Society, broadening out with the organized work of the New University of London, with its special School of Economics and Political Science and of a growing volume of university study in England and America—to the end that this "how?" should be answered....

The broad lines of the process of transition from the present state of affairs to the Socialist state of the future as they are developed by administrative Socialism lie along the following lines.

1. The peaceful and systematic taking over from private enterprise, by purchase or otherwise, whether by the national or by the municipal authorities as may be most convenient, of the great common services of land control, mining, transit, food supply, the drink trade, lighting, force supply and the like.

2. Systematic expropriation of private owners by death duties and increased taxation.

3. The building up of a great scientifically organized administrative machinery to carry on these enlarging public functions.

4. A steady increase and expansion of public education, research, museums, libraries and all such public services. The systematic promotion of measures for raising the school leaving age, for the public feeding of school children, for the provision of public baths, parks, playgrounds and the like.

5. The systematic creation of a great service of public health to take over the disorganized confusion of hospitals and other charities, sanitary authorities, officers of health and private enterprise medical men.

6. The recognition of the claim of every citizen to welfare by measures for the support of mothers and children and by the establishment of old age pensions.

7. The systematic raising of the minimum standard of life by factory and other labour legislation, and particularly by the establishment of a legal minimum wage....

These are the broad forms of the Fabian Socialist's answer to the question of how, with which the revolutionary Socialists were confronted. The diligent student of Socialism will find all these proposals worked out to a very practicable looking pitch indeed in that Bible of Administrative Socialism, the collected tracts of the Fabian Society,[21] and to that volume I must refer him. The theory of the minimum standard and the minimum wage is explained, moreover, with the utmost lucidity in that Socialist classic, Industrial Democracy, by Sidney and Beatrice Webb. It is a theory that must needs be mastered by every intelligent Socialist, but it is well to bear in mind that the method of the minimum wage is no integral part of the general Socialist proposition, and that it still lies open to discussion and modification.

[21] Fabian Tracts. (Fabian Society, 5s.)

II

Every movement has the defects of its virtues, and it is not, perhaps, very remarkable that the Fabian Society of the eighties and nineties, having introduced the conception of the historical continuity of institutions into the Propaganda of Socialism, did certainly for a time greatly over accentuate that conception and draw away attention from aspects that may be ultimately more essential.

Beginning with the proposition that the institutions and formulæ of the future must necessarily be developed from those of the present, that one cannot start de novo even after a revolution; one may easily end in an attitude of excessive conservatism towards existing machinery. In spite of the presence of such fine and original intelligences as Mr. (now Sir) Sydney Olivier and Mr. Graham Wallas in the Fabian counsels, there can be no denial that for the first twenty years of its career, Mr. Webb was the prevailing Fabian. Now his is a mind legal as well as creative, and at times his legal side quite overcomes his constructive element; he is extraordinarily fertile in expedients and skilful in adaptation, and with a real horror of open destruction. This statement by no means exhausts him, but it does to a large extent convey the qualities that were uppermost in the earlier years, at any rate, of his influence. His insistence upon continuity pervaded the Society, was re echoed and intensified by others, and developed into something like a mania for achieving Socialism without the overt change of any existing ruling body. His impetus carried this reaction against the crude democratic idea to its extremest opposite. Then arose Webbites to caricature Webb. From saying that the unorganized people cannot achieve Socialism, they passed to the implication that organization alone, without popular support, might achieve Socialism. Socialism was to arrive as it were insidiously.

To some minds this new proposal had the charm of a school boy's first dark lantern. Socialism ceased to be an open revolution, and became a plot. Functions were to be shifted, quietly, unostentatiously, from the representative to the official he appointed; a bureaucracy was to slip into power through the mechanical difficulties of an administration by debating representatives; and since these officials would by the nature of their positions constitute a scientific bureaucracy, and since Socialism is essentially scientific government as distinguished from haphazard government, they would necessarily run the country on the lines of a pretty distinctly undemocratic Socialism.

The process went even further than secretiveness in its reaction from the large rhetorical forms of revolutionary Socialism. There arose even a repudiation of "principles" of action, and a type of worker which proclaimed itself "Opportunist Socialist." It was another instance of Socialism losing sight of itself, it was a process quite parallel at the other extreme with the self contradiction of the Anarchist Socialist. Socialism as distinguished from mere Liberalism, for example, is an organized plan for social reconstruction, while Liberalism relies upon certain vague "principles"; Socialism declares that good intentions and doing what comes first to hand will not suffice. Now Opportunism is essentially benevolent adventure and the doing of first hand things.

This conception of indifference to the forms of government, of accepting whatever governing bodies existed and using them to create officials and "get something done," was at once immediately fruitful in many directions, and presently productive of many very grave difficulties in the path of advancing Socialism. Webb himself devoted immense industry and capacity to the London County Council—it is impossible to measure the share he has had in securing such great public utilities as water supply, traction and electric supply, for example, from complete exploitation by private profit seekers, but certainly it is a huge one—and throughout England and presently in America, there went on a collateral activity of Fabian Socialists. They worked like a ferment in municipal politics, encouraging and developing local pride and local enterprise in public works. In the case of large public bodies, working in suitable areas and commanding the services of men of high quality, striking advances in Social organization were made, but in the case of smaller bodies in unsuitable districts and with no attractions for people of gifts and training, the influence of Fabianism did on the whole produce effects that have tended to discredit Socialism. Aggressive, ignorant and untrained men and women, usually neither inspired by Socialist faith nor clearly defining themselves as Socialists, persons too often of wavering purpose and doubtful honesty, got themselves elected in a state of enthusiasm to undertake public functions and challenge private enterprise under conditions that doomed them to waste and failure. This was the case in endless parish councils and urban districts; it was also the case in many London boroughs. It has to be admitted by Socialists with infinite regret that the common borough council Socialist is too often a lamentable misrepresentative of the Socialist idea.

The creation of the London Borough Councils found English Socialism unprepared. They were bodies doomed by their nature to incapacity and waste. They represented neither natural communities nor any practicable administrative unit of area. Their creation was the result of quite silly political considerations. The slowness with which Socialists have realized that for the larger duties that they wish to have done collectively, a new scheme of administration is necessary; that bodies created to sweep the streets and admirably adapted to that duty may be conspicuously not adapted to supply electric power or interfere with transit, is accountable for much disheartening bungling. Instead of taking a clear line from the outset, and denouncing these glorified vestries as useless, impossible and entirely unscientific organs, too many Socialists tried to claim Bumble as their friend and use him as their tool. And Bumble turned out to be a very bad friend and a very poor tool....

In all these matters the real question at issue is one between the emergency and the implement. One may illustrate by a simple comparison. Suppose there is a need to dig a hole and that there is no spade available, a Fabian with Mr. Webb's gifts becomes invaluable. He seizes upon a broken old cricket bat, let us say, uses it with admirable wit and skill, and presto! there is the hole made and the moral taught that one need not always wait for spades before digging holes. It is a lesson that Socialism stood in need of, and which henceforth it will always bear in mind. But suppose we want to dig a dozen holes, it may be worth while to spend a little time in going to beg, borrow or buy a spade. If we have to dig holes indefinitely, day after day, it will be sheer foolishness sticking to the bat. It will be worth while then not simply to get a spade, but to get just the right sort of spade in size and form that the soil requires, to get the proper means of sharpening and repairing the spade, to insure a proper supply. Or to point the comparison, the reconstruction of our legislative and local government machinery is a necessary preliminary to Socialization in many directions. Mr. Webb has very effectually admitted that, is in fact himself leading us away from that by taking up the study of local government as his principal occupation, but the typical "Webbite" of the Fabian Society, who is very much to Webb what the Marxist is to Marx, entranced by his leader's skill, still clings to a caricature distortion of this earlier Fabian ideal. He dreams of the most foxy and wonderful digging by means of box lids, table spoons, dish covers—anything but spades designed and made for the job in hand—just as he dreams of an extensive expropriation of landlords by a legislature that includes the present unreformed House of Lords....

III

It was only at the very end of the nineteenth century that the Fabian Socialist movement was at all quickened to the need of political reconstruction as extensive as the economic changes it advocated, and it is still far from a complete apprehension of the importance of the political problem. To begin with, Mr. and Mrs. Webb, having completed their work on Labour Regulation, took up the study of local government and commenced that colossal task that still engages them, their book upon English Local Government, of which there has as yet appeared (1907) only one volume out of seven. (Immense as this service is, it is only one part of conjoint activities that will ultimately give constructive social conceptions an enormous armoury of scientifically arranged fact.)

As the outcome of certain private experiences, the moral of which was pointed by discussion with Mr. and Mrs. Webb, the present writer in 1902 put before the Fabian Society a paper on Administrative Areas,[22] in which he showed clearly that the character and efficiency and possibilities of a governing body depend almost entirely upon the suitability to its particular function of the size and quality of the constituency it represents and the area it administers. This may be stated with something approaching scientific confidence. A local governing body for too small an area or elected upon an unsound franchise cannot be efficient. But obviously before you can transfer property from private to collective control you must have something in the way of a governing institution which has a reasonably good chance of developing into an efficient controlling body. The leading conception of this Administrative Area paper appeared subsequently running through a series of tracts, The New Heptarchy Series, in which one finds it applied first to this group of administrative problems and then to that.[23] These tracts are remarkable if only because they present the first systematic recognition on the part of any organized Socialist body of the fact that a scientific reconstruction of the methods of government constitutes not simply an incidental but a necessary part of the complete Socialist scheme, the first recognition of the widening scope of the Socialist design that makes it again a deliberately constructive project.[24]

[22] See Appendix to Mankind in the Making. (Chapman and Hall, 1905.)

[23] 1. Municipalization by Provinces. 2. On the Reform of Municipal Service. 3. Public Control of Electric Power and Transit. 4. The Revival of Agriculture: a National Policy for Great Britain. 5. The Abolition of Poor Law Guardians. Others to follow. (Fabian Society, 1905 6.)

[24] This generalization is a sweeping one, and would need, were one attempting to give more than a very broad impression of the sequence of Socialist ideas, considerable modification. Such earlier tracts as The New Reform Bill, Facts for Londoners, Facts for Bristol, dealt mainly with the question of machinery.

It is only an initial recognition, a mere first raid into a great and largely unexplored province of study. This province is in the broadest terms, social psychology. A huge amount of thought, discussion, experiment, is to be done in this field—needs imperatively to be done before the process of the socialization of economic life can go very far beyond its present attainments. Except for these first admissions, Socialism has concerned itself only with the material reorganization of Society and its social consequences, with economic changes and the reaction of these changes on administrative work; it has either accepted existing intellectual conditions and political institutions as beyond its control or assumed that they will obediently modify as economic and administrative necessity dictates. Declare the Social revolution, we were told in a note of cheery optimism by the Marxist apostles, and political institutions will come like flowers in May! Achieve your expropriation, said the early Fabians, get your network of skilled experts spread over the country, and your political forms, your public opinion, your collective soul will not trouble you.

The student of history knows better. These confident claims ignore the psychological factors in government and human association; they disregard a jungle of difficulties that lie directly in our way. Socialists have to face the facts; firstly, that the political and intellectual institutions of the present time belong to the present condition of things, and that the intellectual methods, machinery and political institutions of the better future must almost inevitably be of a very different type; secondly, that such institutions will not come about of themselves—which indeed is the old superstition of laissez faire in a new form—but must be thought out, planned and organized just as completely as economic socialization has had to be planned and organized; and thirdly, that so far Socialism has evolved scarcely any generalizations even, that may be made the basis of new intellectual and governmental—as distinguished from administrative—methods. It has preached collective ownership and collective control, and it has only begun to recognize that this implies the necessity of a collective will and new means and methods altogether for the collective mind.

The administrative Socialism which Mr. Webb and the Fabian Society developed upon a modification of the broad generalizations of the Marx phase, is as it were no more than the first courses above those foundations of Socialism. It supplies us with a conception of methods of transition and with a vision of a great and disciplined organization of officials, a scientific bureaucracy appointed by representative bodies of diminishing activity and importance, and coming to be at last the real working control of the Socialist State. But it says nothing of what is above the officials, what drives the officials. It is a palace without living rooms, with nothing but offices; a machine, as yet unprovided with a motor. No doubt we must have that organization of officials if we mean to bring about a Socialist State, but the mind recoils with something like terror from the conception of a State run and ruled by officials, terminating in officials, with an official as its highest expression. One has a vision of a community with blue books instead of a literature, and inspectors instead of a conscience. The mystical democracy of the Marxist, though manifestly impossible, had in it something attractive, something humanly and desperately pugnacious and generous, something indeed heroic; the bureaucracy of the Webbite, though far more attainable, is infinitely less inspiring. But that may be because the inspiring elements remain to be stated rather than that these practical constructive projects are in their nature, and incurably, hard and narrow. Instead of a gorgeous flare in the darkness, we have the first cold onset of daylight heralding the sun. If the letter of the teaching of Mr. and Mrs. Webb is bureaucracy, that is certainly not the spirit of their lives.

The earlier Socialists gave Socialism substance, rudis indigestaque moles, but noble stuff; Administrative Socialism gave it a physical structure and nerves, defined its organs and determined its functions; it remains for the Socialist of to day to realize in this shaping body of the civilized State of the future the breath of life already unconfessedly there, to state in clear terms the reality for which our plans are made, by which alone they can be realized, that is to say, the collective mind of humanity, the soul and moral being of mankind.

CHAPTER XIII

CONSTRUCTIVE SOCIALISM

I

Such a group of ideas and motives as Socialism, fundamentally true as it is to the needs of life, and arising as it does from the inevitable suggestion of very widely dispersed evils and insufficiencies, does not spring from any one source, nor develop along any single line. It appears as a smouldering fire appears, first here, then there, first in one form of expression and then another, now under this name and now under that.

The manifest new possibilities created by the progress of applied science, the inevitable change of scale and of the size and conception of a community that arises out of them, necessitate at least the material form of Socialism—that is to say, the replacement of individual action by public organization, in spite of a hundred vested interests. The age that regarded Herbert Spencer as its greatest philosopher, for example, was urged nevertheless, unwillingly and protestingly but effectually, through phase after phase of more and more co ordinated voluntary effort, until at last it had to undertake a complete system of organized free public primary education. There the moving finger of change halts not a moment; already it is going on to secondary education, to schemes for a complete public educational organization from reformatory school up to professorial chair. The practical logic of the case is invincible.

So, too, the public organization of scientific research goes on steadily against all prejudices and social theories, and, in a very different field, the plain inconveniences of a private control of traffic in America and England alike, force the affected property owners whose businesses are hampered and damaged towards the realization that freedom of private property, in these services at least, is evil and must end. As the proofs of these pages pass through my hands comes the news of Mr. Lloyd George's settlement of the dispute between railway directors and employés by the establishment of a method of compulsory arbitration. Then, again, the movement for public sanitation and hygiene spreads and broadens, and the natural alarm of even the most conservative at the falling birth rate and the stationary infantile death rate is evidently ripening for an advance towards public control and care even in the relation of child to parent, the most intimate of all personal affairs.

Inevitably all such movements must coalesce—their spirit is one, the spirit of construction—and inevitably their coalescence will take the form of a wide and generous restatement of Socialism. Nothing but a broader understanding of the broadening propositions of Socialism is needed for that recognition now.

Socialism, indeed, does not simply look, it appeals to the constructive professions at the present time, to the medical man, the engineer, the architect, the scientific agriculturist.

Each of these sorts of men, in just so far as he is concerned with the reality of his profession, in just so far as he is worthy of his profession, must resent the considerations of private profit, of base economies, that constantly limit and spoil his work and services in the interests of a dividend or of some financial manœuvre. So far they have been antagonized towards Socialism by the errors of its adherents, by the impression quite wantonly created, that Socialism meant either mob rule or the rule of pedantic, unsympathetic officials. They have heard too much of democracy, too much of bureaucracy, and not enough of construction. They have felt that on the whole the financial exploiter, detestable master as he often is, was better than the rule of either clamour on the one hand or red tape on the other. But, as I have been seeking to suggest, mob rule and official rule do not exhaust the possible alternatives. Neither ignorant democracy nor narrow bureaucracy can be the destined rulers of a Socialist State. The only conceivable rule in a Socialist civilization is through the operation of a collective mind that must be by its nature constructive and enterprising, because only through the creation of such a mind can Socialism be brought about. A Socialist State cannot exist without that mind existing also, and a collective mind can scarcely appear without some form of Socialism giving it a material body. Now it is only under an intelligent collective mind that any of the dreams of these constructive professions can attain an effective realization. Where will the private profit in a universal sanitation, for example, be found, in the abolition of diseases, in the planned control of the public health, in the abolition of children's deaths? What thought of private gain will ever scrap our obsolescent railroads and our stagnating industrial monopolies for new clean methods? So long as they pay a dividend they will keep on upon their present lines. The modern architect knows, the engineer knows we might build ourselves perfectly clean, smokeless magnificent cities to day, as full of pure water as ancient Rome, as full of pure air as the Engadine, if private ownership did not block the way. Who can doubt it who understands what a doctor, or an electrical engineer, or a real architect understands? Surely all the best men in these professions are eager to get to work on the immense possibilities of life, possibilities of things cleared up, of things made anew, that their training has enabled them to visualize! What stands in their way, stands in our way; social disorganization, individualist self seeking, narrowness of outlook, self conceit, ignorance.

With that conception they must surely turn in the end, as we Socialists turn, to the most creative profession of all, to that great calling which with each generation renews the world's "circle of ideas," the Teachers!

The whole trend and purpose of this book from the outset has been to insist upon the mental quality of Socialism, to maintain that it is a business of conventions about property and plans of reorganization, that is to say, of changes and expansions of the ideas of men, changes and expansions of their spirit of action and their habitual circles of ideas. Unless you can change men's minds you cannot effect Socialism, and when you have made clear and universal certain broad understandings, Socialism becomes a mere matter of science and devices and applied intelligence. That is the constructive Socialist's position. Logically, therefore, he declares the teacher master of the situation. Ultimately the Socialist movement is teaching, and the most important people in the world from the Socialist's point of view are those who teach—I mean of course not simply those who teach in schools, but those who teach in pulpits, in books, in the press, in universities and lecture theatres, in parliaments and councils, in discussions and associations and experiments of every sort, and, last in my list but most important of all, those mothers and motherly women who teach little children in their earliest years. Every one, too, who enunciates a new and valid idea, or works out a new contrivance, is a teacher in this sense.

And these Teachers collectively, perpetually renew the collective mind. In the measure that in each successive generation they apprehend Socialism and transmit its spirit, is Socialism nearer its goal.

II

At the present time in America and all the western European countries, there is a collective mind, a public opinion made up of the most adventitious and interesting elements. It is not even a national or a racial thing, it is curiously international, curiously responsive to thought from every quarter; a something, vague here, clear there, here diffused, there concentrated. It demands the closest attention from Socialists this something, this something which is so hard to define and so impossible to deny—civilized feeling, the thought of our age, the mind of the world. It has organs, it has media, yet it is as hard to locate as the soul of a man. We know that somewhere in the brain and body of a man lives his Self; that you must preserve that brain entire, aërate it, nourish it lest it die and his whole being die, and yet you cannot say it is in this cell—or in that. So with an equal mystery of diffusion the mind of mankind exists. No man, no organization, no authority, can be more than a part of it. Twice at least have there been attempts of parts to be the whole; the Catholic Church and the Chinese Academy have each in varying measure sought to play the part of a collective mind for all humanity and failed. All individual achievement, fine books, splendid poems, great discoveries, new generalizations, lives of thought, are no more than flashes in this huge moral and intellectual being which grows now self conscious and purposeful, just as a child grows out of its early self ignorance to an elusive, indefinable, indisputable sense of itself. This collective mind has to be filled and nourished with the Socialist purpose, to receive and assimilate our great idea. That is the true work of Socialism.

Consider the organs and media of the collective mind as one finds them in England or America now, how hazardous they are and accidental! At the basis of this strange thought process is the intelligence of the common man, once illiterate and accessible only to the crude, inarticulate influences of talk and rumour, now rapidly becoming educated, or at any rate educated to the level of a reader and writer, and responding more and more to literary influences. The great mass of the population is indeed at the present time like clay which has hitherto been a mere deadening influence underneath, but which this educational process, like some drying and heating influence upon that clay, is rendering resonant, capable of, in a dim answering way, ringing to the appeals made upon it. Reaching through this mass, appealing to it in various degrees at various levels and to various ends, there are a number of systems of organizations of unknown value and power. Its response, such as it is, robbed by multitudinousness of any personality or articulation, is a broad emotional impulse.

Above this fundamental mass is the growing moiety which has a conscious thought process, of a sort. Its fundamental ideas, its preconceptions, are begotten of a mixture of social traditions learnt at home and in school and from the suggestions of contemporary customs and affairs. But it reads and listens more or less. And scattered through this, here and there, are people really learning, really increasing and accumulating knowledge, really thinking and conversing—the active mind cells, as it were, of the world. Their ideas are conveyed into the mass much as impulses are conveyed into an imperfectly innervated tissue, they are conveyed by books and pamphlets, by lecturing, by magazine articles and newspaper articles, by the agency of the pulpit, by organized propaganda, by political display and campaigns. The gross effect is considerable, but it is just as well that the Socialist should look a little closely at the economic processes that underlie these intellectual activities at the present time. Except for the universities and much of the public educational organization, except for a few pulpits endowed for good under conditions that limit freedom of thought and expression, except for certain needy and impecunious propagandas, the whole of this apparatus of public thought and discussion to day has been created and is sustained by commercial necessity.

For example, consider what is I suppose by far the most important vehicle of ideas at the present time, which for a huge majority of adults is the sole vehicle of ideas, the newspaper. It is universal because it is cheap, and it is cheap because the cost of production is paid for by the advertisements of private enterprise. The newspaper is to a very large extent parasitic upon competition; its criticism, its discussion, its correspondence, are, from the business point of view, written on the backs of puffs of competing tobaccos, soaps, medicines and the like. No newspaper could pay upon its sales alone, and the same thing is true of most popular magazines and weekly publications. It is highly probable that whatever checks public advertisement in other directions, the prohibition of bill posting upon hoardings, for example, the protection of scenery, railway carriages and architecture from the advertiser, stimulates the production of attractive literature. Necessarily what is published in newspapers and magazines must be acceptable to advertising businesses and not too openly contrary to their interests. With that limitation the newspapers provide a singularly free and various arena for discussion at the present time. It must, however, be obvious that to advance towards Socialism is, if not to undermine the newspaper altogether, at least to change very profoundly this material vehicle of popular thought....

The newspaper disseminates ideas. So, too, does the book and the pamphlet, and so far as these latter are concerned, their distribution does not at present rest in the same degree upon their value as vehicles of advertisement. They are saleable things unaided. The average book of to day at its nominal price of six shillings pays in itself and supports its producers. So in a lesser degree does the sixpenny pamphlet, but neither book nor pamphlet reach so wide a public as the halfpenny and penny press. The methods and media of the book trade have grown up, no man designing them; they change, and no one is able to foretell the effect of their changes. At present there is a great movement to cheapen new books, and it would seem the cheapening is partly to be made up for in enhanced sales and partly by an increased use of new books for advertisement. Many people consider this cheapening of new books as being detrimental to the interests of all but the most vulgarly popular authors. They believe it will increase the difficulty of new writers, and hopelessly impoverish just the finest element in our literary life, those original and exceptional minds who demand educated appreciation and do not appeal to the man in the street. This may or may not be true; the aspect of interest to Socialists is that here is a process going on which is likely to produce the most far reaching results upon the collective mind, upon that thought process of the whole community which is necessary for the progressive organization of Society. It is a process which is likely to spread one type of writer far and wide, which may silence or demoralize another, which may vulgarize and debase discussion, and which will certainly make literature far more dependent than it is at present upon the goodwill of advertising firms. Yet as Socialists they have no ideas whatever in this matter; their project of activities ignores it altogether....

Books and newspapers constitute two among the chief mental organs of a modern community, but almost, if not equally important is that great apparatus for the dissemination of ideas made up of the pulpits and lecture halls of a thousand sects and societies. Towards all these things Socialism has hitherto maintained an absurd attitude of laissez faire....

So far I have looked at the collective mind as a thought process only, but it has much graver and more immediate functions in a democratic State. It has, one must remember, to will social order and development. In every country the machinery for determining and expressing this will is complex. The common method in the modern western State is through the voting of a numerous electorate, which tends, it would seem, to become more and more the entire manhood, if not the entire adult population of the country. It is a curious but perhaps inevitable method. Practically thought has to percolate down to the common man through all those strange and accidental channels, newspapers which are advertisement sheets, books which may be boycotted in a "Book War," pulpits pledged to doctrine and lecture halls kept open by rich people's subscriptions; it has to reach him, to mingle itself with generalized emotional forces in the heat of mysteriously subsidized election campaigns, and then return as a collective determination. For the Statesman and the Socialist there could hardly be any study more important, one might think, than the science of these processes and methods. Yet the world has still to produce even the rudimentary generalizations of this needed science of collective psychology.

III

Now, I ask the reader to consider very carefully how the Socialist movement, using that expression now in its wider sense, stands to this very vague and very real outcome of social evolution, the Collective Mind; what it is really aspiring to do in that Collective Mind.

One has to recognize that this mind is at present a mind in a state of confusion, full of warring suggestions and warring impulses. It is like a very disturbed human mind, it is without a clear aim, it does not know except in the vaguest terms what it wants to do, it has impulses, it has fancies, it begins and forgets. In addition it is afflicted with a division within itself that is strictly analogous to that strange mental disorder, which is known to psychologists as multiple personality. It has no clear conception of the whole of itself, it goes about forgetting its proper name and address. Part of it thinks of itself as one great being, as, let us say, Germany; another thinks of itself as Catholicism, another as the White Race, or Judæa. At times one might deem the whole confusion not so much a mind as incurable dementia, a chaos of mental elements, haunted by invincible and mutually incoherent fixed ideas. This you will remember is the gist of that melancholy torso of irony, Flaubert's Bouvard et Pécuchet.

In its essence the Socialist movement amounts to this; it is an attempt in this warring chaos of a collective mind to pull itself together, to develop and establish a governing idea of itself. It is like a man saying to himself resolutely, "What am I? What am I doing with myself? Where am I drifting?" and making an answer, hesitating at first, crude at first, and presently clear and lucid.

The Socialist movement is from this point of view, no less than the development of the collective self consciousness of humanity. Necessarily, therefore, it must be international as well as outspoken, making no truce with prejudices against race and colour. These national and racial collective consciousnesses of to day are things as vague, as fluctuating as mists or clouds, they melt, dissolve into one another, they coalesce, they split. No clear isolated national mind can ever maintain itself under modern conditions; even the mind of Japan now comes into the common melting pot of thought. We Socialists take up to day the assertion the early Christians were the first to make, that mankind is of one household and one substance; the Samaritan who stoops to the wounded stranger by the wayside our brother rather than that Levite....

In a very different sense indeed the Socialist propaganda must be the germ of the collective self consciousness of mankind in the coming time. If the purpose of Socialism is to prevail, its scattered writings, its dispersed, indistinct and confused utterances must increase in height and breadth and range, increase in power and service, gather to themselves every means of expression, grow into an ordered system of thought, art, literature and will. The Socialist Propaganda of to day must beget the whole Public Opinion of to morrow or fail, the Socialists must play the part of a little leaven to leaven the whole world. If they do not leaven it then they are altogether defeated....

IV

Now, this conception of Socialism as being ultimately a moral and intellectual synthesis of mankind from which fresh growth may come, sets a fresh test of value upon all the activities of the Socialist— and opens up altogether new departments for research. Let us face the peculiar difficulty of the Socialist position. We propose to destroy the competitive capitalistic system that owns and sustains our present newspapers, gives and leaves money to universities, endows fresh pulpits, publishes, advertises, and buys books; we have to ask, as reasonable creatures, what new media we propose to give in the place of these accidental and unsatisfactory methods of distributing and exchanging thought. It would almost seem as though current Socialism breathes public opinion as the Middle Ages breathed air, without realizing that it existed, that it might be vitiated or withheld. And so we are beyond the range of prepared and digested Socialist proposals here altogether. It is still open to the Anti Socialist to allege that Socialism may incidentally destroy itself by choking the channels of its own thinking, and the Socialist has still to reply in vague general terms.

We must insure the continuity of the collective mind; that is manifestly a primary necessity for Socialism. The attempt to realize the Marxist idea of a democratic Socialism without that, might easily fail into the abortive birth of an acephalous monster, the secular development of administrative Socialism give the world over to a bureaucratic mandarinate, self satisfied, interfering and unteachable, with whom wisdom would die. And yet we Socialists can produce in our plans no absolute bar to these possibilities. Here I can suggest only in the most general terms methods and certain principles. They need to be laid down as vitally necessary to Socialism, and so far they have not been so laid down. They have still to be incorporated in the Socialist creed. They are essentially principles of that Liberalism out of whose generous aspirations Socialism sprang, but they are principles that even to day, unhappily, do not figure in the fundamental professions of any Socialist body.

The first of these is the principle of freedom of speech; the second, freedom of writing; and the third, universality of information. In the civilized State every one must be free to know, knowledge must be patent and at hand, and any one must be free to discuss, write, suggest and persuade. These freedoms must be guarded as sacred things. It is not in the untutored nature of man to respect any of these freedoms; it is not in the bureaucratic habit of mind. Indeed, the desire to suppress opinions adverse to our own is almost instinctive in human nature. It is an instinct we have to conquer. Fair play in discussion is sustained by a cultivated respect, by a correction of natural instinct; men need to be trained to be jealous of obscurantism, of unfair argument, of authoritative interference with opinion when that opinion is against them. In England such a jealousy does already largely exist, it has been cultivated with us since the seventeenth century at least; America, it seemed to me during my short visit to the States, has somewhat retrograded from its former British standard in this respect, there is a crude majority tyranny in the matter of publication, an un English disposition to boycott libraries, books, authors and publications upon petty issues, a growing disposition to discriminate in the mails against unpopular views. These interferences with open statement and discussion are decivilizing forces.

Given a clear public understanding of these necessities as primary, then one may point out that the next necessity for the mental existence of a Socialist State is an extension and cheapening of the impartial universal distributing activity of the public post so that it becomes not only the means of correspondence, but also of distributing books and newspapers, pamphlets and every form of printed matter. The post office must become bookseller and newsagent. In France this is already the case with the press, and newspapers are handed in not by the newsboy but by the public mail. In England Messrs. Smith and Mudie, and so forth, may censor what they like among periodicals or books. The remedy is more toilsome and vexatious than the injury. Neither England nor America has any security against finding its public supply of magazines or literature suddenly choked by the manœuvres of some blackmailing Book or News Trust squalidly "fighting" author or publisher for an increase in its proportion of profits, or interested in financial exploitations liable to exposure. Neither country is secure against the complete control of its channels of thought by some successful monopolistic adventurer....

The Socialist State will not for a moment permit such risks as these; it must certainly be a ubiquitous newsvendor and bookseller; the ordinary newsvendor and bookseller must become an impartial State official, working for a sure and comfortable salary instead of for precarious profits. And this amplification of the book and news post and the book and news trades will need to be not simply a municipal but a State service of the widest range.

Distribution, however, is only the beginning of the problem. There is the more difficult issue of getting books and papers printed and published. And here we come to an intricate puzzle in reconciling the indisputable need for untrammelled individual expression on the one hand with public ownership on the other, and also with the difficult riddle how authors may be supported under Socialist conditions. It is not within the design of this book to do more than indicate a possible solution. These are problems the Socialist has still to work out. At present authors with business shrewdness and the ability to be interesting get an income from the sale of their books, and it seems possible that they might continue to be paid in that way under Socialism. It is difficult outside the field of specialist work (which under any social system has to be endowed in relation to colleges and universities) to find any other just way of discriminating between the author who ought to get a living from writing, and the author who has no reasonable claim to do so. But under Socialism, in addition to the private publisher or altogether replacing him, there will have to be some sort of public publisher.

Here again difficulties arise. It is difficult to see how, if there is only one general State publishing department, a sort of censorship can be altogether avoided, and even if, for example, one insists upon the right of every one who cares to pay for it to have matter printed, bound and issued by the public presses and binders, it still leaves a disagreeable possibility of uniformity haunting the mind. But the whole trend of administrative Socialism is towards a conception of great local governments, of land, elementary education, omnibus transit, power distribution and the like, vesting in the hands of municipalities as great as mediæval principalities; and it seems possible to look to these great bodies and to the municipal patriotism and inter municipal rivalries that will develop about them, for just that spirited and competitive publishing that is desirable, just as one looks now to their rivalries as a stimulus for art and architecture and public dignity and display.[25] Already, as I have pointed out in a previous chapter (Chapter IX., § 5), the decorative arts had to be rescued from the degrading influence of private enterprise; no one wants to go back now to the early Victorian state of affairs, and so it is reasonable to hope that out of the municipal art and technical schools, which teach printing, binding and the like, public presses, public binderies and all the machinery of book production may be developed in a natural and convenient manner. So, too, the municipalities might publish, seek out, maintain and honour writers and sell the books they produced, against each other all over the world. It would be a matter of pride for authors still unrecognized to go forth to the world with the arms of some great city on their covers, and it would be a matter of pride for any city to have its arms upon work become classic and immortal. So at least one method of competition is possible in this matter....

[25] I visited Liverpool and Manchester the other day for the first time in my life, and was delighted to find how the inferiority of the local art galleries to those of Glasgow rankled in people's minds.

This, however, is but one passing suggestion out of many possibilities. But in all these issues of the intellectual life, it is manifest that public ownership must be so contrived, and can be so contrived as to avoid centralization and a control without alternatives. Moreover, whatever public publishing is done, it must be left open to any one to set up as an independent publisher or printer, and to sell and advertise through the impartial public book and news distributing organization.

I lay some stress upon this matter of book issuing because I think it is a remarkable and regrettable thing about contemporary Socialist discussion that it does not seem to be in the least alive to the great public disadvantage of leaving this vitally important service to private gain getting. Municipal coal, municipal milk, municipal house owning, the Socialists seem prepared for, and even municipal theatres, but municipal publication they still do not take into consideration. They leave the capitalist free to contrive the control of their book supply and to check and determine all the provender of their minds....

The problem of the press is perhaps to be solved by some parallel combination of individual enterprise and public resources. All sorts of things may happen to the newspaper of to day even in the near future, it cannot but be felt that in its present form it is an extremely transitory phenomenon, that it no longer embodies and rules public thought as it did in the middle and later Victorian period, and that a separation of public discussion from the news sheet is already in progress. Both in England and America the popular magazine seems taking over an increasing share of the public thinking. The newspaper appears to be in the opening throes of a period of fundamental change.

But I will not go into the future of the newspaper here. All these suggestions are merely thrown out in the most tentative way to indicate the nature of the field for study that lies open for any intelligent worker to cultivate, and that Socialists have so far been too busy to consider....

The same truth that controls must be divided and a competition at least for honour and repute kept alive under Socialism, needs also to be applied to schools and colleges, and all the vast machinery of research. It is imperative that there should be overlapping and competing organizations. An educated and prosperous community such as we postulate for the Socialist State will necessarily be more alert for interest and intellectual quality than our present "driven" multitude; its ampler leisure, its wider horizons, will keep it critical and exacting of what claims its attention. The rivalries of institutions and municipalities will be part of the drama of life. Under Socialism, with the extension of the educational process it contemplates, universities and colleges must become the most prominent of facts; nearly every one will have that feeling for some such place which now one finds in a Trinity man for Trinity; the sort of feeling that sent the last thoughts of Cecil Rhodes back to Oriel. Everywhere, balanced against the Town Hall or the Parliament House, will be the great university buildings and art museums, the lecture halls open to all comers, the great noiseless libraries, the book exhibitions and book and pamphlet stores, keenly criticized, keenly used, will teem with unhurrying, incessant, creative activities.

And all this immense publicly sustained organization will be doing greatly and finely what now our scattered line of Socialist propagandists is doing under every disadvantage, that is to say it will be developing and sustaining the social self consciousness, the collective sense of the State.

V

I am naturally preoccupied with the Mind of that Civilized State we seek to make; because my work lies in this department. But while the writer, the publisher and printer, the bookseller and librarian, and teacher and preacher must chiefly direct himself to developing this great organized mind and intention in the world, other sorts of men will be concerned with parallel aspects of the Socialist synthesis. The medical worker or the medical investigator will be building up the body of a new generation, the Body of the Civilized State, and he will be doing all he can not simply as an individual, but as a citizen, to organize his services of cure and prevention, of hygiene and selection. And the specialized man of science—he will be concerned with his own special synthesis, the Knowledge of the Civilized State, whether he measure crystals or stain microtome sections or count stars. A great and growing multitude of men will be working out the Apparatus of the Civilized State; the students of transit and housing, the engineers in their incessantly increasing variety, the miners and geologists estimating the world's resources in metals and minerals, the mechanical inventors perpetually economizing force. The scientific agriculturist, again, will be studying the food supply of the world as a whole, and how it may be increased and distributed and economized. And to the student of law comes the task of rephrasing his intricate and often quite beautiful science in relation to the new social assumptions we have laid down. All these and a hundred other aspects are integral to the wide project of Constructive Socialism as it shapes itself now.

And to the man or woman who looks at these issues not as one specialized in relation to some constructive calling but as a common citizen, a mere human being eager to make and do from the standpoint of personal liberty and personal affections, the appeal of this great constructive project is equally strong. You want security and liberty! Here it is, safe from the greed of trust and landlord; here is investment with absolute assurance and trading with absolute justice; this is the only safe way to build your own house in perfect security, to make your own garden safe for yourself and for your children's children, the only way in which you can link a hundred million kindred wills in loyal co-operation with your own, and that is to do it not for yourself alone and for your children alone, but for all the world—all the world doing it also for you—to join yourself to this great making of a permanent well being for mankind.

And here, finally, let me set out a sort of programme of Constructive Socialism, as it seems to be shaping itself in the minds of contemporary Socialists out of the Fabianism of the eighties and nineties, in order that the reader may be able to measure this fuller and completer proposition against the earlier Administrative Socialism whose propositions are set out in Chapter XI., § 1. All those are incorporated in this that follows—there is no contradiction whatever between them, but there is amplification; new elements are taken into consideration, once disregarded difficulties have been faced and partially resolved.

First, then, the Constructive Socialist has to do whatever lies in his power towards the enrichment of the Socialist idea. He has to give whatever gifts he has as artist, as writer, as maker of any sort to increasing and refining the conception of civilized life. He has to embody and make real the State and the City. And the Socialist idea, constantly restated, refreshed and elaborated, has to be made a part of the common circle of ideas; has to be grasped and felt and assimilated by the whole mass of mankind, has to be made the basis of each individual's private morality. That mental work is the primary, most essential function of Constructive Socialism.

And next, Constructive Socialism has in every country to direct its energies and attention to political reform, to the scientific reconstruction of our representative and administrative machinery so as to give power and real expression to the developing collective mind of the community, and to remove the obstructions to Socialization that are inevitable where institutions stand for "interests" or have fallen under the sway of aggressive private property or of narrowly organized classes. Governing and representative bodies, advisory and investigatory organizations of a liberal and responsive type have to be built up, bodies that shall be really capable of the immense administrative duties the secular abolition of the great bulk of private ownership will devolve upon them.

Thirdly, the constructive Socialist sets himself to forward the resumption of the land by the community, by increased control, by taxation, by death duties, by purchase and by partially compensated confiscation as circumstances may render advisable, and so to make the municipality the sole landlord in the reorganized world.

And meanwhile the constructive Socialist goes on also with the work of socializing the main public services, by transferring them steadily from private enterprise to municipal and State control, by working steadily for such transfers and by opposing every party and every organization that does not set its face resolutely against the private exploitation of new needs and services.

There are four distinct systems of public service which could very conveniently be organized under collective ownership and control now, and each can be attacked independently of the others. There is first the need of public educational machinery, and by education I mean not simply elementary education, but the equally vital need for great colleges not only to teach and study technical arts and useful sciences, but also to enlarge learning and sustain philosophical and literary work. A civilized community is impossible without great public libraries, public museums, public art schools, without public honour and support for contemporary thought and literature, and all these things the constructive Socialist may forward at a hundred points.

Then next there is the need and opportunity of organizing the whole community in relation to health, the collective development of hospitals, medical aid, public sanitation, child welfare, into one great loyal and efficient public service. This, too, may be pushed forward either as part of the general Socialist movement or independently as a thing in itself by those who may find the whole Socialist proposition unacceptable or inconvenient.

A third system of interests upon which practical work may be done at the present time lies in the complex interdependent developments of transit and housing, questions that lock up inextricably with the problem of re planning our local government areas. Here, too, the whole world is beginning to realize more and more clearly that private enterprise is wasteful and socially disastrous, that collective control, collective management, and so on to collective enterprise and ownership of building land, houses, railways, tramways and omnibuses, give the only way of escape from an endless drifting entanglement and congestion of our mobile modern population.

The fourth department of economic activity in which collectivism is developing, and in which the constructive Socialist will find enormous scope for work, is in connection with the more generalized forms of public trading, and especially with the production, handling and supply of food and minerals. When the lagging enterprise of agriculture needs to be supplemented by endowed educational machinery, agricultural colleges and the like; when the feeble intellectual initiative of the private adventure miner and manufacturer necessitates a London "Charlottenburg," it must be manifest that State initiative has altogether out distanced the possibilities of private effort, and that the next step to the public authority instructing men how to farm, prepare food, run dairies, manage mines and distribute minerals, is to cut out the pedagogic middleman and undertake the work itself. The State education of the expert for private consumption (such as we see at the Royal School of Mines) is surely too ridiculous a sacrifice of the community to private property to continue at that. The further inevitable line of advance is the transfer from private to public hands by purchase, by competing organizations or what not, of all those great services, just as rapidly as the increasing capacity and experience of the public authority permits.

This briefly is the work and method of Constructive Socialism to day. Under one or other head it can utilize almost every sort of capacity and every type of opportunity. It refuses no one who will serve it. It is no narrow doctrinaire cult. It does not seek the best of an argument, but the best of a world. Its worst enemies are those foolish and litigious advocates who antagonize and estrange every development of human Good Will that does not pay tribute to their vanity in open acquiescence. Its most loyal servants, its most effectual helpers on the side of art, invention and public organization and political reconstruction, may be men who will never adopt the Socialist name.

CHAPTER XIV

SOME ARGUMENTS AD HOMINEM

I

Before I conclude this compact exposition of modern Socialism, it is reasonable that the reader should ask for some little help in figuring to himself this new world at which we Socialists aim.

"I see the justice of much of the Socialist position," he will say, "and the soundness of many of your generalizations. But it still seems to remain—generalizations; and I feel the need of getting it into my mind as something concrete and real. What will the world be like when its state is really a Socialist one? That's my difficulty."

The full answer to that would be another book. I myself have tried to render my own personal dream in a book called A Modern Utopia,[26] but that has not been so widely read as I could have wished, it does not appeal strongly enough, perhaps, to the practical every day side of life, and here I may do my best to give very briefly some intimation of a few of the differences that would strike a contemporary if he or she could be transferred to the new order we are trying to evolve.

[26] Chapman & Hall.

It would be a world and a life in no fundamental respect different from the world of to-day, made up of the same creatures as ourselves, as limited in capacity if not in outlook, as hasty, as quick to take offence, as egotistical essentially, as hungry for attention, as easily discouraged—they would indeed be better educated and better trained, less goaded and less exasperated, with ampler opportunities for their finer impulses and smaller scope for rage and secrecy, but they would still be human. At bottom it would still be a struggle for individual ends, albeit ennobled individual ends; for self gratification and self realization against external difficulty and internal weakness. Self gratification would be sought more keenly in self development and self realization in service, but that is a change of tone and not of nature. We shall still be individuals. You might, indeed, were you suddenly flung into it, fail to note altogether for a long time the widest of the differences between the Socialist State and our present one—the absence of that worrying urgency to earn, that sense of constant economic insecurity, which afflicts all but the very careless or the very prosperous to day. Painful things being absent are forgotten. On the same principle certain common objects of our daily life you might not miss at all. There would be no slums, no hundreds of miles of insanitary, ignoble homes, no ugly health destroying cheap factories. If you were not in the habit of walking among slums and factories you would scarcely notice that. Din and stress would be enormously gone. But you would remark simply a change in the atmosphere about you and in your own contentment that would be as difficult to analyze as the calm of a Sunday morning in sunshine in a pleasant country.

Let me put my conception of the Socialist world to a number of typical readers, as it were, so that they may see clearly just what difference in circumstances there would be for them if we Socialists could have our way now. Let me suppose them as far as possible exactly what they are now save for these differences.

Then first let us take a sample case and suppose yourself to be an elementary teacher. So far as your work went you would be very much as you are to day; you would have a finer and more beautiful school room perhaps, better supplied with apparatus and diagrams; you would have cleaner and healthier, that is to say brighter and more responsive children, and you would have smaller and more manageable classes. Schools will be very important things in the Socialist State, and you will find outside your class room a much ampler building with open corridors, a library, a bath, refectory for the children's midday meal, and gymnasium, and beyond the playground a garden. You will be an enlisted member of a public service, free under reasonable conditions to resign, liable under extreme circumstances to dismissal for misconduct, but entitled until you do so to a minimum salary, a maintenance allowance, that is, and to employment. You will have had a general education from the State up to the age of sixteen or seventeen, and then three or four years of sound technical training, so that you will know your work from top to bottom. You will have applied for your present position in the service, whatever it is, and have been accepted, much as you apply and are accepted for positions now, by the school managers, and you will have done so because it attracted you and they will have accepted you because your qualifications seemed adequate to them. You will draw a salary attached to the position, over and above that minimum maintenance salary to which I have already alluded. You will be working just as keenly as you are now, and better because of the better training you have had, and because of shorter hours and more invigorating conditions, and you will be working for much the same ends, that is to say for promotion to a larger salary and wider opportunities and for the interest and sake of the work. In your leisure you may be studying, writing, or doing some work of supererogation for the school or the State—because under Socialist conditions it cannot be too clearly understood that all the reasons the contemporary Trade Unionist finds against extra work and unpaid work will have disappeared! You will not in a Socialist State make life harder for others by working keenly and doing much if you are so disposed. You will be free to give yourself generously to your work. You will have no anxiety about sickness or old age, the State, the universal Friendly Society, will hold you secure against that; but if you like to provide extra luxury and dignity for your declining years, if you think you will be amused to collect prints or books, or travel then, or run a rose garden or grow chrysanthemums, the State will be quite ready for you to pay it an insurance premium in order that you may receive in due course an extra annuity to serve that end you contemplate.

You will probably live as a tenant in a house which may either stand alone or be part of a terrace or collegiate building, but instead of having a private landlord, exacting of rent and reluctant of repairs, your house landlord will very probably be, and your ground landlord will certainly be, the municipality, the great Birmingham or London or Hampshire or Glasgow or such like municipality; and your house will be built solidly and prettily instead of being jerry built and mean looking, and it will have bathroom, electric light, electrically equipped kitchen and so forth, as every modern civilized house might have and should have now. If your taste runs to a little close garden of your own, you will probably find plenty of houses with one; if that is not so, and you want it badly, you will get other people of like tastes to petition the municipality to provide some, and if that will not do, you will put yourself up as a candidate for the parish or municipal council to bring this about. You will pay very much the sort of rent you pay now, but you will not pay it to a private landlord to spend as he likes at Monte Carlo or upon foreign missions or in financing "Moderate" bill posting or what not, but to the municipality, and you will pay no rates at all. The rent will do under Socialism what the rates do now. You cannot grasp too clearly that Socialism will abolish rates absolutely. Rates for public purposes are necessary to day because the landowners of the world evade the public obligations that should, in common sense, go with the rent.

Light, heating, water and so on will either be covered by the rent or charged for separately, and they will be supplied just as near cost price as possible. I don't think you will buy coals, because I think that in a few years' time it will be possible to heat every house adequately by electricity; but if I am wrong in that, then you will buy your coals just as you do now, except that you will have an honest coal merchant, the Public Coal Service, a merchant not greedy for profit nor short in the weight, calculating and foreseeing your needs, not that it may profit by them but in order to serve them, storing coal against a demand and so never raising the price in winter.

I am assuming you are going to be a house occupier, but if you are a single man, you will probably live in pleasant apartments in an hotel or college and dine in a club, and perhaps keep no more than a couple of rooms, one for sleep and one for study and privacy of your own. But if you are a married man, then I must enlarge a little further upon your domestic details, because you will probably want a "home of your own."...

II

Now, just how a married couple lives in the Socialist State will depend very much, as indeed it does now, on the individual relations and individual taste and proclivities of the two people most concerned. Many couples are childless now, and indisposed for home and children, and such people will also be found in the Socialist State, and in their case the wife will probably have an occupation and be a teacher, a medical practitioner, a government clerk or official, an artist, a milliner, and earn her own living. In which case they will share apartments, perhaps, and dine in a club and go about together very much as a childless couple of journalists or artists or theatrical people do in London to day. But of course if either of them chooses to idle more or less and live on the earnings of the other, that will be a matter quite between themselves. No one will ask who pays their rent and their bills; that will be for their own private arrangement.

But if they are not childless people, but have children, things will be on a rather different footing. Then they will probably have a home all to themselves, and that will be the wife's chief affair; only incidentally will she attend to any other occupation. You will remember that the State is to be a sort of universal Friendly Society supplying good medical advice and so forth, and so soon as a woman is likely to become a mother, her medical adviser, man or woman as the case may be, will report this to the proper officials and her special income as a prospective mother in the State will begin. Then, when her child is born, there will begin an allowance for its support, and these payments will continue monthly or quarterly, and will be larger or smaller according first to the well being of the child, and secondly to the need the State may have for children—so long as the children are in their mother's care. All this money for maternity will be the wife's independent income, and normally she will be the house ruler—just as she is now in most well contrived households. Her personality will make the home atmosphere; that is the woman's gift and privilege, and she will be able to do it with a free hand. I suppose that for the husband's cost in the household the present custom of cultivated people of independent means will continue, and he will pay over to his wife his share of the household expenses....

After the revenue in the domestic budget under Socialism one must consider the expenditure. I have already given an idea how the rent and rates, lighting and water are to be dealt with under Socialist conditions. For the rest, the housewife will be dealing on very similar lines to those she goes upon at present. She will buy what she wants and pay cash for it. The milkman will come in the morning and leave his "book" at the end of the week, but instead of coming from Mr. Watertap Jones' or the Twenty per cent. Dairy Company, he will come from the Municipal Dairy; he will have no interest in giving short measure, and all the science in the State will be behind him in keeping the milk clean and pure. If he is unpunctual or trying in any way, the lady will complain just as she does now, but to his official superiors instead of his employer; and if that does not do, she and her aggrieved neighbours (all voters, you will understand) will put the thing to their representative in the parish or municipal council. Then she will buy her meat and grocery and so on, not in one of a number of inefficient little shops with badly assorted goods under unknown brands as she does now if she lives in a minor neighbourhood, but in a branch of a big, well organized business like Lipton's or Whiteley's or Harrod's. She may have to go to it on a municipal electric car, for which she will probably pay a fare just as she does now, unless, perhaps, her house rent includes a season ticket. The store will not belong to Mr. Lipton or Mr. Whiteley or Mr. Harrod, but to the public—that will be the chief difference—and if she does not like her service she will be able to criticize and remedy it, just as one can now criticize and remedy any inefficiency in one's local post office. If she does not like the brands of goods supplied she will be able to insist upon others. There will be brands, too, different from the household names of to day in the goods she will buy. The county arms of Devon will be on the butter paper, Hereford and Kent will guarantee her cider, Hampshire and Wiltshire answer for her bacon—just as now already Australia brands her wines and New Zealand protects her from deception (and insures clean, decent slaughtering) in the matter of Canterbury lamb. I rather like to think of the red dagger of London on the wholesome bottled ales of her great (municipalized) breweries, and Maidstone or Rochester, let us say, boasting a special reputation for jam or pickles. Good honest food all of it will be, made by honest unsweated women and men, with the pride of broad vales and uplands, counties, principalities and great cities behind it. Each county and municipality will be competing freely against its fellows, not in price but quality, the cheeses of Cheshire against the cheeses of France and Switzerland, the beer of Munich against the Kentish brew; bread from the bakeries of London and Paris, biscuits from Reading town, chocolates from Switzerland and Bourneville, side by side with butter from the meadows of Denmark and Russia.

Then, when the provisions have been bought, she will go perhaps to the other departments of the great store and buy or order the fine linen and cotton of the Manchester men, the delicate woollens of the Bradford city looms, the silks of London or Mercia, Northampton or American boots, and so forth, just as she does now in any of the great stores. But, as I say, all these goods will be honest goods, made to wear as well as look well, and the shopman will have no "premiums" to tempt him to force rubbish upon her instead of worthy makes by specious "introduction."

But suppose she wants a hat or a dress made. Then, probably, for all that the world is under Socialism she will have to go to private enterprise; a matter of taste and individuality such as dress cannot be managed in a wholesale way. She will probably find in the same building as the big department store, a number of little establishments, of Madame This, of Mrs. That, some perhaps with windows displaying a costume or so or a hat or so, and here she will choose her particular artiste and contrive the thing with her. I am inclined to think the dressmaker or milliner will charge a fee according to her skill and reputation for designing and cutting and so on, and that the customer will pay the store separately for material and the municipal workshop for the making under the artiste's direction. I don't think, that is, that the milliner or dressmaker will make a trading profit, but only an artiste's fee.

And if the lady wants to buy books, music, artistic bric a brac, or what not, she will find the big store displaying and selling all these things on commission for the municipal or private producers all over the world....

So much for the financial and economic position of an ordinary woman in a Socialist State. But management and economies are but the basal substance of a woman's life. She will be free not merely financially; the systematic development of the social organisation and of the mechanism of life will be constantly releasing her more and more from the irksome duties and drudgeries that have consumed so much of the energies of her sex in the past. She will be a citizen, and free as a man to read for herself, think for herself and seek expression. Under the law, in politics and all the affairs of life she will be the equal of a man. No one will control her movements or limit her actions or stand over her to make decisions for her. All these things are implicit in the fundamental generalization of Socialism, which denies property in human beings.

III

Perhaps now the reader will be able to figure a little better the common texture of the life of a teacher or a housewife under Socialism. And incidentally I have glanced at the position a clever milliner or dressmaker would probably have under the altered conditions. The great mass of the employés in the distributing trade would obviously be living a sort of clarified, dignified version of their present existence, freed from their worst anxieties, the terror of the "swap," the hopeless approach of old age, and from the sweated food and accommodation of the living in system. Under Socialism the "living in" system would be incredible. Their conditions of life would approximate to those of the teacher. Like him they would be enrolled a part of a great public service, and like him entitled to a minimum wage, and over and above that they would draw salaries commensurate with the positions their energy and ability had won. The prosperous merchant of to day would find himself somewhere high in the hierarchy of the distributing service. If, for example, you are a tea merchant or a provision broker, then probably if you like that calling, you would be handling the same kind of goods, not for profit but efficiency, "shipping into the Midlands" from Liverpool, let us say, much as you do now. You would be keener on quality and less keen on deals; that is all. You would not be trying to "skin" a business rival, but very probably you would be just as keen to beat the London distributers and distinguish yourself in that way. And you would get a pretty good salary; modern Socialism does not propose to maintain any dead level to the detriment of able men. Modern Socialism has cleared itself of that jealous hatred of prosperity that was once a part of class war Socialism. You would be, you see, far more than you are now, one of the pillars of your town's prosperity—and the Town Hall would be a place worth sitting in....

So far as the rank and file of the distributing service is concerned the chief differences would be a better education, security for a minimum living, an assured old age, shorter hours, more private freedom and more opportunity. Since the whole business would be public and the customer would be one's indirect master through the polling booth, promotion would be far more by merit than it is now in private businesses, where irrelevant personal considerations are often overpowering, and it would be open to any one to apply for a transfer to some fresh position if he or she found insufficient scope in the old one. The staff of the stores will certainly "live out," and their homes and way of living will be closely parallel to that of the two people I have sketched in §§ 1 and 2.

In the various municipal and State Transit Services, the condition of affairs would be even closer to a broadened and liberalized version of things as they are. The conductors and drivers will no doubt wear uniforms for convenience of recognition, but a uniform will carry with it no association with the idea of a livery as it does at the present time. Mostly this service will be run by young men, and each one, like the private of the democratic French Army, will feel that he has a marshal's batôn in his knapsack. He will have had a good education; he will have short hours of duty and leisure for self improvement or other pursuits, and if he remains a conductor or driver all his life he will have only his own unpretending qualities to thank for that. He will probably remain a conductor if he likes to remain a conductor, and go elsewhere if he does not. He is not obliged to take that batôn out and bother with it if he has quiet tastes.

The great organized industries, mining, cotton, iron, building and the like, would differ chiefly in the permanence of employment and the systematic evasion of the social hardship caused now a days by new inventions and economies in method. There will exist throughout the world an organized economic survey, which will continually prepare and revise estimates of the need of iron, coal, cloth and so forth in the coming months; the blind speculative production of our own times is due merely to the dark ignorance in which we work in these matters, and with such a survey, employment will lose much of the cruel intermittence it now displays. The men in these great productive services, quite equally with teachers and railwaymen, will be permanently employed. They will be no more taken on and turned off by the day or week than we should take on or turn off an extra policeman, or depend for our defence upon soldiers casually engaged upon the battlefield at sixpence an hour. And if by adopting some ingenious device we dispense suddenly with the labour of hundreds of men, the Socialist State will send them, not into the casual wards and colonies as our State does, to become a social burthen there, but into the technical schools to train for some fresh use of their energies. Taken all round, of course, these men, even the least enterprising or able, will be better off than they are now, with a fuller share of the product of their industry. Many will no doubt remain as they are, rather through want of ambition than want of push, because under Socialism life will be tolerable for a poor man. A man who chooses to do commonplace work and spend his leisure upon chess or billiards, or in gossip or eccentric studies, or amusing but ineffectual art, will remain a poor man indeed, but not be made a wretched one. Sheer toil of a mechanical sort there is little need of in the world now, it could be speedily dispensed with at a thousand points were human patience not cheaper than good machinery, but there will still remain ten thousand undistinguished sorts of work for unambitious men....

If you are a farmer or any sort of horticulturist, a fruit or flower grower, let us say, or a seedsman, you will probably find yourself still farming under Socialism—that is to say, renting land and getting what you can out of it. Your rent will be fixed just as it is to day by what people will give. But your landlord will be the Municipality or the County, and the rent you pay will largely come back to you in repairs, in the guiding reports and advice of the Agricultural Department, in improved roads, in subventions to a good electric car service to take your produce to market; in aids and education for your children. You will probably have a greater fixity of tenure and a clearer ownership in improvements than you have to day. I am inclined to think that your dairying and milking and so forth will be done for you wholesale in big public dairies and mills because of the economy of that; you will send up the crude produce and sell it, perhaps, to the county association to brand and distribute. It is probable you will sell your crops standing, and the public authority will organize the harvesting and bring out an army of workers from the towns to gather your fruit, hops and corn. You will need, therefore, only a small permanent staff of labourers, and these are much more likely to be partners with you in the enterprise than wage workers needing to be watched and driven.

In your leisure you will shoot, perhaps, or hunt, if your tastes incline that way—it is quite likely that scattered among the farms of the future countryside will be the cottages and homes of all sorts of people with open air tastes who will share their sports with you. One need not dread the disappearance of sport with the disappearance of the great house.... In the dead winter time you will probably like to run into the nearest big town with your wife and family, stay in an hotel for a few weeks to talk to people in your clubs, see what plays there are in the municipal theatres and so forth. And you will no doubt travel also in your holidays. All the world will know something of the pleasures and freedom of travel, of wandering and the enjoyment of unfamiliar atmospheres, of mountains and deserts and remote cities and deep forests, and the customs of alien peoples.

IV

A medical man or woman, or a dentist or any such skilled professional, like the secondary school master, will cease to be a private adventurer under Socialism, concerned chiefly with the taking of a showy house and the use of a showy conveyance; he or she will become part of one of the greatest of all the public services in the coming time, the service of public health. Either he—I use this pronoun and imply its feminine—will be on the staff of one of the main hospitals (which will not be charities, but amply endowed public institutions), or he will be a part of a district staff, working in conjunction with a nursing organization, a cottage hospital, an isolation hospital and so forth, or he will be an advising specialist, or mainly engaged in research or teaching and training a new generation in the profession.

He must not judge his life and position quite by the lives and position of publicly endowed investigators and medical officers of health to day. At present, because of the jealousy of the private owner who has, as he says, to "find the funds," almost all public employment is badly paid relatively to privately earned incomes. The same thing is true of all scientific investigators and of most public officials. The state of things to which Socialism points is a world that will necessarily be harmonious with these constructive conceptions and free from these jealousies. Whitehall and South Kensington have much to fear from the wanton columns of a vulgarized capitalistic press and from the greedy intrigues of syndicated capital, but nothing from a sane constructive Socialism. To the public official, therefore, of the present time, the Socialist has merely to say that he will probably be better paid, relatively, than he is now, and in the matter of his house rents and domestic marketing, vide supra....

But now, suppose you are an artist—and I use the word to cover all sorts of art, literary, dramatic and musical, as well as painting, sculpture, design and architecture—you want before all things freedom for personal expression, and you probably have an idea that this is the last thing you will get in the Socialist State. But, indeed, you will get far more than you do now. You will begin as a student, no doubt, in your local Municipal Art Schools, and there you will win prizes and scholarships and get some glorious years of youth and work in Italy or Paris, or Germany or London, or Boston or New York, or wherever the great teachers and workers of your art gather thickest; and then you will compete, perhaps, for some public work, and have something printed or published or reproduced and sold for you by your school or city; or get a loan from your home municipality for material—if your material costs money—and set to work making that into some saleable beautiful thing. If you are at all distinguished in quality, you will have a competition among public authorities from the beginning, to act as sponsors and dealers for your work; benevolent dealers they will be, and content with a commission. And if you make things that make many people interested and happy, you may by that fortunate gift of yours, grow to be as rich and magnificent a person as any one in the Socialist State. But if you do not please people at all, either the connoisseurs of the municipal art collection or private associations of art patrons or the popular buyer, well, then your lot will be no harder than the lot of any unsuccessful artist now; you will have to do something else for a time and win leisure to try again.

Theatrical productions will be run on a sort of improvement upon contemporary methods, but there will be no cornering of talent possible, no wild advertisement of favoured stars upon strictly commercial lines, no Theatrical Trust. The theatres will be municipal buildings, every theatre going voter will be keen to see them comfortable and fine; they will, perhaps, be run in some cases by a public repertoire company and in another by a lessee, and this latter may be financed by his own private savings or by subscribers or partners, or by a loan from the public bank as the case may be. This latter method of exploitation by a lessee will probably also work best in the public Music Halls, but it is quite equally possible that these may be controlled by managers under partly elected and partly appointed public committees. In some cases the theatrical lessee might be a kind of stage society organized for the production of particular types of play. The spectators will pay for admission, of course, as they do now, but to the municipal box offices; and I suppose the lessee or the author and artists will divide up the surplus after the rent of the theatre has been deducted for the municipal treasury. In every town of any importance there will be many theatres, music halls and the like, perhaps under competing committees. In all these matters, as every intelligent person understands, one has to maintain variety of method, a choice of avenues, freedom from autocracies; and since the Socialist community will contain a great number of intelligent persons with leisure and opportunity for artistic appreciation, there is little chance of this important principle being forgotten, much less than there is in this world where a group of dealers can often make an absolute corner in this artistic market or that. You will not, under Socialism, see Sarah Bernhardt playing in a tent as she had to do in America, because all the theatres have been closed against her through some mean dispute with a Trust about the sharing of profits....

And if it is not too sudden a transition, it seems most convenient in a Socialist State to leave religious worship entirely to the care of private people; to let them subscribe among themselves, subject, of course, to a reasonable statute of mortmain, to lease land, and build and endow and maintain churches and chapels, altars and holy places and meeting houses, priests and devout ceremonies. This will be the more easily done since the heavy social burthens that oppress religious bodies at the present time will be altogether lifted from them; they will have no poor to support, no schools, no hospitals, no nursing sisters, the advance of civilization will have taken over these duties of education and humanity that Christianity first taught us to realize. So, too, there seems no objection and no obstacle in Socialism to religious houses, to nunneries, monasteries and the like, so far as these institutions are compatible with personal freedom and the public health, but of course factory laws and building laws will run through all these places, and the common laws and limitations of contract override their vows, if their devotees repent. So that you see Socialism will touch nothing living of religion, and if you are a religious minister, you will be very much as you are at the present time, but with lightened parochial duties. If you are an earnest woman and want to nurse the sick and comfort the afflicted, you will need only, in addition to your religious profession, to qualify as a nurse or medical practitioner. There will still be ample need of you. Socialism will not make an end of human trouble, either of the body or of the soul, albeit it will put these things into such comfort and safety as it may.

V

And now let me address a section to those particular social types whose method of living seems most threatened by the development of an organized civilization, who find it impossible to imagine lives at all like their own in the Socialist State....

But first it may be well to remind them again of something I have already done my best to make clear, that the modern Socialist contemplates no swift change of conditions from those under which we live, to Socialism. There will be no wonderful Monday morning when the old order will give place to the new. Year by year the great change has to be brought about, now by this socialization of a service, now by an alteration in the incidence of taxation, now by a new device of public trading, now by an extension of education. This problem at the utmost is a problem of adaptation, and for most of those who would have no standing under the revised conceptions of social intercourse, it is no more than to ask whether it is wise they should prepare their sons or daughters to follow in their footsteps or consent to regard their callings as a terminating function.

So far as many professions and callings go, this matter may be dismissed in a few words. Under Socialism, while the particular trade or profession might not exist, there would probably be ample scope in the public machine for the socially more profitable employment of the same energies. A family solicitor, such as we know now, would have a poor time in a Socialist State, but the same qualities of watchful discretion would be needed at a hundred new angles and friction surfaces of the State organization. In the same way the private shopkeeper, as I have already explained, would be replaced by the department managers and buyers of the public stores, the rent collector, the estate bailiff—one might make long lists of social types who would undergo a parallel transformation.

But suppose now you are a servant, I mean a well trained, expert, prosperous servant; would the world have no equivalent of you under the new order? I think probably it would. With a difference, there will be room for a vast body of servants in the Socialist State. But I think there will be very few servants to private people, and that the "menial" conception of a servant will have vanished in an entirely educated community. The domestic work of the ordinary home, one may prophesy confidently, will be very much reduced in the near future whether we move toward Socialism or no; all the dirt of coal, all the disagreeableness attendant upon lamps and candles, most of the heavy work of cooking will be obviated by electric lighting and heating, and much of the bedroom service dispensed with through the construction of properly equipped bath dressing rooms. In addition, it is highly probable that there will be a considerable extension of the club idea; ordinary people will dine more freely in public places, and conveniences for their doing so will increase. The single handed servant will have disappeared, and if you are one of that class you must console yourself by thinking that under Socialism you would have been educated up to seventeen or eighteen and then equipped for some more interesting occupation. But there will remain much need of occasional help of a more skilled sort, in cleaning out the house thoroughly every now and then, probably with the help of mechanisms, in recovering and repairing furniture, and in all this sort of "helping" which will be done as between one social equal and another, many people who are now, through lack of opportunity and education, servants, will no doubt be employed. But where the better type of service will be found will probably be in the clubs and associated homes, where pleasant mannered, highly paid, skilful people will see to the ease and comfort of a considerable clientèle without either offence or servility. There still remains, no doubt, a number of valets, footmen, maids and so on, who under Socialism would not be servants at all, but something far better, more interesting and more productive socially.

But this writing of servants brings me now to another possibility, and that is that perhaps you are, dear reader, one of that small number of fortunate people, rich and well placed in the world, who even under existing conditions seem to possess all that life can offer a human being. You live beautifully in a great London house, waited upon by companies of servants, you have country seats with parks about them and fine gardens, you can travel luxuriously to any part of the civilized world and live sumptuously there. All things are done for you, all ways are made smooth for you. A skilled maid or valet saves you even the petty care of your person; skilled physicians, wonderful specialists intervene at any threat of illness or discomfort; you keep ten years younger in appearance than your poorer contemporaries and twice as splendid. And above all you have an immense sense of downward perspectives, of being special and apart and above the common herd of mankind.

Now frankly Socialism will be incompatible with this patrician style. You must contemplate the end of all that. You may still be healthy, refined, free, beautifully clothed and housed; but you will not have either the space or the service or the sense of superiority you enjoy now, under Socialism. You would have to take your place among the multitude again. Only a moiety of your property will remain to your sort of person if any revolution is achieved. The rents upon which you live, the investments that yield the income that makes the employment of that army of butlers and footmen, estate workers and underlings possible, that buys your dresses, your jewels, your motorcars, your splendid furnishings and equipments, will for the most part be public property, yielding revenue to some national or municipal treasury. You will have to give up much of that. There is no way out of it, your way to Socialism is through "the needle's eye." From your rare class and from your class alone does Socialism require a real material sacrifice. You must indeed give up much coarse pride. There is no help for it, you must face that if you face Socialism at all. You must come down to a simpler and, in many material aspects, less distinguished way of living.

This is so clearly evident that to any one who believes self seeking is the ruling motive, the only possible motive in mankind, it seems incredible that your class ever will do anything than oppose to the last the advancement of Socialism. You will fight for what you have, and the Have nots will fight to take it away. Therefore it is that the Socialists of the Social Democratic Federation preach a class war; to my mind a lurid, violent and distasteful prospect. We shall have to get out of the miseries and disorder of to day, they think, if not by way of chateau burning and tumbrils, at least by a mitigated equivalent of that. But I am not of that opinion. I have a lurking belief that you are not altogether eaten up by the claims of your own magnificence. While there are no doubt a number of people in your class who would fight like rats in a corner against, let us say, the feeding of poor people's starving children or the recovery of the land by the State to which it once belonged, I believe there is enough of nobility in your class as a whole to considerably damp their resistance. Because you have silver mirrors and silver hairbrushes, it does not follow that you have not a conscience. I am no believer in the theory that to be a sans culotte is to be morally impeccable, or that a man loses his soul because he possesses thirty pairs of trousers beautifully folded by a valet. I cherish the belief that your very refinement will turn—I have seen it in one or two fine minds visibly turning—against the social conditions that made it possible. All this space, all this splendour has its traceable connection with the insufficiencies and miseries from which you are so remote. Once that realization comes to you the world changes. In certain lights, correlated with that, your magnificence can look, you will discover—forgive the word!—a little vulgar....

Once you have seen that you will continue to see it. The nouveau riche of the new Plutocratic type comes thrusting among you, demonstrating that sometimes quite obtrusively. You begin by feeling sorry for his servants and then apologetic to your own. You cannot "go it" as the rich Americans and the rich South Africans, or prosperous book makers or rich music hall proprietors, "go it," their silver and ivory and diamonds throw light on your own. And among other things you discover you are not nearly so dependent on the numerous men in livery, the spaces and enrichments, for your pride and comfort, as these upstart people.

I trust also to the appeal of the intervening spaces. You cannot so entirely close your world in from the greater world without that, in transit at least, the other aspects do not intrude. Every time you leave Charing Cross for the Continent, for example, there are all those horrible slums on either side of the line. These things are, you know, a part of your system, part of you; they are the reverse of that splendid fabric and no separate thing, the wide rich tapestry of your lives comes through on the other side, stitch for stitch in stunted bodies, in children's deaths, in privation and anger. Your grandmothers did not realize that. You do. You know. In that recognition and a certain nobility I find in you, I put my hope, much more than in any dreadful memories of 1789 and those vindictive pikes.

Your class is a strangely mixed assembly of new and old, of base and fine. But through it all, in Great Britain and Western Europe generally, soaks a tradition truly aristocratic, a tradition that transcends property; you are aware, and at times uneasily aware, of duty and a sort of honour. You cannot bilk cabmen nor cheat at cards; there is something in your making forbids that as strongly as an instinct. But what if it is made clear to you (and it is being made clear to you) that the wealth you have is, all unwittingly on your part, the outcome of a colossal—if unpremeditated—social bilking?

Moreover, though Socialism does ask you to abandon much space and service, it offers you certain austere yet not altogether inadequate compensations. If you will cease to have that admirable house in Mayfair and the park in Kent and the moorlands and the Welsh castle, yet you will have another ownership of a finer kind to replace those things. For all London will be yours, a city to serve indeed, and a sense of fellowship that is, if you could but realize it, better than respect. The common people will not be common under Socialism. That is a very important thing for you to remember. But better than those thoughts is this, that you will own yourself too, more than you do now. All that state, all that prominence of yours—do you never feel how it stands between you and life?

So I appeal from your wealth to your nobility, to help us to impoverish your class a little relatively and make all the world infinitely richer by that impoverishment. And I am sure that to some of you I shall not appeal in vain....

VI

And lastly, perhaps you are chiefly a patriot and you are concerned for the flag and country with which your emotions have interwoven. You find that the Socialist talks constantly of internationalism and the World State, and that presents itself to your imagination as a very vague and colourless substitute for a warm and living reality of England or "these States" or the Empire. Well, your patriotism will have suffered a change, but I do not think it need starve under Socialist conditions. It may be that war will have ceased, but the comparison and competition and pride of communities will not have ceased. Philadelphia and Chicago, Boston and New York are at peace, in all probability for ever at peace, so far as guns and slaughter go, but each perpetually criticizes, goads and tries to outshine the other. And the civic pride and rivalry of to day will be nothing to that pride and rivalry when every man's business is the city and the city's honour and well being is his own. You will have, therefore, first this civic patriotism, your ancient pride in your city, a city which will be like the city of the ancient Athenian's, or the mediæval Italian's, the centre of a system of territories and the property and chief interest of its citizens. I, for instance, should love and serve, even as I love to day, my London and my Cinque Ports, these Home Counties about London, the great lap of the Thames valley and the Weald and Downland, my own country in which all my life has been spent; for you the city may be Ulster or Northumbria, or Wales or East or West Belgium, or Finland or Burgundy, or Berne or Berlin, or Venetia, Pekin, Calcutta, Queensland or San Francisco. And keeping the immediate peace between these vigorous giant municipal states and holding them together there will still be in many cases the old national or Imperial government and the old flag, a means of joint action between associated and kindred municipalities with a common language and a common history and a common temper and race. The nation and the national government will be the custodian of the national literature and the common law, the controller and perhaps the vehicle of intermunicipal and international trade, and an intermediary between its municipal governments and that great Congress to which all things are making, that permanent international Congress which will be necessary to insure the peace of the world.

That, at least, is my own dream of the order that may emerge from the confusion of distrusts and tentatives and dangerous absurdities, those reactions of fear and old traditional attitudes and racial misconceptions which one speaks of as international relations to day. For I do not believe that war is a necessary condition to human existence and progress, that it is anything more than a confusion we inherit from the less organized phases of social development. I think but a little advancement in general intelligence will make it an impossible thing.

But suppose after all that I am wrong in my estimate in this matter, and that war will still be possible in a Socialist or partly Socialist world; suppose that the Socialist State in which I am imagining you to live is threatened by some military power. Then I don't think the military power that threatens it need threaten very long. Because consider, here will be a State organized for collective action as never a State has been organized before, a State in which every man and woman will be a willing and conscious citizen saturated with the spirit of service, in which scientific research will be at a maximum of vigour and efficiency. What individualist or autocratic militarism will stand a chance against it? It goes quite without saying from the essential principles of Socialism that if war is necessary then every citizen will, as a matter of course, take his part in that war. It is mere want of intellectual grasp that has made a few working class Socialists in England and France oppose military service. Universal military service, given the need for it, is innate in the Socialist idea, just as it is blankly antagonistic to the "private individual" ideas of Eighteenth Century Liberalism. It is innate in the Socialist idea, but equally innate in that is the conception of establishing and maintaining for ever a universal peace.

CHAPTER XV

THE ADVANCEMENT OF SOCIALISM

I

And here my brief exposition of the ideals of Modern Socialism may fitly end.

I have done my best to set out soberly and plainly this great idea of deliberately making a real civilization by the control and subordination of the instinct of property, and the systematic development of a state of consciousness out of the achievements and squalor, out of the fine forces and wasted opportunities of to day. I may have an unconscious bias perhaps, but so far as I have been able I have been just and frank, concealing nothing of the doubts and difficulties of Socialism, nothing of the divergencies of opinion among its supporters, nothing of the generous demands it makes upon the social conscience, the Good Will in man. Its supporters are divergent upon a hundred points, but upon its fundamental generalizations they are all absolutely agreed, and some day the whole world will be agreed. Their common purport is the resumption by the community of all property that is not justly and obviously personal, and the substitution of the spirit of service for the spirit of gain in all human affairs.

It must be clear to the reader who has followed my explanations continuously, that the present advancement of Socialism must lie now along three several lines.

FIRST, and most important, is the primary intellectual process, the elaboration, criticism, discussion, enrichment and enlargement of the project of Socialism. This includes all sorts of sociological and economic research, the critical literature of Socialism, and every possible way—the drama, poetry, painting, music—of expressing and refining its spirit, its attitudes and conceptions. It includes, too, all sorts of experiments in living and association. In its widest sense it includes all science, literature and invention.

SECONDLY, comes the propaganda; the publication, distribution, repetition, discussion and explanation of this growing body of ideas, until this conception of a real civilized State as being in the making, becomes the common intellectual property of all intelligent people in the world; until the laws and social injustices that now seem, to the ordinary man, as much parts of life as the east wind and influenza, will seem irrational, unnatural and absurd. This educational task is at the present time the main work that the mass of Socialists have before them. Most other possibilities wait upon that enlargement of the general circle of ideas. It is a work that every one can help forward in some measure, by talk and discussion, by the distribution of literature, by writing and speaking in public, by subscribing to propagandist organizations.

And THIRDLY, there is the actual changing of practical things in the direction of the coming Socialized State, the actual socialization, bit by bit and more and more completely, of the land, of the means of production, of education and child welfare, of insurance and the food supply, the realization, in fact, of that great design which the intellectual process of Socialism is continually making more beautiful, attractive and worthy. Now this third group of activities is necessarily various and divergent, and at every point the conscious and confessed Socialist will find himself co operating with partial or unintentional Socialists, with statesmen and officials, with opportunist philanthropists, with trade unionists, with religious bodies and religious teachers, with educationists, with scientific and medical specialists, with every sort of public spirited person. He should never lose an opportunity of explaining to such people how necessarily they are Socialists, but he should never hesitate to work with them because they refuse the label. For in the house of Socialism as in the house of God, there are many mansions.

These are the three main channels for Socialist effort, thought, propaganda and practical social and political effort, and between them they afford opportunity for almost every type of intelligent human being. One may bring leisure, labour, gifts, money, reputation, influence to the service of Socialism; there is ample use for them all. There is work to be done for this idea, from taking tickets at a doorway and lending a drawing room for a meeting, to facing death, impoverishment and sorrow for its sake.

II

Socialism is a moral and intellectual process, let me in conclusion reiterate that. Only secondarily and incidentally does it sway the world of politics. It is not a political movement; it may engender political movements, but it can never become a political movement; any political body, any organization whatever, that professes to stand for Socialism, makes an altogether too presumptuous claim. The whole is greater than the part, the will than the instrument. There can be no official nor pontifical Socialism; the theory lives and grows. It springs out of the common sanity of mankind. Constructive Socialism shapes into a great system of developments to be forwarded, points to a great number of systems of activity amidst which its adherents may choose their field for work. Parties and societies may come or go, parties and organizations and names may be used and abandoned; constructive Socialism lives and remains.

There is a constantly recurring necessity to insist on the difference between two things, the larger and the lesser, the greater being the Socialist movement, the lesser the various organizations that come and go. There is this necessity because there is a sort of natural antagonism between the thinker and writer who stand by the scheme and seek to develop and expound it, and the politician who attempts to realize it. They are allies, but allies who often pull against each other, whom a little heat and thoughtlessness may precipitate into a wasteful conflict. The former is, perhaps, too apt to resent the expenditure of force in those conflicts of cliques and personal ambition that inevitably arise among men comparatively untrained for politics, those squabbles and intrigues, reservations and insincerities that precede the birth of a tradition of discipline; the latter is equally prone to think literature too broad minded for daily life, and to associate all those aspects of the Socialist project which do not immediately win votes, with fads, kid gloves, "gentlemanliness," rose water and such like contemptible things. These squabbles of the engineer and the navigating officer must not be allowed to confuse the mind of the student of Socialism. They are quarrels of the mess room, quarrels on board the ship and within limits, they have nothing to do with the general direction of Socialism. Like all indisciplines they hinder but they do not contradict the movement. Socialism, the politicians declare, can only be realized through politics. Socialism, I would answer, can never be narrowed down to politics. Your parties and groups may serve Socialism, but they can never be Socialism. Scientific progress, medical organization, the advancement of educational method, artistic production and literature are all aspects of Socialism, they are all interests and developments that lie apart from anything one may call—except by sheer violence to language—politics.

And since Socialism is an intellectual as well as a moral thing, it will never tolerate in its adherents the abnegation of individual thought and intention. It demands devotion to an idea, not devotion to a leader. No addicted follower of so and so or of so and so can be a good Socialist any more than he can be a good scientific investigator. So far Socialism has produced no great leaders at all. Lassalle alone of all its prominent names was of that romantic type of personality which men follow with enthusiasm. The others, Owen, Saint Simon, and Fourier, Proudhon, Marx, and Engels, Bebel, Webb, J. S. Mill, Jaurès, contributed to a process they never seized hold upon, never made their own, they gave enrichment and enlargement and the movement passed on; passes on gathering as it goes. Kingsley, Morris, Ruskin—none are too great to serve this idea, and none so great they may control it or stand alone for it. So it will continue. Socialism under a great leader, or as a powerfully organized party would be the end of Socialism. No doubt it might also be its partial triumph; but the reality of the movement would need to take to itself another name; to call itself "constructive civilization" or some such synonym, in order to continue its undying work. Socialism no doubt will inspire great leaders in the future, and supply great parties with ideas; in itself it will still be greater than all such things.

III

But here, perhaps, before the finish, since the business of this book is explanation, it may be well to define a little the relation of Socialism to the political party that is most closely identified with it in the popular mind. This is the Labour Party. There can be no doubt of the practical association of aim and interest of the various Labour parties throughout modern civilized communities with the Socialist movement. The Social democrats of Germany are the Labour Party of that country, and wherever the old conception of Socialism prevails, those "class war" ideas of the Marxist that have been superseded in English Socialism for nearly a quarter of a century, there essentially the Socialist movement will take the form of a revolutionary attack upon the owning and governing sections of the community. But in Great Britain and America the Labour movement has never as a whole been revolutionary or insurrectionary in spirit, and in these countries Socialism has been affected from its very beginnings by constructive ideas. It has never starkly antagonized Labour on the one hand, and the other necessary elements in a civilized State on the other; it has never—I speak of the movement as a whole and not of individual utterances—contemplated a community made up wholly of "Labour" and emotionally democratic, such as the Marxist teaching suggests. The present labouring classes stand to gain enormously in education, dignity, leisure, efficiency and opportunity by the development of a Socialist State, and just in so far as they become intelligent will they become Socialist; but we all, all of us of Good Will, we and our children, of nearly every section of the community stand also to gain and have also our interest in this development. Great as the Labour movement is, the Socialist movement remains something greater. The one is the movement of a class, the other a movement of the best elements in every class.

None the less it remains true that under existing political conditions it is to the Labour Party that the Socialist must look for the mass and emotion and driving force of political Socialism. Among the wage workers of the modern civilized community Socialists are to be counted now by the hundred thousand, and in those classes alone does an intelligent self interest march clearly and continuously in the direction of constructive civilization. In the other classes the Socialists are dispersed and miscellaneous in training and spirit, hampered by personal and social associations, presenting an enormous variety of aspects and incapable, it would seem, of co operation except in relation to the main Socialist body, the Labour mass. Through that, and in relation and service to that, they must, it would seem, spend their political activities (I am writing now only of political activities) if they are not to be spent very largely to waste. The two other traditional parties in British politics are no doubt undergoing remarkable changes and internal disruptions, and the constructive spirit of the time is at work within them; but it does not seem that either is likely to develop anything nearly so definitely a Socialist programme as the Labour Party. The old Conservative Party, in spite of its fine aristocratic traditions, tends more and more to become the party of the adventurous Plutocracy, of the aggressive nouveau riche, inclines more and more towards the inviting financial possibilities of modern "Imperialism" and "Tariff Reform." The old Liberal Party strains between these two antagonists and its own warring and conflicting traditions of Whiggery and Radicalism. There can be no denying the great quantity of "Good Will" and constructive intention that finds a place in its very miscellaneous ranks, but the strong strain of obstinate and irreconcilable individualism is equally indisputable.

But the official Liberal attitude is one thing, and a very unsubstantial and transitory thing, and the great mass of Good Will and broad thinking in the ranks of Liberalism and the middle class quite another. Socialists are to be found not only in every class, but in every party. There can be no "Socialist" party as such. That is the misleading suggestion of irresponsible and destructive adventurers. It is impossible to estimate what forces of political synthesis may be at work at the present time, or what ruptures and coalitions may not occur in the course of a few years. These things belong to the drama of politics. They do not affect the fact that the chief Interest in the community on the side of Socialism is Labour; through intelligent Labour it is that Socialism becomes a political force and possibility, and it is to the Labour Party that the Socialist who wishes to engage in active political work may best give his means and time and energy and ability.

I write "political work," and once more I would repeat that it is to the field of electioneering and parliamentary politics under present conditions that this section refers. The ultimate purpose of Socialism can rely upon no class because it aims to reconstitute all classes. In a Socialist State there will be no class doomed to mere "labour," no class privileged to rule and decide. For every child there will be fair opportunity and education and scope to the limit of its possibilities. To the best there will be given difficulty and responsibility, honour and particular rewards, but to all security and reasonable work and a tolerable life. The interests and class traditions upon which our party distinctions of to day rely must necessarily undergo progressive modification with every step we take towards the realization of the Socialist ideal.

IV

So this general account of Socialism concludes. I have tried to put it as what it is, as the imperfect and still growing development of the social idea, of the collective Good Will in man. I have tried to indicate its relation to politics, to religion, to art and literature, to the widest problems of life. Its broad generalizations are simple and I believe acceptable to all clear thinking minds. And in a way they do greatly simplify life. Once they have been understood they render impossible a thousand confusions and errors of thought and practice. They are in the completest sense of the word, illumination.

But Socialism is no panacea, no magic "Open Sesame" to the millennium. Socialism lights up certain once hopeless evils in human affairs and shows the path by which escape is possible, but it leaves that path rugged and difficult. Socialism is hope, but it is not assurance. Throughout this book I have tried to keep that before the reader.

Directly one accepts those great generalizations one passes on to a jungle of incurably intricate problems, through which man has to make his way or fail, the riddles and inconsistencies of human character, the puzzles of collective action, the power and decay of traditions, the perpetually recurring tasks and problems of education. To have become a Socialist is to have learnt something, to have made an intellectual and a moral step, to have discovered a general purpose in life and a new meaning in duty and brotherhood. But to have become a Socialist is not, as many suppose, to have become generally wise. Rather in realizing the nature of the task that could be done, one realizes also one's insufficiencies, one's want of knowledge, one's need of force and training. Here and in this manner, says Socialism, a palace and safety and great happiness may be made for mankind. But it seems to me the Socialist as he turns his hand and way of living towards that common end knows little of the nature of his task if he does so with any but a lively sense of his individual weakness and the need of charity for all that he achieves.

In that spirit, and with no presumption of finality, this little book of explanations is given to the world.

H G WELLS – A SHORT BIOGRAPHY

Herbert George Wells was born on September 21st, 1866 at Atlas House, 46 High Street, Bromley, Kent. He was the youngest of four siblings and his family affectionately knew him as 'Bertie'.

At the time of his birth his father, Joseph Wells, was a professional cricketer playing for the Kent county team. While this afforded him some seasonal income, it was far too little to raise a family and so he and his wife Sarah, a former domestic servant, acquired a shop on Bromley high street selling sporting goods and chinaware. It was in their accommodation above this shop that H. G. Wells was born.

The first few years of his childhood were spent fairly quietly, and Wells didn't display much literary interest until, in 1874, he accidentally broke his leg and was left to recover in bed, largely entertained by the library books his father regularly brought him. Through these Wells found he could escape the boredom and misery of his bed and convalescence by exploring the new worlds he encountered in these books.

Very quickly his vivid and fertile imagination began an interest in creating his own worlds, and from then on he was motivated to write.

Later that year the young Wells entered Thomas Morley's Commercial Academy, a private school. An earlier version of the school had gone bankrupt some years before. And perhaps not without good reason; the teaching was erratic, the curriculum mostly focused, as Wells later said, on producing copperplate handwriting and doing the sort of sums useful to tradesmen. However, despite that, Wells remained a pupil there for six years until 1880.

In 1877, his father fractured his thigh and effectively put an end to Joseph's career as a cricketer. His subsequent earnings as a shopkeeper were not enough to compensate for the loss of the primary source of family income.

No longer able to support themselves financially, the family instead sought to place their sons as apprentices in various occupations. From 1880 to 1883, Wells had a miserable apprenticeship as a draper at the Southsea Drapery Emporium, Hyde's. The hours were long, usually thirteen hours a day, and board was provided by a dormitory shared with the other apprentices. These experiences were valuable in one respect. They would later inspire such classic novels as *The Wheels of Chance* and *Kipps*, which portray the life of a draper's apprentice as well as providing much of the factual evidence for his writings on society's unequal distribution of wealth.

Wells' parents had a turbulent marriage, mainly caused by the friction of his mother being a Protestant and his father a freethinker. When his mother returned to work as a lady's maid (at Uppark, a country house in Sussex), one of the conditions of work was that she would not be permitted to have living space for her husband and children. Thereafter, she and Joseph lived separate lives, though they never divorced and remained faithful to each other. As a probable extension of this the young Well's personal troubles increased as he subsequently failed as a draper and also, later, as a chemist's assistant.

Fortunately for him Uppark had a magnificent well stocked library in which he immersed himself, reading many from the many classic works; from Plato's Republic to More's Utopia.

In October 1879 Sarah secured Wells a position through a distant relative as pupil-teacher at the National School at Wookey, in Somerset, where, as a senior pupil of the school, he would teach the younger children. This was a regular practice at the time and, for Wells, a valuable experience.

But the career plan did not go as hoped. A few months later in December his relative, Arthur Williams, was dismissed for "irregularities in his qualifications" and so Wells was also dismissed. It was yet another obstacle for him to overcome.

He moved to Midhurst Grammar School, though his time there was brief lasting only a year.

Whilst there he gained a scholarship to the Normal School of Science, which would later become the Royal College of Science in South Kensington.

Here he studied biology under the tuition of Thomas Henry Huxley, the famous advocate of the theory of evolution and known as "Darwin's Bulldog" for his ferocity.

The scholarship also gave him twenty-one shillings per week upon which to live, and helped him to remain at the College until 1887. The College also had a debating society which quickly aroused Wells's interest, and he joined it within his first year.

Drawing on his learnings from his time in the library at Uppark, he soon became interested and involved with societal matters, including that of reformation and revolution. Though his initial involvement was founded on his understanding of *The Republic*, it wasn't long before he began to consider socialist matters from a more contemporary perspective, encouraged by his fellows and recently expressed by the Fabian Society, a newly established socialist organism seeking reform by gradualist means. He attended lectures given at the home of the artist and socialist William Morris at Kelmscott House.

Wells was numbered amongst the co-founders of *The Science School Journal*, for which he began to write about his own views on society, and literature. The journal also provided an environment in which he could relatively safely experiment with fiction writing, and the earliest version of *The Time Machine* (1895) was published in the journal, under the name *The Chronic Argonauts*.

Unfortunately for Wells he experienced another obstacle when he lost his scholarship in 1887 when he failed to pass his geology exams, owing to a marked lack of interest, though he had successfully passed exams in biology and physics.

Wells moved to Stoke-on-Trent in 1888, staying in both Basford and in Burslem in the Leopard Hotel. In a letter to a friend he wrote that "the district made an immense impression on me", and it is widely thought that he took inspiration from the Potteries, the furnaces and industry of the area in his imagining of the landscape of *The War of the Worlds*. While here he wrote *The Cone*, a macabre short story, which was published in 1895 alongside *The Time Machine*. It is set in the north of Stoke-on-Trent.

He spent some time teaching at Henley House School where he taught A.A. Milne (the future and famed author of Winnie the Pooh), and after some time decided to further his knowledge of the methodology and principles of the practice of education. In order to do so, he enrolled at the College of Preceptors, now the College of Teachers, and went on to receive his Licentiate and Fellowship FCP diplomas.

Two years later, in 1890, Wells finally received a Bachelor of Science degree, in zoology, from the University of London External Programme.

Having now left London he found himself without accommodation until he moved to his aunt Mary's house, where he courted his cousin, Isabel Mary Wells, whom he married in 1891.

Wells was still teaching at Henley House School throughout the courtship and marriage, and gradually he became romantically interested with Amy Catherine Robbins, one of his students. Wells separated from Isabel in favour of Amy, who later became known as Jane, and they married in 1895.

The same year saw the publication of *The Time Machine*. Interestingly, Wells was initially expecting to reuse the material from *The Chronic Argonauts*, the first version he had written for his College journal, in a series of articles for the *Pall Mall Gazette*. However, upon that magazine's publisher's request he instead expanded and serialised the novel on the agreement of a sum of £100 on publication by Heinemann (this is roughly equivalent today to £10,000), was significantly more money than he expected or had, and he readily agreed.

It ran from January to May in *The New Review*, and then was published in its first book edition by Henry Holt and Company in New York on May 7th of the same year. Shortly thereafter Heinemann produced an English book edition, which became available on May 29th. The two editions differ slightly, but the English version has now established itself as the preferred version.

In this classic book Wells first uses the term 'time machine', and introduces and popularises the concept of purposeful and deliberate travel through time. Along with the novel's significance for the genre of science fiction is its importance as a text of social commentary and criticism, exploring

Wells's views of abundance and the industrial revolution. Written at the time of a growing British Empire where great strides were being made in real life across many fields it tunes in to his unique ability to slightly distort reality and make our fears and dreams believable and achievable.

Buoyed by his success with *The Time Machine*, Wells proceeded with his next major work, *The Wonderful Visit*. It was published in the same year, by MacMillan and Co., to critical acclaim. It is purportedly based on a famous quotation from John Ruskin, the painter and critic, who wrote that, were an angel to appear in Victorian England, it would be shot on sight. Wells introduces themes of contemporary fantasy and satire, and was highly praised for the book; Joseph Conrad wrote to him praising his "imagination so unbounded and so brilliant". Alongside these two more prominent works of 1895 were two others, *Select Conversations With An Uncle* and *The Stolen Bacillus and Other Incidents*.

In 1896 *The Island of Doctor Moreau*, was published by Heinemann, Stone and Kimball. In it Wells imagines our narrator, Edward Prendrick, marooned on the island of Doctor Moreau who uses the vivisection of animals to construct macabre representations of human beings. Using this model Wells is able to explore a number of philosophical ideas about morality, ethics and pain. The book was written at a time of increasing and vested interest in vivisection across Europe, and in the succeeding few years several interest groups were established, notable amongst which was the British Union for the Abolition of Vivisection.

In a change of literary direction and tone Wells finished 1896 with *The Wheels of Chance*, a satirical comedy, much in the vein of Jerome K. Jerome's more famous and celebrated *Three Men in a Boat*. It was written at the height of the cycling craze in Great Britain, when bicycles became cheap to manufacture and available to the masses, and imagines the escapist holiday of a frustrated draper whose calamitous expedition by bicycle to the South coast to explore new areas of his country. Indeed a famous Wells quote of the time was "Every time I see an adult on a bicycle, I no longer despair for the future of the human race."

The next year saw his published work return to its more philosophical grandeur with the publication by C. Arthur Pearson of *The Invisible Man*. Firmly in his now established vein of early science fiction, it explores the moral and social implications of scientific experiment and the consequences when the experiment malfunctions.

This same year, 1897, Wells completed what is arguably his most famous, most influential and most recognisable work, *The War of the Worlds*. He had been working on the idea since 1895, and when it was published it was classified along with his earlier work, *The Time Machine*, as 'scientific romance'.

Romance seems a stretch as the Martian invasion lays waste to southern England. But Wells was able to explore some of the popular superstitions of Victorian society as well as ideas about British Imperialism as the Empire approached its zenith.

Though it had been serialised the year before in *Pearson's Magazine*, for which he was paid £200 on the condition that he tell the publisher how it ends before receipt of payment, it was more successful the following year when it was published in book form by Heinemann. It has become a never ending source of media inventions, from books to Radio, TV and of course, film.

Part of its success is arguably attributable to the fascination with an increasing interest by the general population in what has become known as 'invasion literature', this genre, most prominent between 1871 and 1914, had a focus largely directed towards the increasing hostilities between the

British Empire and her European rivals, and the ramifications of the widespread nature of the British Empire both commercial, culturally and military.

Between 1898 and 1899, Wells serialised a novel entitled *When The Sleeper Awakes*, concerning a man who, after experimenting with drugs to alleviate his insomnia, enters a sort of coma for 203 years and wakes up in the year 2100 to find that his wealth, with compound interest from the bank, accumulated to such an extent over the course of his coma that he is now the richest man in the world. Meanwhile, a sinister organisation called the White Council has invested his money and used his status as a demi-god to justify their actions in order to establish a plutocracy. Graham awakes and is presented with a dystopian reality over which he effectively has dominion. The novel sought to explore the nature of greed and oppression and, though it was fairly successful in its time, Wells revisited it in 1910 to far greater commercial and critical acclaim with *The Sleeper Awakes*. Wells followed the first version of this novel with *Love and Mr Lewisham*, a departure from his now established science fiction genre, and with a protagonist who bears striking resemblance to Wells in several ways. Mr Lewisham is a teacher at the age of eighteen, he falls in love in circumstances which cause the loss of his teaching post, and he progresses to study at the Normal School of Science, where Wells himself had studied. Wells himself spoke of the differences between this and his earlier work, stating that "the writing was an altogether more serious undertaking than I have ever done before".

In 1901, and with his health poor, Wells moved near Folkestone to Sandgate where he built a large home, which he named Spade House, for his family in anticipation of his first son, George Philip, who was born in the same year on July 17th.

H G Wells had by now established himself as a significant proponent of the scientific romance genre, now becoming better known as science fiction, his works reaching and thrilling a wide commercial audience as did those of Jules Verne who, although in his last days, was equally instrumental in bringing life to this new literary genre.

Wells wrote a novel almost every year until 1941 when he published his last novel, *You Can't Be Too Careful*, and in each he explores his various progressive, and progressing, political and social ideas.

Alongside his significant output of serialised novels, he was a prolific writer of shorter stories and non-fiction, whether that be social and political commentary or scientific journalism, literary criticism or autobiography. His attendance at the Fabian Society continued, and it was through connections made there that he had several affairs, with Jane's consent, with writers, political thinkers and most ironically an American birth control activist named Margaret Sanger.

Despite these affairs, his marriage to Jane continued and remained strong enough that they had another child, Frank Richard, in 1903, and the marriage continued until 1927 when Jane died. Some of the affairs seemed rather more complicated and, given society's morals at the time, must have caused problems with his wife. Having met the parents of novelist Amber Reeves at the Fabian Society, he began an affair with her which resulted in a child, born in 1909, named Anna-Jane. Five years later, in 1914, he had a son, Anthony West, with the feminist and novelist Rebecca West, who at the time was twenty-six years younger than him. Wells remained in fairly regular contact with his lovers and his children.

While continuing to write at his regular pace of one or two novels, short stories or essays per year, a glance at the bibliography below will give some idea of the scope, quality and output he was able to write with.

Wells also managed to put more time into politics and religion, though he was increasingly outspoken in his criticism of the Catholic church in his final years.

He ran as a Labour Party candidate for London University in the 1922 and 1923 general elections though it appears his views on the Party were diverging from theirs at the time.

In 1933 Wells predicted in *The Shape of Things to Come* that the world war he feared would begin in January 1940. It was another example of his predictive skills that had brought so many new ideas once thought fantastic to become almost everyday events.

By now Wells had become widely read almost everywhere both in the English language and through the myriad of translated works also in print through many other languages. With the rise of the Nazi party and his direct and confrontational criticism of it on May 10th, 1933, Wells' books were burned by the Nazi youth in Berlin's Opernplatz, and his works banned from libraries and bookstores.

Wells, who was president of PEN International (Poets, Essayists, Novelists), further angered the Nazis by overseeing the expulsion of the German PEN club from the international body in 1934 following the German PEN's refusal to admit non-Aryan writers to its membership.

It was later discovered after the war that he was one of almost three thousand names listed in "The Black Book" and slated for immediate arrest by the SS should the invasion of Britain have been successful.

Having suffered from diabetes throughout his life, in 1934 he decided to set up the charity which became Diabetes UK, which has now become the UK's leading diabetes charity.

On October 28th, 1940, on radio station KTSA in San Antonio, Texas, Wells took part in a radio interview with his near namesake, Orson Welles, who two years previously had performed a famous radio adaptation of *The War of the Worlds* which had caused utter panic and mass evacuation in America. During the interview Wells admitted his surprise at the events that resulted from the broadcast, but acknowledged his debt to Welles for increasing sales of one of his "more obscure" titles.

An immense talent Wells not only wrote prolifically and to a large audience but he was always much admired both for this thinking on various subjects including social issues, such as governments and race relations, but also for his literary ideas which pushed the boundaries for both contemporary science and future generations.

Additionally, his work received major recognition by being nominated for the Nobel Prize in Literature in 1921, 1932, 1935, and 1946.

Herbert George Wells died at home, 13 Hanover Terrace, Regent's Park, London, August 13th, 1946. His death is recorded as being of 'unspecified causes'. He was 79 years of age.

Wells had stated that his epitaph should be: "I told you so. You damned fools".

He was cremated at Golders Green Crematorium on August 16th, 1946, his ashes scattered at sea near Old Harry Rocks at Handfast Point, on the Isle of Purbeck in Dorset

The literary papers and correspondence from his estate were purchased in 1954 by the University of Illinois at Urbana–Champaign.

Novels
The Time Machine (1895)
The Wonderful Visit (1895)
The Island of Doctor Moreau (1896)
The Wheels of Chance (1896)
The Invisible Man (1897)
The War of the Worlds (1898)
When the Sleeper Wakes (1899)
Love and Mr Lewisham (1900)
The First Men in the Moon (1901)
The Sea Lady (1902)
The Food of the Gods and How It Came to Earth (1904)
Kipps (1905)
A Modern Utopia (1905)
In the Days of the Comet (1906)
The War in the Air (1908)
Tono-Bungay (1909)
Ann Veronica (1909)
The History of Mr Polly (1910)
The Sleeper Awakes (1910) – revised edition of When the Sleeper Wakes (1899)
The New Machiavelli (1911)
Marriage (1912)
The Passionate Friends (1913)
The Wife of Sir Isaac Harman (1914)
The World Set Free (1914)
Bealby: A Holiday (1915)
Boon (1915)
The Research Magnificent (1915)
Mr Britling Sees It Through (1916)
The Soul of a Bishop (1917)
Joan and Peter: The Story of an Education (1918)
The Undying Fire (1919)
The Secret Places of the Heart (1922)
Men Like Gods (1923)
The Dream (1924)
Christina Alberta's Father (1925)
The World of William Clissold (1926)
Meanwhile (1927)
Mr. Blettsworthy on Rampole Island (1928)
The Autocracy of Mr. Parham (1930)
The Bulpington of Blup (1932)
The Shape of Things to Come (1933)
The Croquet Player (1936)
Brynhild (1937)
Star Begotten (1937)
The Camford Visitation (1937)

Apropos of Dolores (1938)
The Brothers (1938)
The Holy Terror (1939)
Babes in the Darkling Wood (1940)
All Aboard for Ararat (1940)
You Can't Be Too Careful (1941)

Non Fiction
Cover of Little Wars (1913).
Text-Book of Biology (1893)
Honours Physiography (1893) – with R. A. Gregory
Certain Personal Matters (1897)
Anticipations of the Reactions of Mechanical and Scientific Progress upon Human Life and Thought (1901)
Mankind in the Making (1903)
The Future in America (1906)
This Misery of Boots (1907)
Will Socialism Destroy the Home? (1907)
New Worlds for Old (1908)
First and Last Things (1908)
Floor Games (1911)
The Great State (1912)
Great Thoughts From H. G. Wells (1912)
Thoughts From H. G. Wells (1912)
Little Wars (1913)
The War That Will End War (1914)
An Englishman Looks at the World (1914); US title: Social Forces in England and America
The War and Socialism (1915)
The Peace of the World (1915)
What is Coming? (1916)
The Elements of Reconstruction (1916) – published under the pseudonym D. P.
God the Invisible King (1917)
War and the Future (a.k.a. Italy, France and Britain at War) (1917)
Introduction to Nocturne (1917)
In the Fourth Year (1918)
The Idea of a League of Nations (1919) – with Viscount Edward Grey, Lionel Curtis, William Archer, H. Wickham Steed, A. E. Zimmern, J. A. Spender, Viscount Bryce and Gilbert Murray
The Way to the League of Nations (1919) – with Viscount Edward Grey, Lionel Curtis, William Archer, H. Wickham Steed, A. E. Zimmern, J. A. Spender, Viscount Bryce and Gilbert Murray
The Outline of History (1920)
Russia in the Shadows (1920)
Frank Swinnerton (1920) – with Arnold Bennett, Grant Overton
The Salvaging of Civilization (1921)
A Short History of the World (1922)
Washington and the Hope of Peace (aka Washington and the Riddle of Peace) (1922)
Socialism and the Scientific Motive (1923)
The Story of a Great Schoolmaster: Being a Plain Account of the Life and Ideas of Sanderson of Oundle (1924) – a biography of Frederick William Sanderson
A Year of Prophesying (1925)
A Short History of Mankind (1925)

Mr. Belloc Objects to "The Outline of History" (1926)
Wells' Social Anticipations (1927)
The Way the World is Going (1928)
The Book of Catherine Wells (1928)
The Open Conspiracy (aka What Are We To Do With Our Lives?) (1928)
The Science of Life (1930) – with Julian S. Huxley and G. P. Wells
Divorce as I See It (1930)
Points of View (1930)
The Work, Wealth and Happiness of Mankind (1931)
The New Russia (1931)
Selections From the Early Prose Works of H. G. Wells (1931)
After Democracy (1932)
Experiment in Autobiography (1934)
The New America: The New World (1935)
The Anatomy of Frustration (1936)
World Brain (1938)
The Fate of Homo Sapiens (a.k.a. The Fate of Man) (1939)
The New World Order (1939)
Travels of a Republican Radical in Search of Hot Water (1939)
The Common Sense of War and Peace (1940)
The Rights of Man (1940)
The Pocket History of the World (1941)
Guide to the New World (1941)
The Outlook for Homo Sapiens (1942)
The Conquest of Time (1942)
Modern Russian and English Revolutionaries (1942) – with Lev Uspensky
Phoenix: A Summary of the Inescapable Conditions of World Reorganization (1942)
Crux Ansata: An Indictment of the Roman Catholic Church (1943)
'42 to '44: A Contemporary Memoir (1944)
Reshaping Man's Heritage (1944) – with J. B. S. Haldane, Julian S. Huxley
The Happy Turning (1945)
Mind at the End of Its Tether (1945)
Marxism vs Liberalism (1945) – with J. V. Stalin
H.G. Wells: Early Writings in Science and Science Fiction (1975)

Stories
A Family Elopement (1884)
A Tale of the Twentieth Century (1887)
A Talk with Gryllotalpa (1887) – published under the pseudonym Septimus Browne
A Vision of the Past (1887)
The Chronic Argonauts (1888)
The Devotee of Art (1888)
The Flying Man (aka The Advent of the Flying Man) (1893)
Æpyornis Island (1894)
A Deal in Ostriches (1894)
The Diamond Maker (1894)
The Flowering of the Strange Orchid (aka The Strange Orchid) (1894)
The Hammerpond Park Burglary (1894)
The Lord of the Dynamos (1894)
How Gabriel Became Thompson (1894)

In the Avu Observatory (1894)
In the Modern Vein: An Unsympathetic Love Story (aka A Bardlet's Romance) (1894)
The Jilting of Jane (1894)
The Man With a Nose (1894)
A Misunderstood Artist (1894)
Mr. Ledbetter's Vacation (1894) (aka Mr. Leadbetter's Vacation)
The Stolen Bacillus (1894)
The Thing in No. 7 (1894)
Through a Window (aka At a Window) (1894)
The Thumbmark (1894)
The Treasure in the Forest (1894)
The Triumphs of a Taxidermist (1894)
The Argonauts of the Air (1895)
A Catastrophe (1895)
The Cone (1895)
How Pingwill Was Routed (1895)
Le Mari Terrible (1895)
The Moth" (aka A Moth – Genus Novo) (1895)
Our Little Neighbour (1895)
Pollock and the Porroh Man (1895)
The Reconciliation (aka The Bulla) (1895)
The Remarkable Case of Davidson's Eyes (aka The Story of Davidson's Eyes) (1895)
The Sad Story of a Dramatic Critic (aka The Obliterated Man) (1895)
The Temptation of Harringay (1895)
Wayde's Essence (1895)
The Apple (1896)
In the Abyss (1896)
The Plattner Story (1896)
The Purple Pileus (1896)
The Rajah's Treasure (1896)
The Red Room (1896) (aka The Ghost of Fear)
The Sea Raiders (1896)
A Slip Under the Microscope (1896)
The Story of the Late Mr. Elvesham (1896)
Under the Knife (aka Slip Under the Knife) (1896)
The Crystal Egg (1897)
The Lost Inheritance (1897)
Mr Marshall's Doppelganger (1897)
A Perfect Gentleman on Wheels (1897)
The Presence by the Fire (1897)
The Star (1897)
A Story of the Days To Come (1897)
A Story of the Stone Age (aka. Stories of the Stone Age) (1897)
Jimmy Goggles the God (1898)
The Man Who Could Work Miracles (1898)
Miss Winchelsea's Heart (1898)
The Stolen Body (1898)
Walcote (1898)
Mr. Brisher's Treasure (1899)
A Vision of Judgment (1899)
A Dream of Armageddon (1901)

Filmer (1901)
Mr. Skelmersdale in Fairyland (1901)
The New Accelerator (1901)
The Inexperienced Ghost (aka The Story of the Inexperienced Ghost) (1902)
The Loyalty of Esau Common (1902)
The Land Ironclads (1903)
The Magic Shop (1903)
The Truth About Pyecraft (1903)
The Valley of Spiders (1903)
The Country of the Blind (1904)
The Empire of the Ants (1905)
The Door in the Wall (1906)
The Beautiful Suit (aka. A Moonlight Fable) (1909)
Little Mother Up the Morderberg (1910)
My First Aeroplane (1910)
The Story of the Last Trump (1915)
The Wild Asses of the Devil (1915)
Peter Learns Arithmetic (1918)
The Grisly Folk (1921)
The Pearl of Love (1924)
The Queer Story of Brownlow's Newspaper (1932)
Answer to Prayer (1937)
The Country of the Blind (revised) (1939)

Story Collections
Select Conversations with an Uncle (Now Extinct) and Two Other Reminscences (1895)
The Stolen Bacillus and Other Incidents (1895)
The Red Room (1896)
Thirty Strange Stories (1897)
The Plattner Story and Others (1897)
Tales of Space and Time (1899)
A Cure For Love (1899)
Twelve Stories and a Dream (1903)
The Country of the Blind and Other Stories (1911)
The Door in the Wall and Other Stories (1911)
The Star (1913)
Boon, The Mind of the Race, The Wild Asses of the Devil, and The Last Trump (1915) – first edition published under the pseudonym Reginald Bliss
Tales of the Unexpected (1922)
Tales of Wonder (1923)
Tales of Life and Adventure (1923)
The Empire of the Ants and Other Stories (1925)
The Short Stories of H. G. Wells (1927)
Selected Short Stories (1927)
The Adventures of Tommy (1929)
The Valley of Spiders (1930)
The Stolen Body and Other Tales of the Unexpected (1931)
The Famous Short Stories of H. G. Wells (aka The Favorite Short Stories of H. G. Wells) (1937)
Short Stories by H. G. Wells (1940)
The Inexperienced Ghost (1943)

The Land Ironclads (1943)
The New Accelerator (1943)
The Truth About Pyecraft and Other Short Stories (1943)
Twenty-Eight Science Fiction Stories (1952)
Seven Stories (1953)
Three Prophetic Science Fiction Novels of H. G. Wells (1960)
The Cone (1965)

Published versions of film scripts and scenarios written by Wells
The King Who Was a King: The Book of a Film (1929 – scenario for a film which was never made)
Things to Come (1935 – adaptation of The Shape of Things to Come and The Work, Wealth and Happiness of Mankind)
The Man Who Could Work Miracles (1936)
The New Faust (in Nash's Pall Magazine, December 1936 – adaptation of The Story of the Late Mr Elvesham)

Zoological Retrogression (1891)
The Rediscovery of the Unique (1891)
Ancient Experiments in Co-Operation (1892)
On Extinction (1893)
The Man of the Year Million (1893)
The Sun God and the Holy Stars (1894)
Province of Pain (1894)
Life in the Abyss (1894)
Another Basis for Life (1894)
The Rate of Change in Species (1894)
The Biological Problem of To-day (1894)
The 'Cyclic' Delusion (1894)
Flat Earth Again (1894)
Bio-Optimism (1895)
Bye-Products in Evolution (1895)
Death (1895)
The Duration of Life (1895)
The Visibility of Change in the Moon (1895)
The Limits of Individual Plasticity (1895)
Human Evolution, an Artificial Process (1896)
Intelligence on Mars (1896)
Concerning Skeletons (1896)
The Possible Individuality of Atoms (1896)
Morals and Civilisation (1897)
On Comparative Theology (1898)
The Discovery of the Future (1902)
The English House of the Future (1903; several other authors)
Skepticism of the Instrument (1903)
The Things that Live on Mars (illustrated by William Robinson Leigh) (1908)
The Grisly Folk (1921)
Mr. Wells and Mr. Vowles (1926)

The Red Dust a Fact! (1927)
Democracy Under Revision (1927)
Wells Speaks Some Plain Words to us, New York Times, October 16, 1927
Common Sense of World Peace (1929)
Foretelling the Future (1938)